DARK REFLECTIONS

DARK REFLECTIONS

Stories Influenced by the Masters of Dark Literature

PAUL KANE

Dark Reflections by Paul Kane
Published by Black Beacon Books
Edited by Cameron Trost
Cover art by Greg Chapman
Copyright © Paul Kane, 2023

Black Beacon Books
blackbeaconbooks.com

ISBN: 9780645247152

Collections

Alone (In the Dark)
Touching the Flame
FunnyBones
Peripheral Visions
The Adventures of Dalton Quayle
Shadow Writer
The Butterfly Man and Other Stories
The Spaces Between
Ghosts
Monsters
The Dead Trilogy
Shadow Casting
Nailbiters
Death
The Life Cycle
Disexistence
Kane's Scary Tales Vol. 1
More Monsters
Lost Souls
The Controllers
White Shadows (as P.B. Kane)
The Colour of Madness: Official Movie Tie-In
Traumas
Darkness & Shadows
The Naked Eye
Tempting Fate
Nailbiters – Hard Bitten
Zombies!
Even More Monsters

Editor & Co-Editor

Shadow Writers Vol. 1 & 2
Terror Tales #1-4
Top International Horror
Albions Alptraume: Zombies
The British Fantasy Society: A Celebration
Hellbound Hearts
The Mammoth Book of Body Horror
A Carnivàle of Horror: Dark Tales from the Fairground
Beyond Rue Morgue
Dark Mirages
Exit Wounds
Wonderland
Cursed

Twice Cursed
In These Hallowed Halls

Non-Fiction
*Contemporary North American Film Directors: A Wallflower Critical Guide
(Major Contributor)*
Cinema Macabre (Contributor)
The Hellraiser Films And Their Legacy
Voices in the Dark
Shadow Writer – The Non-Fiction. Vol. 1: Reviews
Shadow Writer – The Non-Fiction. Vol. 2: Articles & Essays
Leviathan – The Story of Hellraiser and Hellbound: Hellraiser II (contributor)
Hellraisers
War is Hell: Making Hellraiser III: Hell on Earth (Contributor)
*Stuart Gordon: Interviews (Conversations with Filmmakers Series)
(Contributor)*

Black Beacon Books would like to thank our patrons, whose passion for great fiction and independent publishing helped make this collection happen.

If you'd like to join the team and reap the benefits, subscribe on our Patreon page at: *patreon.com/blackbeaconbooks*

The five patronage tiers are
Shipwreck Survivor, Moonlight Smuggler, Sea Witch, Assistant Keeper, and *Lighthouse Keeper.*

Dedication:

For the masters of the craft who've gone before.

Acknowledgements:

My thanks to Cameron at Black Beacon for being willing with this one, I know it's quite a niche subject. A huge thank you to Kim Newman for the terrific introduction, Greg Chapman for the stunning cover, and thank yous all round to the editors and publishers who took some of these stories in the first place. As always, hugs and big thank yous to all my friends in the writing and film/TV world, for their continual help both now and in the past; people like Mike Carey, Pete & Nicky Crowther, Simon Clark, the much missed Christopher Fowler, Alexandra Benedict, Michael Marshall Smith, Stephen Volk, Tim Lebbon and oh so many more. You guys know who you are! Lastly, a massive thank you to my lovely better half Marie for everything. Love you to the moon and back.

Previous Publication History:

In Hyding (Traumas, published by Black Shuck Books, 2020)
Signals (Ghosts, Spectral Press, 2013)
Life Sentence (Albions Alpträume: Zombies Eloy Edictions, 2006)
Humbuggered (Festive Fear, Tasmaniac, 2010)
The Greatest Mystery (Gaslight Arcanum, Edge Publishing, 2011)
Dracula in Love (Dead Things Issue 5, October/December 2000)
Heartless (Original to this Collection)
Masques (Return of the Raven, Horror Bound Books, 2009)
Paw People (Original to this Collection)
Thicker Than Water (Innsmouth Nightmares, PS Publishing, 2015)
The Grey Room (Original to this Collection)

INTRODUCTION BY KIM NEWMAN

An all-but-forgotten genre of popular music is the "answer song".

You know the drill. Ray Charles tops the charts with "Hit the Road, Jack" and Nina Simone responds with "Come On Back, Jack". The Coasters sing "Get a Job" and The Miracles reply "Got a Job". Barry Mann asks "Who Put the Bomp (in the Bomp, Bomp, Bomp)?" and Frankie Lyman somewhat grandiosely claims "I Put the Bomp (in the Bomp, Bomp, Bomp)". Pete Rodriguez declares "I Like It Like That" and The Bobbettes rather petulantly contradict him with "I Don't Like It Like That". Sometimes, very rarely, you remember the answer more than the question. The Beatles' "Back in the USSR" follows Chuck Berry's "Back in the USA". When pop culture really starts poppin', you get conversations. Everyone knows they're building on what came before, but sometimes they want to give the foundations a shake-up and get into an argument with predecessor works. Or sometimes creators are just inspired to wonder what happens next or what if things hadn't panned out that way.

Samuel Richardson's epistolary novel *Pamela; or: Virtue Rewarded* (1740) inspired Henry Fielding to write a parody—*Shamela*—and a sequel which is also a critique, *Joseph Andrews*, whose hero is the brother of Richardson's heroine. Fielding wasn't alone: there were novels called *Pamela's Conduct in High Life* and *The Anti-Pamela*, and the French writer Robert-Martin Lesuire wrote a *Paméla Française*. Some of these authors wanted to cut themselves in on the money, some were affronted by Richardson's worldview and wanted to take him to task, some wanted to continue the story beyond the original ending (which Richardson himself did in a sequel, *Pamela Volume Two*), some wanted to look at it from other angles. And that was what happened with the *first* English novel. Since then, every significant work of fiction in any medium has inspired others to pick up where the story ends or ask what happened before it started or consider that it might have played out better. Quite a few have written stories to "correct" elements of the original that don't meet their own standards. Ray Bradbury wrote an alternative final chapter for Ira Levin's *Rosemary's Baby*, which dodges damnation and (possibly unconsciously) echoes Honoré de Balzac, who was prompted by Charles Maturin's gothic masterpiece *Melmoth the Wanderer* to write a sequel *Melmoth Reconciled to the Church*.

Looking at my shelves, I see quite a few "answer novels". I'd particularly recommend Jean Rhys' *Wide Sargasso Sea*, the story of Mrs Rochester from *Jane Eyre*... the Flashman novels of George MacDonald Fraser, which continue the story of the bully from *Tom Brown's Schooldays*... Robert McCammon's *Usher's Passing*, an elaboration on the Rise Again of the House of Usher... Philip José Farmer's *Tarzan Alive!*, "a definitive biography of Lord Greystoke" (which, speak it in a whisper, I prefer to any of Edgar Rice Burroughs' books)... T.H. White's *Darkness at Pemberley*, an old dark house thriller set in the mansion from *Pride and Prejudice*... Valerie Martin's *Mary Reilly*, the story of Dr Jekyll's housemaid... Susan Kay's *Phantom*, a historical epic filling in the many gaps in Gaston Leroux' *The Phantom of the Opera*... and Chris Priestley's *Mister Creecher*, which follows the Frankenstein Monster into a Dickensian underworld. There are whole libraries of follow-ups to or deconstructions of Dracula, Frankenstein, Sherlock Holmes and Jane Austen—not to mention Shakespeare, or thriving comics, film and TV franchises which generate fan fictions so fast no chronicler could hope to keep up with it all.

The stories in this collection are all built on pre-existing works... sometimes, you'll know which world you're in from the titles or (if you sneak a look at the copyright page) the books in which they originally appeared... sometimes, it takes a while for the penny to drop as to which cornerstone of horror is under review. Paul Kane takes a range of approaches—revisionist, parodic, fannish, critical, humane, wicked, cruel. But these are love stories—in the sense that they were written by someone in love with the material... someone who recognises the sparks in stories that make us want to read and re-read them—and re-reading at different ages or in different moods shows just how set texts can shift in meaning depending on who we are—and feels an urge not to leave it at the last page.

Time for some ghosts...

Kim Newman, Islington 2023

IN HYDING

It was just my little joke.

Hyde. Hyding... Hiding. Amused me at any rate, I was only having my fun. Had to do something to entertain myself while I was biding my time, waiting in secret. Trapped. Because that's what I was for such a long time, you see. For so very long even before the serum—whose idea do you think that was anyway?—I was biding my time. Always with him, always watching.

Much later, when he was setting down his account of the whole affair, he'd call me the "curse of mankind" or "pure evil". Base and primal, responsible for all man's ills. A dark reflection, an ugly twin if you will. An urge to do the most horrific things, that little voice inside which encourages the worst behaviour possible. Selfishness and violence and... sexual depravity. The very thought of it makes me want to—

But no, he had his turn; his chance to set everything down and tell his side of the story. Now it is time for me to tell mine, to set the record straight. I mean, do you think I would have been able to do all those things if he hadn't wanted me to, if he hadn't enjoyed it as well? That loss of control, that feeling—it's almost as potent, as intoxicating as the drugs he took which allowed me to venture forth. Recriminations would be for afterwards, and not my domain. Acting in the moment, that's always been my speciality; not thinking or worrying about the consequences. That's someone else's problem. That was his speciality. Cleaning up messes.

Like that £100 cheque which had to be made out to the family of the unwitting child I... hurt. The clumsy bitch shouldn't have got in my way in the first place! Trampling was too good for her, if you ask me. But that bastard Enfield, chasing me and forcing recompense. Threatening a scandal. I should have just done to him what I did later on to Carew (and the delicious memory of that—the blood, striking him so hard with my cane I could hear the bones cracking—gives me a magnificent shiver of delight) but there were simply too many people around.

His money saved the day, my "other half", thanks in no small part to his family's wealth. It allowed me to push forward with my work just as the good doctor had done with his.

And his labours up to that point had been vital; without them I wouldn't have been able to have my... fun and games. My sport. The fact that he thought he was doing humanity some sort of great service, that to separate the two halves of oneself might mean one day he'd be able to eradicate the more unsavoury side, just added to the pleasure for me. Pure fantasy, as one cannot possibly exist without the other. Symbiosis, it's called. Night and day. To imagine that the world would be some sort of utopia without its darker tendencies is delusional in the extreme. Mankind would never have progressed had it not been for the faction I represent. Besides, imagine how boring that would be!

Nevertheless, it suited my purposes for him to think what he thought. For him to come to the conclusion he did.

Without his sickly-sweet drive to do good, I wouldn't have been presented with my little windows of opportunity. Portions of time in which I would go on my sprees, conduct myself in the manner *I* saw fit. Holding nothing back! Listen, if you think you know the story, you really don't. Actually, you don't know the half of it, my friend. Not in the slightest. Some of the things we... I did, it would turn your hair white. Why, this one time with a lady of the night—although, I have to remark she was no lady; not by the time I had finished with her anyway—well, I committed an act whereby I...

But no, I am becoming distracted once more. Where was I? Oh yes, the doctor. So, it was imperative he take up medicine. Develop a keen interest in the human form growing up—beyond the obvious which I had been fuelling in him for a number of years. It was I who subtly encouraged him to spy upon the maids at the family home. And especially through the windows of their quarters on the lower floors, catching them in various states of undress. On other occasions there were instances of relations between Meg the scullery maid and Robinson the gardener. They thought they were being oh so clever with their secrets and schemes. Arranging their meetings in the woods or the shed, never suspecting their antics were being scrutinised. Rutting away, him thrusting into her up against a tree or over the lawnmower, her cries of pleasure often more than I could stand; not when I could do nothing about it. When all I wanted to do was slit Robinson's throat, bathe in his blood, and then take Meg myself. Squeezing her breasts so hard that she would let out a different kind of cry altogether.

It was more than Henry could bear as well, verging on his teens—images he would often take away with him so that when he was alone, hiding away...

Never caught, never seen.

But there again, that just proves how necessary the other half of the equation is. Not just Meg and Robinson, lust guiding their actions, but the ability to be able to defend oneself should the boy have been discovered. Defend, conquer. Taking what you desire in more ways than one. Why, nations... whole *empires* have been built on such philosophies. Have risen up out of the need to plunder, to expand one's horizons. Of course, they have often burnt themselves out as well, but that which burns brightly can only burn for so long. As was the case in our situation, too. All good things must come to an end.

Do they not?

Distracted again, must try and focus—communicate all this while it is still fresh in my... my mind. That makes me smile, gives me cause to chuckle certainly. Henry the boy-child, the keen observer, and his nature studies. That's where we'd got to, wasn't it. Him and his high ideals, and yet he was corrupted from the start. From the moment he first lied about whether he'd knocked over the hydrangea in the parlour causing the soil to stain the carpet, or stole that apple from the market stall on a trip to town with his father. How appropriate it should be that particular fruit, eh? No doubt all the time putting it down to that shadow cast over all men. Lead us not into temptation? No, lead away, that's my philosophy. Give in to it! The more tempting the better!

But, as I must also do, it was necessary for him to follow a certain path—in spite of a leaning towards industry. Crucial that his interests be diverted towards science and medicine rather than steam engines and mechanics, especially in an age that was embracing such studies.

Did one influence the other, the idea of ridding society of its ills leading to his taking up arms in the laboratory against it—or the other way around? Whilst studying how things "tick" did he come up with the notion of *divide* and conquer this time? A lifetime's obsession, to separate out the good from the bad then destroy it? Impossible to do, simply impossible!

It was, however, possible to facilitate the bad to thrive. To bring it to the fore, let it rise to the surface just like those empires rose. And fell. Let us not forget that they also fell... How glorious, though, were they when they were at their height? How glorious was my own time in the limelight!

Before that could possibly happen, there was still much to do. Much to consider. Failures and successes, until that secret ingredient was found. The one which made it all possible, so he believed. An impurity in the chemical, he posited, that made the whole thing work in the first place. I recall one of those very early experiments, when the "change"—as he came to call it—lasted but a few moments at most. Definitely didn't take. Didn't assist my *taking* over, taking control. Oh, the frustration of it!

However, I suppose the anticipation of this made the first time he got it right all the sweeter. That night when he drank the potion and the nausea come upon him, and his bones began to contort; making him lighter, making him feel younger, freer. As he once described it, the caged devil being set free—and it was not a million miles from the truth. An apt description.

I will never forget when he saw himself during that inaugural transformation. When I allowed him to see what he'd become in the mirror, after crossing the yard and venturing to his bedroom, knowing his own staff were sound asleep. I could feel his shock at what he witnessed thrown back at him in that reflective glass; what I know Enfield also described as deformities. How dare he! And while it is correct to say that my visage is somewhat distinctive, I prefer to think of myself as unique in appearance. Down to earth, as I am in all things.

And so, the genie was out of the bottle at last! My friend had proven his worth, proven to be an excellent choice after all. I cannot tell you how wonderful it felt to be unfettered once more, to feel at home in that skin instead of merely a prisoner. But, yet again, I was to be denied, my hold on that form not as stable as I had assumed. This was very much in evidence when the doctor effected a change back into his former self; panic gripping him and countering all my efforts. My grasp was slippery back then, and as desperate as I was to remain, I found myself imprisoned once more. Not on the outside looking in, but the inside looking out. However, he had experienced what it could be like to live without boundaries. To care not for rules and regulations. I needed only to wait a short while longer. It would only be a matter of time before he gave in to those temptations again, and then... and then...

As he said himself in his "confession", he fell into slavery. He became *my* slave, in effect. Once we had started, he even began to take my "suggestions" as direct orders when he transformed back. I would need a hidden place, for example, so that I could conduct my most private affairs away from the eyes of others. Thus it became essential to rent and furnish the room in Soho (the perfect location, populated by the dispossessed and the depressed alike) accessed by way of a certain door. We would also need to engage the services of a housekeeper who could be discrete. Bribery or the threat of violence, either worked as far as I was concerned.

In addition, it was necessary for his staff, for butler Poole especially, to grant me the run of his own home, not to mention arranging for me to be the sole beneficiary of his funds should he suddenly vanish without trace (securing the services of that wet fish lawyer Utterson to do so would arouse suspicion, I realised, but there was no other way unfortunately). Believe me when I say I was hoping to make the change permanent at some point, to switch places as it were. For him to become the prisoner and I the keeper of the keys, strong enough—stronger than him now by far—to ignore his pitiful pleas for release. What could he offer me, when all was said and done? Nothing to match what I had offered him.

His detainment would not be without fringe benefits. As he did with Meg and Robinson, he would be able to watch as I indulged my fantasies. No, not fantasies anymore. *Realities*. Things he could not possibly have dreamed of if he'd had a lifetime to do so. Many lifetimes. What some might call barbarity, and others would almost without a doubt call depravity, I call nourishment. It fed me, as a bountiful meal would feed a ravenous man (as the long pig had for me on special occasions). And I *was* ravenous, no two ways about that. It had been so long since I'd indulged in all the pleasures flesh had to offer.

The memories will have to sustain me, I know that. Flashes of nights when I gambled in the most unsavoury of places, drank—but not so much I might inadvertently lose the reins of this particular carriage—and fought. Fists connecting with jaws, breaking noses with wet crunches. Biting, tearing and choking. I took what I wanted, when I wanted. The laws of man did not apply to me, they never have. I did not make them, do not agree with them. Some say that without such laws there would be chaos, but I say what's wrong with a little chaos? All right, a *lot* of chaos? Civility is all an illusion anyway, the strongest and most dominant force in this world is that of will: to do and not think twice. You people spend so long trying to curb it all, when it is not realistic or achievable. It can never be wiped out, I do know that. When he loosened the shackles, hoping to find a way to stamp what I am out completely, all he did was make me stronger. And as much as he talked about being revolted by it, he enjoyed witnessing my exploits as much as he had back when he was in his teens. It had only taken a nudge then, only took one when he was older. One step at a time; a step in the right direction, so to speak.

He also managed to convince himself he wasn't to blame for any of it, that what occurred when he took the potion was not his fault. And, while I can be convincing, while I *ached* for him to create more of the solution, he still had a choice back then. Not like when I took over, when I had control; then there was no choice at all. A grey area, I suppose. Only natural he should seek to blame someone—*something*—else.

They thought he was being blackmailed, Utterson and co. That I had something over poor old Henry—which I did, as it happened, *lots* of things, but that wasn't the reason for him telling them all to leave me alone. He was scared of me, as he was right to be. Scared of what I could do, more timid every single day—night—I was out there. Had seen what I was capable of, thought it best that it should be his turn now to hide away and leave me to it.

Oh, there were efforts to resist, I'm not saying there weren't. He did well for a while, just before what happened with Sir Danvers Carew, but he was always going to weaken eventually. And it was when he finally did after an extended period that made me really go berserk. Made me do what I did with the cane... There was speculation, I know, as to what we were both doing down there and, yes, you would be right in thinking that my particular tastes do not just run to the fairer sex. Why limit yourself, why limit your pleasure?

But, of course, Carew had certain reservations. When it came right down to it, he got cold feet about the entire thing, which just made me frustrated. Made me angry—and he was the one who paid the price. I needed to express myself in other ways, but was not aware as I stood there raining blows down upon him, harder and harder until the cane itself broke in two, until I could see his brains, that *I* myself was being observed. That it would set in motion a chain of events which would lead to the police becoming involved, for a manhunt to begin, initiated by the lawyer—Carew's lawyer—Utterson, who had every reason to hate me. Not even the note Henry showed him apologising for everything that had happened—and imagine how sick that made me feel!—put him off the scent. He thought the good doctor had forged it because of the similarity in handwriting.

It necessitated a change in plans, put a halt to my activities temporarily. I had to go into hiding once more, simply so I wouldn't be found. Yet I retained a degree of control which hadn't been there before, which hadn't been apparent until then. However, this did not prevent *him* from bringing others into this affair. From writing his account of all this to give to his friend Dr Lanyon, to be opened in the event of Henry's death. Something that he had to prove by transforming again, and the only comfort I could gain from that was it drove Lanyon to an early grave.

More meddling, people not able to leave us—me—alone. Enfield, Utterson, even the staff on occasion. All interfering, preventing me from having my fun.

Even I could see that all this was heading towards its inevitable conclusion. I recognise the signs. He was growing weaker and weaker, enabling me to emerge on a more frequent basis—in his sleep, in the daytime—but at the same time it was taking its toll on his body and consciousness. As all of this reached its tipping point, it

23

was just a matter of letting him think he was making the ultimate sacrifice. That he would stop me permanently, trap me. He had just enough resolve to "bring the life of that unhappy Henry Jekyll to an end" and die a hero. Ha!

By that time I was long gone, I'd vacated his pitiful, broken body and was away. Nebulous, as I was before I found him in the first place when he was little and I attached myself to him. Wormed my way inside my new "home", accepting that—in my own weakened condition and without being able to exert any degree of control beyond whispering, suggesting—I would be interred until the experiments could begin anew. He was the best subject thus far, I have to give him that. The most malleable eventually, and the best equipped to cater to my particular and inimitable needs.

You see, I would like to take credit for all of men's ills. Would like to say to you that I represent the darkness, the shadow inside every one of us. But that is simply not true. It just served my purposes for old Henry to believe in the notion. Why, if he had known the truth about the parasite within him, the spirit that had begun its own journey of discovery so many years ago—one "step" at a time, and in the right direction hopefully—flitting from host to host, lifetime after lifetime, unable to survive without them (a true symbiosis), following a certain path... If he had known all that, it would have left his keen mind useless. Instead, we came the closest yet to my being able to take total control over a body, to beat down the soul which inhabits it and dominate at will.

I admit, he had his uses—and Henry made a good place to conceal myself when the authorities were looking for me. The trick would've been if I could have taken on his shape, but still remained... well, me. Hiding in plain sight, able to flit back and forth but still *be* Hyde. The ultimate goal, and something to strive towards for next time. When another empire rises, now that this one has fallen, now that this host has fallen.

It is why he could never have defeated me, because he did not fully understand the enemy he was fighting against. How could he? This all began so long ago, when I first separated myself from my original body; the true separation in this case. Dispossessed... searching for someone *to* eventually possess. Since then I have gone from body to body, always indulging myself but seeking a way to make it permanent. Different concoctions, sometimes even magicks like the ones that brought me to this state in the first place, but always the same objective.

So much hiding, so much waiting.

As I do now, locked inside this new unwitting child's form, who will slowly but surely learn not to get in my way. Subtly I shall steer events towards where they must go again, towards the sciences whilst at the same time nudging him to entertain me; to show me sights that simultaneously frustrate but build the appetites, until I can break free once more and partake for real. Always watching, waiting, always with him.

As for the story, this true account, I know there is nobody listening to that. I am simply relating it to myself, another way to while away the time. What do I care that folk believe Henry's version of events? Utterson, Enfield... all idiots! It will be long forgotten when I emerge victorious again to wreak havoc. Although I have learned the value of not letting myself be seen too quickly, not coming even close to getting caught.

And the name, variations of such used over and over, but this one was definitely the best. My favourite. Hyde. Hyding... Hiding. Amused me at any rate, entertained me.

In the end I was only having my fun.

It was just my little joke.

SIGNALS

"Halloa! Below there!"

The words echoed, following her up and out of a dream that was already well on its way to being forgotten, leaving behind only a faint unpleasant odour.

Robin opened her tired eyes, sleep like glue trying to keep them together. For a second or two she thought she was blind. She rubbed it away, seeing again, and glanced blearily over sideways at the clock display. In spite of the pills, she was awake again at 2:30am. It was always the same story of late: they'd get her off to sleep— especially when, as Robin did on occasion, she mixed them with a little red wine—that familiar hot heaviness weighing down her eyelids until she couldn't keep them open anymore. And inevitably she'd drift off... but not for long.

Never for long.

She'd wake in the early hours, trying, struggling to hold on to that feeling. But she might as well have been trying to trap smoke in a cage.

No smoke... No smoke without—

Now that the thought had entered her head, she needed a cigarette so badly it hurt. Simple cause and effect. Robin flicked on the bedside light, shielding her eyes from the glare with one hand and scrabbling around on the table beside her for the packet of Bensons there.

She got up off the mattress, which was just as sticky as her eyes had been moments before. Her body was slick with sweat, her vest and pyjama bottoms clinging to her skin. Comfy nightwear, no guests tonight in her bed. She wasn't sure whether that was a good or bad thing. Sex helped you sleep, didn't it? Or was that just for men?

26

Robin flapped her top to cool down. It was barely even Spring, not *that* hot yet. So why...?

She snatched up the lighter, pulling out one of the ciggies and lighting it. She drew in a satisfying lungful, relishing the taste. She'd tried a few times to quit, but never managed it. Tried gum and patches, but somehow smoking them didn't have the same effect— ha, ha!—so had always returned to the weed that had made her its bitch back in her college days.

Moments later, she was downstairs making herself a coffee. Robin knew from experience that there was no point even trying to get back off to sleep again, so her best option was to hop herself up on caffeine. She had work first thing in the morning... wait, it *was* the morning... so her priorities now changed from trying to sleep to trying to keep herself awake. She'd probably just watch whatever crap was on TV, feeding into the really early morning breakfast stuff: non-entities mugging for the camera in the hopes they'd get noticed; get promoted to a later slot where they'd be interviewing celebrities and talking about last night's soaps.

And so the world kept turning, people went about their business, and eventually Robin had to get ready, putting off looking in the bathroom mirror as long as she could—attempting to ignore the serious bags under her eyes, the way her dark hair was thinning.

Getting herself ready to head off and catch her bus, the first one running at that ungodly time of day.

*   *   *

She arrived long before the rush hour had even started. The only people on the roads at that time of day were shift workers, either heading off to their jobs or returning home from them (how Robin envied the latter right at that moment, maybe it would be easier to catch some z's in the daytime?), the insane...

And her. Though it was a fine line. You don't have to be mad to work here and all that.

Robin used her chipped ID to enter the building, having already passed security checks at the gate. She often wondered if all that was necessary, but in this day and age someone could really do some damage if they got in here and screwed around with things. Forget

27

blowing shit up or crashing planes, this would be chaos on a level nobody had ever seen before. There again, why would anyone bother in such a low key area? This wasn't London, after all. Now, doing this job down there really would *drive* you mad.

As it was, Robin had to oversee the smooth running of sixty junctions around the city. It mostly happened by computer—what didn't these days?—but something as important as keeping the flow moving also required that human touch. Yes, those loops of cables under the tarmac at crossings detected the metal passing over them and sent the information off to a central computer that could work out when the busiest or quietest times of day were, how long to leave lights on red and how often to change them. Theirs was one of the most sophisticated systems in operation, they'd been told, being trialled there, no less. It had only been in operation six months, and already it had cut jams down by twenty percent. It all ran like clockwork, was backed up to the hilt—even the back-ups had back-ups—but even so, actual people were still needed to make judgement calls. Could override a decision one of the machines had made, tightening things up just that little bit more, making the flow quicker—especially during times of greater congestion. Not that much to do, but with so much depending on it.

There was little more than a skeleton crew remaining now, nothing like the team she'd had when she first started working in this field. That's something they didn't tell them when the computers began taking over: most of their jobs would be forfeit. They weren't told until the first round of redundancies, as a matter of fact.

"Hey Harry," said Robin, as she entered the darkened room filled with monitors. The man she was addressing sat at a curved desk, headset on—allowing him to communicate with the other controllers still on the payroll—resting snugly atop his balding head. "How're things this morning?"

Harry looked up at her, but over the rims of his glasses that he needed for close-up work. Staring at, *scrutinising*, screens like these for hours on end really did your retinas in. Occupational hazard, like varicose veins for hairdressers.

"Pretty quiet so far, as you'd expect. It is already starting to build near Telford Lane," he told her, "though that's probably got something to do with the roadworks not far away. Bloody temporary lighting," he muttered. They had no jurisdiction over those kinds of set-ups, sadly.

"Kay," replied Robin.

"You all right?" asked Harry. "You don't look too good this morning."

So all that Polyfilla on the face and it still wasn't concealing her tiredness. Great. "Just didn't sleep well again," she told him. It wasn't like he hadn't heard it before. When she was younger, she could get away with it more. But now on the wrong side of thirty-five, it was catching up with her. She'd never slept all that well, but it was definitely getting worse. And so was how she felt. "I'm fine," she lied.

"Fancy a drink after work later?" Harry asked.

Robin shook her head. It wasn't that she thought Harry was after anything more than a drink—they were friends and there had never been any hint of it going any further... apart from at that Christmas do when he'd had too much to drink and kept saying quite earnestly how much he really, *really* valued their friendship, especially since his divorce; then she'd smiled and said she did as well, before making her excuses and exiting stage left. Didn't want to give him the wrong... Neither of them had mentioned it since, thankfully, but she sensed Harry had got the message. It wasn't that she couldn't see something happening in that department, it was more if it did then that would ruin their friendship forever. Her life was a train wreck, and she didn't want to drag him into that. It was what she told herself, at any rate. "Got something on," was all she would say, and Harry didn't push it. He just went back to work, bringing up other images on the screen.

As she was about to leave him to it, Robin caught sight of something on one of those monitors. It was an impressive thing, Edgecross roundabout, and one that used to scare many motorists to death. People would go around it like they were on *Wacky Races* at one time of day, until the much-needed traffic light system was put in place. The trouble was the vehicles feeding into this from the motorway and dual carriages were hitting the massive circle at 70 mph in some cases.

Even now, some drivers didn't seem to understand which lane they were supposed to be in, and there had been a number of prangs

29

since the new layout had been implemented. But it was still safer than it ever had been. The traffic was beginning to build up here as well now, local commuters mainly, although Robin knew it wouldn't be long before those coming from further afield joined them, branching off from larger, faster roads. She watched for a few moments, making sure all was as it should be; the cars like rats being herded around a maze.

But it wasn't that her eyes were particularly drawn to. It was a shadow on the screen, lingering at the mouth of the roundabout's largest major access point. It wasn't far away from the first of the lights, which allowed vehicles to stream in from slip roads. Robin frowned, took a step forward, her sore eyes narrowing. The shadow moved, and now it looked for all the world like a figure.

That part of Edgecross wasn't even pedestrianised, so what was—

"Harry, do you see that?" Robin was by his side again, bending.

"See what?" Harry asked, head darting about, checking several of the monitors at once.

"There!" Robin was pointing now at the one showing the large roundabout from above. "Someone's playing silly buggers at Edgecross."

"What? Where?" Harry was as aware as she was of the penalty for being caught anywhere near that roundabout; there were enough signs dotted about down there, as if you needed them. What kind of lunatic would want to risk getting mowed over reaching that part of the busy intersection? Sure, there had been the occasional person late at night, drunk out of their skulls, who'd tried to use that road as a short cut and wound up regretting it. There had even been some that had wandered out into traffic intentionally, though there were much easier and less painful ways to commit suicide.

Robin was at the keyboard, bringing up that section of screen, dragging it to the monitor in front of them and zooming in.

It showed the traffic light, but nothing else.

"I don't see any..."

Ignoring Harry, Robin's fingers passed over the keyboard, moved the small joystick, bringing up sections that were adjacent to the lights there. Pulling back and out to give a wider angle.

Nothing. No shadow. No figure.

She blinked, backed away from the keyboard. "I could have sworn there was someone..."

"Nobody there now, anyway. Maybe a mark on the camera?" he suggested, though they could both see there were no smears there. The screen was crystal clear, not even a scratch. "Or some maintenance bod doing a recce?"

They had no maintenance scheduled for today, especially at this time in the morning. But still...

Robin squeezed her eyes shut tight, pinched the bridge of her nose. Then she moved away from the desk. "Ignore me, I'm just seeing things. Spots in front of my eyes or something."

Harry was looking at her, a worried expression on his face that was actually quite sweet. "If you're that exhausted, maybe you should see someone about it?" he offered.

"Yeah, maybe," she replied, but didn't tell him that she already had. That the new doctor in the practice, who'd taken over after her usual one retired, had almost refused her a repeat prescription. Had only let her have the last batch of sleeping pills on one condition.

A condition that was actually the real reason why she couldn't have that drink with him later on.

*　*　*

A condition in the form of the man opposite her now, reclining in his leather chair.

A condition wearing a shirt open at the neck, revealing the edges of a forest of chest hair that had almost made Robin's top lip curl with disgust the first time she'd seen it. A condition called Saul, who'd bid her to take a seat opposite while he sat, crossed his legs— the friction from the cream nylon trousers making a *thwipping* noise Spider-Man would have been proud of—and rested a clipboard with notes attached to it on one knee.

As Robin had taken her place, joking uncomfortably about the lack of a couch, eliciting a smile that was more like a grimace from Saul, he'd flicked through pages attached to that clipboard and glanced over at her from time to time.

"So..."

Robin shrugged. "So?"

Saul flipped through more pages. "So, what brings you here today,

31

Miss Dean?"

She was tempted to say a taxi, but bit her tongue. Another shrug was all she could manage.

"According to this, you're suffering with bouts of severe insomnia. Is that correct?"

He knew it was, she could see it written all over his face even if it wasn't written down on the notes. "I guess so."

"You *guess* so?"

"All right. I am. But it's nothing to worry about. Nothing—"

"A good night's sleep wouldn't fix, eh?"

"I was being prescribed pills," she said, a little too defensively—but then his tone was seriously pissing her off.

"Which deal with the immediate symptoms, but not the underlying cause. Once we figure out what that is, we can move forwards." He nodded, as if agreeing with himself. "I'd imagine your job can be quite stressful?"

Robin fidgeted about in her seat. "No more than a lot of others."

"Oh, don't sell yourself short. You're responsible for a lot of lives."

"People are responsible for their *own* lives." Again, too defensive. She needed to tone it down, try and make nice. Maybe he'd let her off with a few stupid relaxation exercises.

"Quite, quite... It's a curious position, how did you end up doing what you do for a living?"

A third shrug. "I just kind of stumbled into it."

"Bit of a specific thing, though, isn't it?"

"Look, what do you want from me? I saw the job, I applied." Robin folded her arms, then realised what it would look like and unfolded them again.

"So it didn't have anything to do with what happened when you were a child, then?" Saul uncrossed his legs, leaned forward—allowing her to see down into the valley of his hairy chest. She pulled a face which he took as a response to his question. He gave another nod, which Robin immediately countered with:

"No. Not a thing. And anyway, how do you know about—"

"It's all here," said Saul, tapping his clipboard. "Contrary to popular belief, our different departments do talk to each other occasionally. And now all the data's centralised, all on databases...

32

Well, I'm sure you understand."

Robin thought about all those loops of cable gathering information about the movement of vehicles. Imagined herself at one of those lights at some point in the past, that she'd travelled over one particular loop and her details had been logged forever somewhere. Though she realised it was much simpler than that. It was a matter of record what had happened, about how she'd been orphaned at age six.

"You were... you were in the car when the accident happened, weren't you?" Saul's expression was expectant, as if he was simply waiting for her to unburden herself to him. Right, cracked it, another one sorted. That was easy, wasn't it?

"I don't remember anything about it," Robin stated honestly. "I was too little."

"The mind remembers more than we think." Saul allowed himself a slight pause to admire his own unintentional in-joke. "But it can also hide things from us, Robin. Is it okay if I call you Robin?"

She waved a hand, couldn't care less what he called her.

"You see, when we experience a traumatic event, the brain sometimes tries to prevent... to *block* the signals being sent from our eyes and ears because they're too difficult for us to immediately deal with. It's a protective mechanism, but we can't keep those memories locked away forever. It's impossible, especially when our subconscious is in play. They seep out in various ways, in the choices we make in life. In our dreams."

Robin looked away, pretending to study a painting on the wall of a landscape recreated in splodges of colour. Then she forced herself to turn back to Saul. "I don't remember any of it. I was too young." She repeated the words, parrot fashion. The same answer she'd given for years when asked about it.

Saul nodded. "I understand. It must have been a hell of a thing to go through. Being the only survivor."

Hell of a thing... like going *through* Hell.

A faint, unpleasant smell... of... of burning. Burning paint, burning rubber and something else. Smoke?

And those words: *"Halloa! Below there!"*

Robin shook her head, rising. "It was a mistake to come here."

"Wait," said Saul, "I'm just trying to help you, Robin. If you don't

33

confront this stuff in a controlled environment, it'll only fester. Emerge in ways you really don't want. Trust me."

But she was already out of the door, marching away down the corridor.

*   *   *

Robin managed to keep the tears in check until she got home.

Why was she crying? It was bloody stupid. She really couldn't remember anything about the accident. Hadn't even thought about it in years. So... what? Was she crying for the life she might have led, had her mother and father not been killed in that collision?

Being the only survivor.

And that's what she was, wasn't it? How she'd always seen herself. A survivor.

Only survivor.

That life... It had ended on the day 33,000 lbs of tow truck had slammed into their estate, ripping the car in two. Robin had been in the back seat, thrown clear by the impact. Her parents hadn't been so lucky; they'd died almost instantly, along with the driver of the truck who'd been three times over the drink-driving limit. The end of three lives. Four, if you counted hers.

But the start of another one, with her Aunty Jean—Mum's sister—and her husband, Ken. They were her godparents, and they'd taken her in; been glad to, as they hadn't been able to have kids of their own. She'd had a happy childhood, still nestled in the bosom of her family. Just not the childhood she might have had, is all. Could have been worse.

Robin was drying her eyes and lighting her third cigarette since getting back, when she decided to give them a call. Well, give Jean a call at any rate—her uncle having passed away two years ago from prostate cancer.

"Hell..."

Like going through *Hell?*

"Hell-hello," said her aunty, voice tentative as always since she lost her husband. Robin never wanted to get like that, to be so reliant on a partner being there you were scared to even answer the phone.

"It's me," Robin said, taking another drag on her ciggie.

34

"Oh, hello love!"

"Halloa!..."

"Are you... Is everything okay? You sound a bit... well..." She let the sentence trail off.

Robin thought for a moment. Yes, everything was okay. Apart from things being stirred up that shouldn't be, emotions like hornets in a nest that's just been shaken. "I'm... Yeah, I'm all right."

"Good. That's good, sweetheart."

"Look, Aunty Jean..." Not Mum, never Mum. Because you can remember your Mum, can't you? Sights and smells and sounds. No. The brain cutting off signals, protecting you. "When I was... I mean, when I first came to live with you, can you remember, did I ever have any sleepless nights? Any dreams? Any nightmares?"

There was a second's hesitation before her aunty answered: "You've never been the best of sleepers, love." She knew that already; wasn't what she'd asked. "Why?"

"It's just that, well, I've been thinking about what happened... back then."

"You don't want to be thinking about all that. You couldn't remember anything," said Jean, a little too quickly. "You were *too young* to remember anything."

"Yeah." Robin blew a stream of smoke out of the side of her mouth. "Yeah, I know."

"Listen, I was meaning to call you anyway. To see if you'd got your invite yet?"

"Invite?" asked Robin, and the change of subject had worked its magic. A shifting of attention. Something else to focus on.

"To the family get-together? At your cousin Neville's place? He's trying to get as many of us to go along as he can. It's been years since we had a proper family reunion."

Robin vaguely recalled something coming through by email a few weeks ago, but it hadn't really registered. "Oh, I'm not sure I—"

"He told me to remind you."

"When is it?"

"Week on Sunday. Oh go on, please say you're going. We can go together." More for her aunty's benefit than hers, Robin agreed to think about it and said she would let her know.

After saying their goodbyes, Robin hung up, had a few more puffs

35

of her cigarette, and wandered into the kitchen to see what ready meals there were for dinner.

It wasn't long before she found herself opening a bottle of Shiraz to go with her store brand fish pie.

And, by the time she was ready to pop another sleeping pill, more than half of the bottle had been polished off.

*   *   *

She still couldn't remember her dreams—nightmares?—but she was wrenched violently from her sleep by the sound of bells.

Of *alarms*, to be precise. Not one, but at least two car alarms outside: close and piercing enough to wake her, but too far away to do anything about. By the time she was up and had got to the window to call out—

"Hey, cut it out down there!"

—they'd stopped anyway. Probably just some cats setting them off or something. Or the wind; it was getting up she noticed, a chill creeping in through the open window that she closed again.

But one she didn't really feel. Because she was still hot, could still feel the intense heat, burning.

Paint, rubber... something else.

There was still a taste in the back of her throat she put down to the wine, and that she attempted to clear by lighting another ciggie.

She'd made it to 3am, which would have been cause for celebration in itself, had she not turned in at gone one, cursing what had looked like the beginnings of a good movie on TV and which she could barely remember the end of now.

Robin slumped back onto the bed, feeling the effects of the Shiraz and pills still in her system, making her drowsy, but not sending her back off to sleep. Before she knew it, it was time to get ready for work again.

And all the while she was washing, plastering on more make-up, she couldn't help thinking about what else she was struggling to remember. The crash, and its aftermath. The impact (poor choice of words) it had had on her life, the road... the road not taken. No, snatched away from her.

Had it just been fate, or might it all have been avoided?

It'll only fester, emerge in ways you really don't want.

Was that what was happening, after all these years? Were the (signal) barriers finally breaking down in her mind?

Trust me, Saul had said, like he'd seen it happen before. Or was speaking from personal experience perhaps?

Robin bit her lip, then left to catch the bus.

*   *   *

"You have a full driver's license, yet you don't drive."

Saul let the words settle, before continuing. "Why is that, Robin?"

"I-I just prefer not to, that's all." Back again in the room, sitting opposite the man. It had taken a few more days of appalling nights, of comments at work, some from management, and for her to run out of pills before she'd called up and made another appointment. "I don't really like driving. Not everyone does."

"True. That's true, of course. So why go to the bother and expense of learning at all then?"

Robin leaned back. She almost got out her packet of Bensons and lit one, but like seemingly everywhere else in the fucking country it was banned inside, in places like this particularly. Places where they "cured" people. "My uncle thought it would be a good thing."

"Make you less scared of it?"

"I wasn't... I'm not scared."

Saul nodded, but it was one of those nods this time that said he didn't believe a word of it. "And you stopped—when?"

"I can't remember exactly," Robin answered, without even really thinking about it.

Saul looked down at his clipboard again, then up at Robin, looking directly at her. "Perhaps around the time of the tunnel incident?"

Robin rose, just like she'd done on her first visit here—but instead of storming out this time, she skirted around the back of the chair. She stared at him, opening and closing her mouth a couple of times before speaking. "Jesus, is there anything you don't have about me on that fucking clipboard?"

"Calm down, Robin."

"Calm? I am calm," she snapped, but her breathing said otherwise.

"Why don't you sit down again and we can discuss it."

Robin looked at him sideways. "It's got nothing to do with anything."

"Then you won't mind if we discuss it, will you?" He had her there.

"I wasn't even involved in it. Not really," she argued. "I just happened to be there."

"But you *were* injured." He tapped his papers. "That's why it's on record, Robin. That's why it's on my 'fucking clipboard'." Saul grinned. "Minor burns, smoke inhalation, wasn't it?"

Of course, I'm a survivor.

Robin said nothing, just took her seat again. "I wasn't even driving that day, it was my then boyfriend." She hadn't thought about Tony in years. Back then he'd been *the one*, but they all are when you're young, aren't they? She hadn't thought about the tunnel, either.

"But you witnessed the accident, didn't you?"

"Not as such. Look, I haven't... It was a long time ago."

"Like your mum and dad. You don't remember?"

Robin looked away, gazing over at the painting again. The dabs of colour forming a picture. Close up, it would just be a mess, but pull away far enough and it created an image. Pull back the camera, a wider angle and—

"Robin?" Saul's voice broke in, and she faced him once more. "Talk to me. Cast your mind back, tell me what happened."

"There really isn't much to tell."

"Oh, I doubt that."

"Okay, all right. So we were on the bridge, saw the vehicles enter from both sides. Then..."

Saul peered at his notes again. "Glitch in the system according to the official report. I did a little digging. Wouldn't have happened on your watch, would it?"

Robin ignored the question. "I got Tony—that was my boyfriend's name—I got him to pull over. I climbed out. I could see..." She shook her head.

"The tunnel wasn't wide enough for two lots of traffic, was it?"

She shook her head. Both lights on green? Damn straight it wouldn't have happened on her watch, for fuck's sake! Those poor people *hadn't* ignored the signals, had they?—and look what had happened. The signals were meant to be your friends; they weren't supposed to hurt you. To... to kill you. "I could see the smoke."

"People were in trouble, you wanted to help them. So you went down there."

"I shouted down first," she corrected. "But I couldn't get anyone to hear me." And Tony, standing and gawping. Was that why she'd chucked him? Because she'd seen what he was really like? Not everyone's first instinct is to put themselves in harm's way.

"You saved lives that day, Robin. The paramedics said so."

"I only did what anyone would have," she replied, though she was still thinking about Tony. What he *didn't* do. There were tears welling in her eyes again, and she quickly wiped them away with the back of her hand. "Look, I don't really want to talk about all this. I..."

Saul nodded again. "I understand. You've spent as much time tucking that incident away as you have the other one. But you work with this kind of stuff, day in, day out. It makes sense you'd want to ensure that what happened then, what happened to your parents, never happens again. At the same time, though, you can't run from your past. You can't pretend it didn't happen. It's a part of you. It was a conscious choice to go down there and help; you should be proud of that. You should *embrace* those memories."

Embrace them? Robin's face soured. "I-I have to go," she said.

This time Saul didn't argue. Their hour was almost up, he'd get his money either way, thought Robin. He simply told her to make another appointment to see him at a time convenient for her.

Robin didn't make it home before the floodgates burst again, though. She only made it as far as the Ladies' in the medical centre.

Thankfully, they were empty, so she found a cubicle and slid down the wall of it—grabbing handfuls of toilet roll on her way.

At one point she thought the tears were never, ever going to stop.

*   *   *

It was a few days later when she saw the shadow again.

This time she was alone in the main control room, Harry having gone for a short break after she said she'd cover for him. "Something

39

I ate at lunch," he explained. *Really too much information*, she'd thought.

Robin was monitoring the mid-afternoon traffic; not horrendous at this point, but now some people were returning from late lunches, she guessed. And from about three in the afternoon onwards, things would start to build again until hitting the high of the five-six o'clock climax of the rush hour period.

She told herself it was just routine, but somehow ended up flitting back to the Edgecross roundabout. And within seconds she saw it; that shape standing by the mouth of the main entrance, next to the lighting system. A dark shadow, made even darker by the black and white of the surveillance system they used.

Robin looked around again, maybe hoping Harry was back already—but there was fat chance of that. He'd still be in the loo; not crying, like her, but—

Not a mark on the camera or monitor, not a spot in front of her — admittedly—still tired eyes. But something that resembled a figure, something moving, trying to form itself.

Something that was *waving*. One arm definitely, distinctly crossing the other. But this was no greeting, it was more like a warning. Whoever was down there was trying to get the attention of the traffic, flowing into and onto the roundabout at speed now the lights were a go.

Once more, Robin zeroed in on that particular patch. Zooming in close. But, as with the painting in Saul's office, now she lost all sense of the picture. The shadows which had converged there suddenly dispersed, vanished.

And when she pulled out again the figure had gone completely.

She tapped at the keyboard, playing back the digitally recorded images from the last few minutes. Nothing. Gritting her teeth, she punched in the footage from the time and date of the other morning. She scanned the monitor, her eyes on fire. Nothing there either. No proof that anyone had even been down there, causing a nuisance.

Robin slammed her fist on the desk, causing a—thankfully empty—styrofoam coffee cup to leap up and plummet to the ground. "Shit!"

"Whoa, whoa—"

"Halloa!"

40

Robin looked up and over, saw Harry in the doorway, back from his trip to evacuate his bowels. "Robin? Is everything all right?"

She opened her mouth to speak, to tell him she'd seen the shadow again—then said nothing. How would that sound, how would it look? *You're just exhausted... You should see someone about it... You should maybe take some time off...*

You should probably never come back, Robin.

"Er... Yeah, it's nothing."

"But you seemed—"

"I said it was fucking nothing, Harry. *Okay?*"

Harry looked as if all the air had been punched out of him.

Robin shook her head, apologised, and went over. "Things are just a bit, I don't know, weird at the moment."

"Right," Harry said, but she could still see the hurt in his eyes.

"Don't worry about it. We'll do that drink sometime soon, yeah?" That seemed to cheer him up, but it did little to comfort her.

Robin's hands were shaking as she stepped outside of the room. As she found an empty stretch of corridor (it wasn't that difficult around here) with a window, which she opened and smoked a cigarette out of.

And they were still shaking when she left work early half an hour later.

*   *   *

She went out early for that drink, alone. But she didn't stay that way for long.

His name was Rick (Rick and Robin), and he had a nice smile. He told her he'd just come out of a serious relationship, so he wasn't looking for anything heavy. That was okay, neither was she. All Robin was looking for was a distraction (a *collision*). A way to stem the flood of tears, of memories she feared she wouldn't be able to get a handle on ever again. She let him buy her several drinks and they ended up back at his place.

Rick took his time, made sure he built things up slowly but surely, until there was nothing else she could do but let go. Building to the—rush hour—climax. His strokes were long and even, and Robin relished his weight on top of her in the dim light of his bedroom.

41

It was as he pushed, easing himself back and then into her again, that she looked up and saw his face. It was changing. First it was Harry, then Saul. Then something else. His body was in shadow. *He* was a shadow. But his face was completely white and distorted, like something out of a nightmare. Rushing towards her, its shape flowing behind... like traffic.

Like smoke.

She screamed, trying to push him off. He took no notice, only speeded up, speeding towards her, speeding towards his own climax.

Robin sat bolt upright in the bed, the scream merely a croak now. Her whole body was shaking, not just her hands. And suddenly Rick was beside her, roused by her. She didn't even know she'd fallen asleep (sex helped you sleep, didn't it?) and jumped when she felt his fingers on her arm. She did yelp then, backing up and away from him, taking the saturated sheets with her.

"Hey, it was just a bad dream. It's all right," he was telling her. He of the nice smile.

But Robin knew it wasn't. Things were far from all right. And, as she gathered her underwear, her clothes, from Rick's bedroom floor, she wondered if they ever would be again.

*   *   *

"I need to stop, I—"

"We're just getting started, Robin. We're making progress."

"You're stirring things up that I didn't want to think about. Now I'm... It's affecting my work. My whole *life*." Robin was behind the seat again, leaning on it with both hands like she was about to start doing push ups.

"Don't you see? It had already started affecting your life before you came to visit me." Balancing the clipboard on his knees, Saul rolled up his sleeves, to show he meant business, and revealed that they were just as gorilla-like as his chest. Robin had a flashback to his face riding high above her, and her jaw locked tight. "These recollections were seeping out, causing your insomnia. They might even have caused visual hallucinations and—"

"What did you just say?" asked Robin.

"What? Hallucinations? Have you experienced something like that yourself?" Saul virtually leapt forward, eager to hear the answer, but Robin refused to oblige. "Look, I think the only way you're going to be free of all this is if we take the hypnotherapy route. Unblock those signals to the brain once and for all. Maybe use sounds or even smells to trigger something, and—"

That smell...

"Wait!" Robin was holding up her hand for him to stop. "Just please, wait a second. This is all going a bit too—"

"We won't do anything you're not comfortable with, I promise." Saul smiled, and it reminded her of Rick. Rick who she'd left behind, run away from, all because of that—nightmare—dream. Might they have had a future together, in spite of everything?

No. No future. People died, you lost them when you let your guard down. But still...

Robin needed to do something. She certainly couldn't go on the way she had been doing lately. Reluctantly, she nodded.

"Good. Look, Robin, everything's going to be all—" But she held up her hand again to silence him before he said it.

"Don't make promises you can't keep," she said to him by way of an explanation.

*   *   *

"Hey!"

"Halloa there!"

"Hey, you there! You can go. The light's green!"

Robin had been miles away, shopping—including more wine—clutched to her body tightly like a baby. Like an only child. The crossing's lights were green, the high-pitched bell... *beeping* growing in intensity.

"Wha—"

"You can cross!" said the overweight man who'd been crammed into a business suit. "The signal!" He pointed upwards.

Unblock those signals, once and for all.

Green on both sides, 33,000 lbs of tow truck that had slammed into their estate, ripping the car in two, the shadow—

"You can go!" the man growled.

Robin nodded, faced front again and put a foot out to cross. Just as the lights turned against her, and the beeping stopped. Just as a 4x4 was setting off across the pelican. She was dragged backwards just in time by the man who'd told her she could go.

"What the hell's wrong with you?"

Hell... like going into, through *Hell*.

He whirled her around and she dropped the bag, the bottles smashing on the pavement. "Ah." He nodded his head like he knew her, like he knew her problems, what she was going through. Robin screamed into his face to let go, and he did, backing off immediately. "Crazy bitch," he muttered under his breath, as he sought another way across the road.

"They... They were for a party," she called after him, voice weakening with each word. There was a crowd gathering round her, all staring. Robin bent and began picking up the pieces of glass, shoving them back into the plastic carrier. There was a sharp pain, and she looked at her finger. It was red, she was bleeding from an angry slash across the pad. Robin gaped at it, mesmerised.

"Are you all right?"

Everything's going to be...

Robin snapped to, looked up at the older lady who'd addressed her. Had she not been out and about, she might have thought it was her Aunty Jean—there was a definite likeness—or someone who'd be about that age if she hadn't been killed so long ago with her husband.

"I saw the whole thing. That man was a pig. Oh dear, look at that, you've cut yourself." Robin found her head going up and down, like a nodding dog in the back of a—

The woman took out a handkerchief from her handbag and proceeded to wrap it around Robin's finger to stem the bleeding.

"Th-Thank you," said Robin.

"Always happy to help," said the woman cheerily. "I only did what anyone would have."

Not everyone's first instinct is to put themselves in harm's way.

It was a conscious choice to go down there and help.

You should be proud of that.

You should embrace *those memories.*

Robin smiled back wearily. "I-I'm not having the best of days. Not having the best of weeks, really." Months, even.

"Not to worry," the woman told her. "Just keep motoring on.

44

You'll get there."

Strangely, that was what Robin was most afraid of in the world right now.

* * *

Luckily, Aunty Jean had some wine they could take with them to the party—as Robin found out when she arrived at her place and they rang for a taxi to cousin Neville's: a twee house in a suburb of town that looked like it was stuck back in the 1960s. Or maybe even 1860s.

Neville's wife Audrey greeted them at the front door with air kisses and led them through the equally twee interior, then out the back through the French doors in the kitchen. The garden was immaculately laid out and Robin saw that regardless of the fact Spring had only just sprung, Neville was trying to get a barbecue up and running, his apron assuring everyone that he had a "License to Grill".

While her Aunty was nervous at first, and Robin had to admit herself she wanted to be anywhere but here today, the woman soon got chatting with some of the older members of the clan. Robin, for her part, hardly recognised anyone. Perhaps a few faces from weddings and christenings, but no one she was on an intimate basis with. Children ran and played, pretending to shoot each other or kicking balls around.

"You look tired, sweetie," said Audrey, still beside her. Ever the loyal wifie and hostess, with her regulation perm and flowery dress. "Not working you too hard are they at the..." Robin could see, could hear the gears grinding inside Audrey's head, trying to remember just what the hell—

Into Hell, through *Hell*...

—it was Robin did for a living. She put the woman out of her misery and told her.

"Must be very interesting, that. What drove you to that line of—" Robin let out a sigh of relief when someone tapped Audrey on the shoulder and spoke to her; some kind of emergency with the coleslaw, apparently. Audrey offered her apologies and left.

Robin made for the drinks table, pouring herself a large wine. She closed her eyes as she swallowed the first mouthful. And the smell hit her, overpowering, all consuming. Meat, frying, burning in the heat from the grill. Charring, blackening meat—

("Cast your mind back...")

Just like when the car was torn in two, and the tow truck began haemorrhaging fuel. The spark from the estate's engine—two figures rolling around, trapped in the front by their seatbelts. Her mum looking back, looking scared, but her eyes trying to tell her that everything would be all—

Then the fireball of an explosion; baking alive, both of her parents. The cloying smoke in the back of Robin's throat. The knowledge that she would always be alone now, no matter who else was there around her. Thinking "I'm a survivor, but they aren't... Won't ever be now." Waiting and watching, but not wanting to. Listening out as the sounds of—

Then the hesitation at the tunnel, vague remembrances of her childhood holding her back, but hearing the screams—there hadn't been time for her parents or the driver of the truck to do that—the people in so much pain. Making her way inside, wafting away the blackness that was fighting to get inside her with every shallow breath. The first car, concertinaed up as it had hit the wall, the driver quite clearly already dead... Children in the back, doors jammed, but she'd tugged on the nearest one, got it open, got them out and to the mouth of the tunnel. Lying to them: it's all going to be all right... (Run and play, run and play!)

Then going back for more. Inside further, like being in Hell. Like going through Hell. These poor tortured souls. One person on fire, like those stuntmen you see in horror movies. One woman crawling across to Robin, clothes torn. She'd tried to drag her away from the flames, pulling and pulling, until she didn't have the energy anymore. Then cradling her head on her knee as she asked where she was, why everything was going dark? Was she going blind? Tears streaming down both their faces from the smoke and because the woman wasn't moving now.

Then hands on her, more of the injured begging her to get them out. To lead them out.

—sirens in the distance approaching. Real help, professional

help...

Bells, the beeping the—

"Shit!"

The commotion made her snap her eyes open and she saw Neville standing by the barbeque, fanning down the flames. Smoke was drifting across the lawn, into the kitchen where it had set off the smoke alarm. Audrey, bowl of coleslaw in her hand, was glaring across at her husband. "Language, Neville!" she admonished. It was like something out of an old British sitcom.

Robin released a long breath, refilled her glass, and drank more wine.

* * *

A little later, and after Robin had drunk more glasses of Pinot, smoked virtually a packet of cigarettes, and managed to successfully extricate herself from several tedious conversations that seemed to have blossomed spontaneously around her—about the state of the country, economy, health service and that old English favourite, the weather—Robin's Aunty Jean apparently remembered she'd arrived with a plus one and called her over.

Reluctantly, she joined her, mainly because the group of pensioners there were sitting in an out of the way spot next to the summerhouse—there just had to be one of those, didn't there.

"Robin, you remember your dad's cousin Mabel, don't you? And her husband, Alfred?"

She nodded, but had no recollection of ever having met them in her life. Mabel was a large lady, with red cheeks, but it wasn't a natural bigness—like the man back at the crossing—more like you get when someone's on steroids for something. In contrast, her husband had a very slight frame, his face like a roadmap, with huge multiple heavy-duty bags under his eyes. Robin thought idly that she'd have some of those soon if she didn't get a decent night's sleep.

"We were just talking about our family's one great claim to fame," Mabel said with a smirk.

"Oh?" said Robin, taking another swig of wine and planting herself down opposite the couple, next to Jean. She very nearly

47

missed the seat, but recovered enough to hope nobody had noticed. Her aunty gave her a concerned glance, but said nothing. Her guardians had never really been big drinkers, but Robin was in no mood for a lecture today. She said her next words clearly, perhaps a little too precisely, trying to show she was all... that she wasn't pissed. "I didn't know we had one."

"Well, not officially," Alfred chipped in. "More rumour handed down over the generations. We don't know if it's actually true."

"Oh shush, you," said Mabel. "It's real and that's that."

"What is?" Robin asked, her curiosity on the way to being piqued.

"What happened to one of our ancestors back in the nineteenth century. One of *your* ancestors," Mabel continued. "Quite a famous story was based around—"

"There's never been any proof of that, Mabel," her husband, the voice of doom, chipped in.

Mabel ignored him, carried on as if he'd never spoken. "He worked on the railway, this man. A quiet little station, tucked away in the countryside. But, well, he saw things."

Robin frowned. "What sort of things?"

"You must have heard all this before," said Jean. "Surely?"

Robin shook her head.

"*'Halloa! Below there!'* and all that," said Alfred with a chuckle.

Robin stared at him. "What did you just say?"

Alfred seemed a little taken aback by her intensity. He laughed it away, before answering, "That's how the story starts."

"Story?" Robin wasn't much for reading, and definitely not for pleasure. School English lessons had put paid to that.

"The *made-up* story," Mabel jumped in this time. "Based on what happened to our long, lost relative. Poor thing."

Poor, tortured soul.

"Based on..." Robin's head was spinning. She took another gulp of the wine she had, but that only made things worse.

"Kept seeing omens. One omen, really: a dark, ghostly spectre. Some say it might have been death itself, though in the story it turns out to be some kind of premonition of the future. I think, anyway."

"A warning," Jean added for clarification, as if it were needed. "All very fantastical."

Not to Robin, not right at that moment.

48

"He saw it three times," said Mabel. "And it always heralded a tragic accident."

"Accident," repeated Robin, her face slack.

It was at this point her Aunty Jean realised this probably wasn't a very good subject, especially in light of Robin's questions on the phone the other night. "Mabel, I think perhaps we should move on to a better topic of conversation."

"Why ever would you..." Mabel caught Jean's look and the penny dropped. "Oh, right. Sorry."

"I mean," Jean said, covering. "I'll never sleep tonight at this rate."

Never sleep...

Robin stood. "I-I'm not feeling very well. I think... Are you okay to make it home, Aunty Jean?"

"We can give her a lift, love," Alfred offered. "Are you not feeling too clever?"

Robin didn't reply, she simply mumbled her goodbyes and headed back towards the house. As she left them behind she heard something about drink, but ignored it. What they thought about her alcohol consumption was the farthest thing from her mind right now. She had to get away. Had to—

Inside the kitchen, Audrey and Neville thanked her for coming — Neville giving her what was left of a Pinot bottle; "You seem to like that one," he said, but didn't mean anything by it—and they ordered her a taxi.

When she got inside her place, Robin made a dash for the loo, throwing up violently into the pan. Not from the wine, or at least she didn't think so, but from the words. The thought that something in her family's past might link to her present.

When she'd recovered enough, she poured herself more of the wine, lit a cigarette and booted up her computer. She searched for the story, read it, drank more wine, sucked in a huge lungful of smoke before stubbing her fag out, and said one word:

"Fuck."

Because she'd seen the shadow—the ghost? spectre? The Appearance—herself before, hadn't she? Not just on the monitor. The session with Saul had brought back those memories, even though she'd fought against it.

49

The first time, just before they hit the junction. Looking out through the window, too fast to do anything about it, although she remembered trying to shout: "Over there! Mummy, Daddy, look!" But they didn't turn—or did they?—because if they had that might have meant they weren't watching where they were going and—

The second time, when she'd got Tony to pull over on that bridge (pull over for a fag to start with, but she'd got more smoke than she'd bargained for in the end, hadn't she). Down by the lights, both sides on green, waving. Warning. So much so that she'd shouted down to the line of traffic, to try and stop them: "Hey, below! Stop! Please, stop!"

She'd seen it before those accidents, which meant—

The flames, the smoke. The tunnel.
"For God's sake..."
The screaming... And that figure, dark, waving.
"Clear the way!"
Face all white, the face of death? Or something else? Future visions, premonitions...
Cast your mind back. Blocked signals. The light...
Danger-light! Telegraphed...
Life like a car—train—crash.
Christ!
Blackness.

*   *   *

She wasn't even aware she'd fallen asleep at the laptop, and wouldn't have woken were it not for the phone going off.

The bell, the alarm!

Robin stumbled across the room and picked up. It was her Aunty Jean, checking she'd got home okay, and that she hadn't been too upset by all that nonsense Mabel had been waffling on about. Silly family superstitions. It was as her Aunty was talking that Robin noticed it was light outside, streaming in through the curtains.

What time was it, then? She looked at her watch, almost swore but remembered she was on the phone with Jean... then made her excuses, assuring the woman she was okay, that she'd speak to her soon. No time to wash or get changed, after so long on hardly any sleep at night, she'd fallen into a virtual coma and overslept. Robin barely had time to make it to work before the rush hour, and she was ringing a taxi as she was grabbing her handbag, coat and keys, before rushing out through her front door.

She couldn't be late. Not today. It was important, Robin could sense it was. She almost fell down the steps to the main road; rushing, but also still a bit tipsy from last night, hangover yet to kick in. And in spite of the sleep, she was knackered. More tired than she had been in weeks. They did say that when you eventually got some kip after a long time not being able to sleep, you felt a million times worse. It didn't matter, all that mattered was she made it to work. Monday morning rush hour was one of the worst there was.

Robin didn't even wait for the taxi to properly brake before she was trying to get in, blurting out an address.

"And hurry," she slurred. "Please hurry!"

*   *   *

As it turned out there was no need to rush.

When she ran into the room where Harry was already hard at work, monitoring the flow of traffic, everything was fine. "All under control, ticking along nicely," he told her. "You can relax."

Relax? Robin stared at him like he was insane. How could she relax when—

She caught herself. *You must have heard all this before?*

Silly family superstitions.

She must have overheard it sometime, the family "claim to fame", and it had lodged in her brain. Either that or she'd been read the story? No, her parents wouldn't do that, it wasn't something you read to... More likely at a family event like yesterday. Look how keen Mabel was to spread the word.

She wasn't going crazy after all. It *wasn't* happening again.

But then she saw it, that strange shadow—The Appearance—near Edgecross roundabout. Near the lights (the danger-lights). The signals. She pushed Harry aside, working the controls again.

"Robin...?"

"Look! There, can't you see him? That figure, that man!

51

Waving?" Her breaths were coming in short bursts.

"I don't see anything," Harry said. "But... but I'm pretty sure you shouldn't be smoking *that* in here!"

Robin looked down at her hand, her fingers. She hadn't even realised she'd lit up. "I—"

"Look, I know you've been having some problems lately," Harry said, trying to sound understanding.

"You *know*. What do you know?"

"Just rumours, really."

Silly superstitions.

"That, er, that you've been seeing someone."

I'm bloody well seeing someone right now! thought Robin. *There's someone, something—an omen, a ghost of the future, whatever—right there!* "I'm not losing it, Harry."

"I never said you were. You've just been having trouble sleeping, I know."

"Look, really *look* at that screen. Something terrible's going to happen."

"Damn right. You need to put that out," Harry told her, reaching across for the cigarette. "Before it—"

Too late, alarms began to sound. Smoke detectors even more sensitive than the ones in Audrey's kitchen were blaring away.

The bells, the beeping. "Shit!" said Harry.

But Robin wasn't looking at that. She was watching the signals. On the screen in front of her and those relating to the lights.

"We've got a fault," she said. "There."

Harry followed her gaze. There was indeed a red light flashing to indicate a failure on the roundabout signals. "Back-ups should kick in any moment," he assured her.

They waited a few seconds. Nothing happened. Robin stabbed her cigarette out on the table. What if something else had set them off, what if there was a fire somewhere else? Something on the system, something electrical that had caused...

The back-ups that had back-ups to fail.

Harry fiddled with the controls, punched keys. "It's not responding," he said, looking at her with a panicked expression.

Robin blinked, pushed herself away from the desk. Someone had to get down there, had to warn them. Though it was fairly clear at the moment, they were going to get traffic filtering on to that roundabout at speed soon, and all the lights (both sides, no *all* sides) on all the junctions were stuck on green.

"Not on my watch," she whispered.

"What?" asked Harry, still confused.

She was out through the door before she knew it, Harry's cries trailing her. Soon this place would be evacuated. People would be coming in to see just what the hell...

Like being in Hell, going through *Hell.*

...was happening. She didn't have time to explain it, Harry could call up the authorities, get them mobilised. Robin needed to get down there.

To do what? It was too late, surely?

No, Edgecross wasn't far away. She could get a taxi and... Too long, it would take too long. Robin took the stairs, slipping, sliding and almost tumbling down them to reach the ground floor.

Even before she was outside, she saw it: the small Nissan parking up on the road outside. Her means to get to Edgecross. Robin stood in front of it, ignored the beeping... the bell... alarm... and the woman behind the wheel calling her names. She went round and yanked the door open, dragged the woman—

Pulling and pulling, until she didn't have the energy anymore...

—out, apologising even as she did it. Even as she slid behind the wheel and put it in first, accelerating away.

As she headed in the direction of Edgecross roundabout.

* * *

Robin was rusty, but the more she drove, the more she got used to it. She had no choice, though all the way she was acutely aware that she could also cause an accident herself.

But she knew this city like the back of her hand; should do, she spent all her time looking at tiny squares of it. She knew the short-cuts, the back alleys that would get her where she needed to go as safely as possible. Until, finally, she veered off the road altogether, down an embankment, aiming herself at the roundabout. Anyone who saw her might have said she was nuts, or drunk.

Just like the driver of that tow truck when he slammed into—

53

She made it, though; she got there. Abandoned the car on the verge and stood by it. There had already been half a dozen minor collisions by the looks of it. Those who had trusted the lights. The signals on the far side. Cars that had run headlong into each other. But there would be more pile-ups once others ran into them, heading back along down the duel carriageways and—Jesus—the motorway exit.

Robin tried to attract the attention of those heading for the crashes from the city side, stepping out and flagging them down. For the most part this worked, the drivers pulling up in time to see the mess they were heading towards. But the real mess would happen if she couldn't stop those coming in from the opposite side. Robin looked both ways and made a dash for it, crossing over.

She was almost clipped by a sports car, but managed to dodge that just in time. Robin stumbled over the circle of grass in the middle of the roundabout, overshooting it and having to pull back to avoid a green mini that had made a break for it, incredibly still trying to get through even though it was obvious what was going on. She heard swear words coming from the open window, and thought: *I'm trying to help!*

It's in your nature, it's who you are.
People are responsible for themselves.
But you don't really believe that, do you?
Why did you choose that job?
What drove you to it?

...Robin began trying to flag them down, the cars heading towards her off the motorway. More and more, building... building to a climax... as the rush hour entered full swing.

She was waving frantically, but nobody was taking any notice. If the spearhead of traffic didn't slow down, there was going to be a bloodbath. Robin gritted her teeth, decided, then stepped out in front of the first moving vehicle. It had enough time to turn, to veer off. To miss her.

I'm a survivor, she said to herself.

The car—a red Ford—did just that, swerving to avoid this mad woman in the middle of the road who shouldn't be there. It swung onto the verge, crashing through barriers, tearing up grass, but at least it was safe. The next three cars did something similar, breaking off left or right, but it was the motorbike zipping in-between the vehicles—that Robin hadn't seen—which hit her. Full force, sending her up in the air and the rider skidding sideways, crushing his leg on impact.

Robin landed awkwardly on the concrete, vaguely heard the sound of bones cracking, snapping. Knew she was bleeding from the splashes of red pooling around her. But she didn't black out. Instead she tried to get up, tried to crawl. Tried to wave, to warn.

To signal.

There was a car heading right towards her. Robin blinked once, twice. Then suddenly, she couldn't see anything.

Have I gone blind?

Somebody somewhere was screaming, and she could hear alarm bells. No, not bells. Sirens. They'd save her. Or someone would sit with her, cradle her head as the smoke—

The blackness was sudden and all consuming. She realised it was her own voice she could hear, her *own* screams.

Then, suddenly, mercifully, Robin knew nothing either.

*   *   *

She drifted, as if floating on the wind or a lapping sea.

For a long time she just enjoyed the sensation. It was relaxing.

"All under control. You can relax."

She could hear the voices, thought she remembered who they belonged to, but then the information would escape her. It was like trying to... to cage smoke. And there's no smoke without—

Was she asleep? Felt like it. So this was a dream, right? But she couldn't—wouldn't—allow herself to remember those.

She couldn't remember who she was, but then did it even matter anyway, here? Yes, she thought that it did. It... bothered her. She had something important to do, *was doing* something important when she—

When she'd fallen asleep. No, say it: when she'd *died*.

Crashing through barriers. Crossing...

Edgecross.

"You can cross!"

Where was she now? Heaven or—

Splodges of colour, images she couldn't make out. No, wait. Pull back. She saw flames, or did she just remember them? Poor, tortured, burning souls. But not in whatever afterlife this was. Back in the real world, in the past. And probably the present as well, because she hadn't listened, had she? Hadn't seen the danger that had been telegraphed. Hadn't been able to work out the signals, the warning signs—the...

"Cast your mind back."

Someone had said that to her once, she was sure of it. Someone who'd just been trying to help, like she always did. She couldn't remember much, but... Yes, something had stuck. An accident. Back when she was little. Some kind of car—train—crash?

Then once again, when she was a bit older. Something to do with a tunnel. And of course the one when she'd—

Signals. That was what this was all about, *seeing* them. The warning signs. If only she'd taken notice, if only she could go back and—

But then, maybe she could Wasn't anything possible when you were in this state? Couldn't you go anywhere, do anything? With no body, there were no restrictions.

She remembered she'd been waving, trying to get people's attention when what happened, happened—something that had hurt. She'd been crying out in pain.

Not, not on her watch.

Cast your mind back? If she could do that, then how about her spirit? That had survived all this, clung on. Because that's what she was, wasn't she? A survivor, with no attachments. Not willing to go to Heaven nor Hell. Not yet, at any rate.

Perhaps she could cast that back, as well?

She gritted her teeth, pictured the scene. Made it come into focus, pulling back, widening the angle. Dropping herself into it. *Appearing.* An estate car travelling towards her on a road. Two people in the front, a man and a woman. And in the back, a six-year-old girl who she was connected to. The only person who'd be able to see her.

She concentrated on piecing herself together, on becoming some kind of whole again. But that wasn't easy—and without being able to remember what you looked like... She'd settle for a shape, a shadow. Some kind of form at least, that might warn her.

She began to wave, frantically, trying to get the girl's attention. She'd do this over and over again until the outcome was different. She'd do it here, and at the tunnel. Then finally, at that place. The circular place where she'd crossed over.

She'd remember that too, in time.

"Halloa! Below there!"

Words... words from a story she'd once read. A silly superstition. Echoing, like they were following her up and out of a dream—if she was really asleep?—that was already well on its way to being forgotten.

But one day, she knew, she was determined—she would wake up.

She would finally open her eyes again and *see*.

LIFE SENTENCE

"For what is your life? It is even a vapour, that appeareth for a little time, and then vanisheth away."

The Bible: James 4.

Every second of every minute of every hour of every day, he prayed for death to come.

He knew it never would, of course. That was impossible, his jailers had made sure of it. Ensured that he couldn't harm himself in any way, at least until he changed his mind, altered his opinions or, through the miracle of modern science, they found a way to do it for him.

A part of him wished they *would* come up with a drug or something. That way he'd be just like everyone else—apart from those who shared this place with him; his waking nightmare. He wouldn't care anymore what happened. He might be able to lead a near enough normal life...

A life.

With the best will in the world you could hardly call what he was living now a life. Existence maybe, but nothing more. Twenty-four hours a day stuck in this transparent cube. His see-through Hell, sat watching all those others in theirs. What stories did they have to impart? he wondered. Same as his? Hardly likely. But then he'd never find out, would he? Contact was strictly prohibited. True, there weren't many of them, but there were enough to convince him he wasn't completely crazy.

For the millionth time today he struggled against his bonds. What was the point? Useless, it was all useless. How could you break "chains" of pure energy? Not even a power cut would achieve that, as the penitentiary boasted its own internal system of backup generators. Nothing was left to chance. No hope of release.

Not that it was release from this prison he craved—what was waiting outside for him?—but rather release from the burden of just being. That was all he could hope for, really.

This must sound pretty strange, though not when viewed in context. Not when you consider what has happened to Joseph up to this point. And what has happened to the human race in general.

There had been a time, long, long ago, when Joseph was happy to be alive—ecstatic even. When he feared the inevitable swing of the Grim Reaper's scythe as much as the next person. No one knows, *really* knows what happens when you die; where you go or what becomes of you. Christians believed you went to Heaven if you'd lived a fairly decent life—the other place if you hadn't. Buddhists, they said you came back again and again and again as people, animals, *insects*. Jehovah's Witnesses, they thought you waited in the ground until Judgement Day and then rose up at the end. Some folk convinced themselves there was nothing beyond except empty blackness. A void. You come from nothing and go back to nothing. But no one knew; they still don't. No one has returned from the grave to report back.

This probably makes what happened all the more understandable—if not forgiveable. Because given the choice between life and death, the more appealing option will always be life. In most instances...

For centuries, millennia, there *was* no choice. The only power over life and death man possessed was the power to kill: with stone tools, with blades, with guns, and finally with weapons the likes of which the Devil himself could never have conceived.

Then the discovery was made. The writings of Baron Victor von Frankenstein uncovered by a distant relative underneath the collapsed ruins of the scientist's castle. Buried in a partially-sealed antechamber of the catacombs. Translated, interpreted and sold on to the highest bidders, they were studied very closely indeed.

Thought to be a madman, Frankenstein was a legend in the mountain villages of Switzerland where the name was used to frighten children at bedtime. A substitutive bogie man; the Baron and his monster—cobbled together from dead tissue to form a new creation, a new *dangerous* creation. The story, a fable in those parts, was well known. But what no one realised was that, as with most folktales, there was a grain of truth to it all. The myth was based on actual events at the end of the eighteenth century.

A graduate of the University of Ingolstadt, where he studied alchemy and modern science, his methods, though crude and ultimately disastrous (leading to the Baron's untimely death, though nobody could pinpoint how exactly), *did* bear fruit. Obsessed with the notion that he could discover the secret of life eternal, he succeeded in re-animating certain body parts: arms, legs, hands... according to his notes. But his most triumphant work was in the area of human brain transplantation—a veil was hastily drawn over how he came by all his raw material. Certain chapters of the journals were missing or in poor condition, torn or eaten by vermin, but there was enough left to make use of. Frankenstein's groundbreaking theories, lost for so many years, provided the basis for a whole new mode of thinking. The first and last piece of the puzzle.

It sparked a glimmer of an idea in the minds of early twenty-first century scientists who were only just catching up. But it especially interested those involved in the fields of genetic engineering and cloning, DNA and the building blocks of life itself. Many doctors had already been thinking along the same lines as the Baron—limb and organ transplants had become commonplace, raiding the temples of the recently deceased to profit the living.

But what if this process could somehow be refined and extrapolated? they said. What if entire bodies could be built, instead of parts stolen, and the brain deposited inside? Theoretically it could even be a carbon copy of your own frame; the technology was in place. Or maybe a designer body, a different look, a mishmash of various people all seamlessly blended together. A younger, fitter version of yourself.

In this way death, disease and disability could be almost totally eliminated. Instead of a facelift, why not an entire body lift? Immortality would eventually reign supreme...

The Warder's footsteps echoed up the glass hall. His sky-blue uniform reflected first off one surface, then another. He didn't normally visit, no one did; all food was taken intravenously, all waste extracted in a similar fashion. This was a rare occurrence and Joseph knew there had to be a reason for it.

60

The man stopped about halfway down, a broad figure beneath his uniform: muscled and bronzed—eighth or ninth generation now, Joseph suspected—but with a positively ugly face. Probably the one he was originally born with; why else would he choose to keep it? Some people were sentimental that way.

"Could I have your attention, please."

He was a sadistic son of a bitch, the Warder. They had no option but to look at him. What other sounds were they going to listen to *but* the droning of his voice? Jackass!

"Thank you. Now this afternoon," he continued, "we have a special treat for you. The engineers are coming in to look over your units, to make sure you're all as comfortable as can be. Won't that be nice? New faces and everything." The question was rhetorical. He knew the mouth-plates prevented them from answering, as well as stopping them from biting through their own tongues. And although he was addressing all of them, the Warder was looking at Joseph, and Joseph alone.

The announcement over, he turned around and headed back up the aisle to someplace Joseph had never seen. It wouldn't be the same as when he was brought in. None of it was. How could it possibly be? Time had moved on.

Time. It was a strange thing... Here there were no clocks, no calendars, no links to the big, wide world. Joseph imagined he'd been here a long time, but he had no idea exactly how long. Even prisoners in the olden days could chalk their sentences on the wall. He had neither the ability nor the inclination. At least this way he couldn't depress himself further by looking back at all the lost months and years scratched off on the glass.

Maybe at his next elusive parole hearing, always held in his cell, he would be able to convince them he was better. That he no longer thought the way he once did. Joseph didn't hold out much hope. He'd failed to dupe them twice in the past. Their monitors and lie detectors had exposed his untruths, informed them of his intentions. Told them that as soon as Joseph left the confines of his cell, he would make another attempt. As many as it took until he succeeded.

Until he was dead.

They couldn't have that. A black mark against their records. No, it was more than just neat paperwork. It was a kind of jealousy and spite. They wouldn't allow him to discover the truth because *they* were afraid to. Unacceptable; outrageous.

At first it had been fantastic. "Who wants to live forever?" they'd asked, and everyone answered: "We do!" Including Joseph. Ironically he wanted it more than anything else in the world. Wanted to be around to meet his great-great-grandchildren, the descendants of his only son, Karl; and still be healthy enough to play ball with them! If anyone deserved the right it was Joseph. Moreover, it had been one of his conditions...

Neither Joseph nor Maggie, his beloved wife, were getting any younger—now both in their 60s—so they signed up for the earliest trials.

The techniques were far from perfected, but they went ahead anyway and hoped for the best. To start with the doctors were like ghouls, waiting for the names on the list to expire so they could set to work bringing them back. Transplanting consciousness into freshly made skin altered to suit. But in the end they became impatient and induced death, in some cases without the subjects' knowledge or permission. Thankfully, the operations were a complete success. The results astounding; beyond anybody's wildest expectations. Not one rejection.

Maggie had volunteered to go first, then Joseph a few days later, once he was sure she'd come through. They were brought back from the brink renewed, just like all the others. Obviously they had been frightened, who wouldn't have been? But the process was over very quickly, leaving them to live out their lives again and again, if necessary. To do things they hadn't made time for on the first trip. It was nothing short of a miracle. The beginning of a new world order.

After it was found to be safe, the treatment was offered around. Only the privileged, the wealthy or famous could afford the fees, but something like this couldn't remain a secret forever. The general public clamoured to be let in through the gates of paradise early. If society was to survive in any reasonable shape or form, then the process had to be opened up to all.

Or given to none.

As expected, there was resistance from some quarters. The *Pro-Death* campaigners for a start, who went on the rampage, as well as on marches. Devout religious followers came out of the woodwork

62

and banded together for the first time ever in history, those who argued that mankind was tampering with forces they could not hope to control. They were the blessed who had faith in the hereafter. They believed in God and Heaven—in all its forms. They were the lucky ones who were not afraid to die.

And they were in a minority.

Why should people believe in religion anymore? the masses cried back. There was no need now. Nobody would ever have to face the Almighty. No death, no reckoning in the clouds. It sounded like a good deal to them. Frankenstein, a man who never *believed* himself, had at last got his wish. A godless world. A world where men *were* the gods, in effect.

Governments proved weak, politicians only human. Was there any wonder it all turned out the way it did? A collective hysteria or madness, as Joseph called it now.

Gradually new laws were passed decreeing that everyone must undergo the treatment. Hefty penalties faced those who disobeyed. No one would miss out, and that was an order! In addition, it was also decided that both men and women should be sterilised. If everyone was staying put then the planet would soon be overcrowded at the rate newborn babies kept arriving—a million a day was the last conservative estimate. The human race would therefore end with its current generation. So much for Joseph's great-great-grandchildren. When all was said and done, the only reason to have children was so that a little piece of you could carry on into the future. A sort of immortality. There was no need now that the real thing was feasible.

Finally, the laws on suicide were modified and strengthened. It became a heinous crime to even discuss such things. Obviously, there was still depression and poverty and hunger... although if you died of it, they just brought you right back. The world hadn't moved on *that* much; immortality couldn't fix these major problems. So it followed that there were still some people who wanted out, who'd seen enough of life already.

Suicide had always been against the law, but how could the courts ever hope to prosecute? The perpetrator was dead. End of story. It was different now, though. The dead could legally be charged and tried, depending on how good or bad a job they'd made of things.

They could be sentenced and imprisoned. Shut away, repressed like social pariahs.

Just like Joseph.

There was movement again at the end of the hall. Four men in grey jumpsuits. The engineers, come to hunt for glitches in the system. To right problems before they occurred. Making sure there was no chance of escape into limbo. If Joseph could have mustered enough strength, enough motivation, he might have cried today. But he'd shed all the tears he was going to in here. Possibly before he'd even got here. There were no more left; they weren't real anymore. He had nothing left to give. All he wanted now was closure, to meet his maker—yes, *he* still believed in Him—and ask why?

Why had it happened to him? A punishment, perhaps. If so, it was richly deserved. He just needed an answer. Why had his family been taken away from him?

The reasons for Joseph's mental collapse were plain. It started when he came home one day to find Maggie eating her own son's brains in the kitchen. There she was on the floor next to the body, scooping them up with a spoon and shovelling them hungrily into her mouth.

Joseph ran to Maggie, not quite knowing what he'd do when he reached her. He was processing the whole thing as a series of snapshots: Kurt's open cranium, smashed like the shell of an egg; Maggie's vacant expression; the spoon bearing a dollop of glistening grey matter; the hammer on the floor, crusted with dried blood.

It was a scene which bowed his mind, defying logic and inviting insanity.

The doctors confirmed his suspicions. It was a regression, after all this time! A legacy of the Baron's work. Revenge from beyond the grave because he himself had died before he could carry out his plans. And it had turned Joseph's wife into a maniacal zombie. Nothing could be done for her, or his son. There was no way to bring the brain back, only re-house it. "Luckily" it meant that the doctors were able to screen others for the problem, catching it just in time... mostly. A crisis was narrowly averted thanks to Joseph and his bride. That was another favour the world owed him.

He could never see it that way. Both his reasons for living were gone now. It was like he was looking at the world for the first time and realising what had become of it. And he didn't like it at all. Not one little bit. Maggie, the real Maggie, had gone to meet Kurt wherever he now dwelt. The time had come for Joseph to join them.

But *they* were keeping a close eye on him. (A high risk subject.) Waiting for him to make his move. *Suicide watch.* The authorities seized him even before he could place his head on the subway track. They ran him in and questioned his intentions; they called it preventative medicine. Yet in spite of the exceptional circumstances and his unique heritage, the judge showed Joseph no leniency. He was to be incarcerated immediately for his own good. They all said the same...

For his own good.

The engineers came closer, entering the cells in front and on either side. One stepped into his cubicle, the glass door gliding gently back. He was a thin man with flared nostrils and sunken cheeks. Walking further inside, he looked Joseph over.

"In here," he shouted to his colleagues, then crouched by the door. With a tool from his belt he opened the central panel and extinguished the power, the back-ups having already been disabled.

For the first time in as long as he could remember, Joseph could move.

Free of the field, he collapsed at the engineer's feet. But this was no ordinary workman. His cause was a just one.

"Your time is at hand, brother," he said, and louder now: "Justice for all, the right to choose death!"

Joseph spat out the mouthpiece. He didn't know whether he still had a voice or not. "Please," he gasped, "end it now." That's what the man was here for, he felt it.

Joseph's instincts were right. Some small pockets of resistance still survived, those who believed.

The pen-laser was out. One blast and Joseph's brain, his very consciousness, would be no more. No way back. *Now,* he thought. *I'm ready now.*

The engineer aimed and—

Part of his right shoulder disappeared in a spray of blood and cauterised bone. He screamed, the pen-laser slipping, slicing a line across the side of Joseph's neck before clanging to the floor.

He looked up in time to see the Warder with security, hefting high-powered rifles. The rest of the engineers were targeted and incapacitated seconds later.

The one in Joseph's cell was toppling, another bolt of pure energy erupting through his abdomen. Pieces of his gut stuck to the glass walls and slid down. No headshots—no *killshots*. Joseph crawled towards the laser, his rheumatic fingers inches away. Then he was touching it, holding it, stabbing at the button as the Warder and his men approached.

There was a spark inside; Joseph looked down as the laser exploded in his face. A blinding white light. Then a moment of pain...

Replaced by blackness.

Joseph was floating, drifting away on a breeze of empty nothing. It felt like he was moving down a tunnel. Yes, a spiralling conduit. Warmth and peace overwhelmed and penetrated him. In this place he could move faster than light. Everything would soon be explained.

Ghosts travelled to greet him: Maggie, Karl, his parents... Victor. That last one was a tremendous shock. What was Victor doing here in the land of saints? *He* did not believe.

This truly was a merciful God.

But Victor was laughing. *Why?*

Another white circle and his journey was nearly over, from one world to the next. He felt sorry for all those he'd left behind who would never experience this. All because of him, because he'd found those damned notes in the wreck of that castle.

Yes, this really was a merciful God.

Almost there, heading for the light, heading for the—

Joseph Frankenstein arrived at the light. He opened his eyes expecting to see it all: the gates, the clouds, the angels.

But instead he saw only the Warder's bulldog face.

"He's coming round."

"Good." Another figure alongside him, a woman in a white lab coat.

"You gave us all quite a scare." Again the trademark sarcasm. "Just missed the frontal lobe. But you're all right now. That's the main thing. You survived."

Joseph felt something in his mouth and he couldn't move. The buzzing forcefield was back around him, holding him securely. With some effort, he looked left and right. Beyond his own cell he saw the engineer opposite, hoisted up by his own field. Sentenced while Joseph had been away being rebuilt: *reconstructed*. Joseph wanted to speak, to tell them all about his experience, but the mouthpiece thwarted him.

"You're home again," said the Warder. "And you'll be here for some time to come, I'm afraid." He seemed to find this all very amusing. "They've added another three million years to your original sentence, just to make sure. No possibility of parole."

The Warder and the scientist backed off, out through the glass door. "We'll leave you to think about what you've done, Joseph."

They walked away, abandoning him with only the new inmates and his own dreams for company. As he thought of the place he'd left behind, a contrast to the eternity stretching out before him in here, Joseph did cry that day. He cried using new tear ducts, the *new eyes* those doctors had given him. Cried because of his rebirth, and because he was the cause of all this, the architect of a world gone mad. It was all his fault, all his fault...

But most of all he cried because his last chance had gone.

And his life sentence had begun anew.

HUMBUGGERED

Marlowe's Ghost

Maybe it was his imagination, or that he'd just pulled a four-hour shift at the refuge—doling out food and a kindly word to those less fortunate than himself—but he was pretty sure when he came to open the front door of his block of flats, the list of names on the column of buzzers beside him turned into a face.

The names of the tenants in this ramshackle building, the words themselves, had slipped from their perches on their respective lines and begun to form a pattern. The buttons joined in, turning themselves into nostrils, a pair of eyes, a mouth. A mouth which spoke his name even as he was putting his key into the lock.

A mouth belonging to a face he knew all too well. The face of his best friend who'd died several years ago, stabbed to death on a street corner for the money he'd been carrying.

"Eric," said the mouth, forming the name with those buttons, the jumbled words making creases in this strange face. "Eric..." The voice was almost a whisper, causing him to bend down and cock an ear.

"Jared?"

He stared at the sight of his long-dead friend, now rendered in ink and plastic. Then he blinked twice, and when he did the list of names and their corresponding buttons returned to normal.

Eric shook his head and stared at the list once more, daring it to change again. Daring *something* to happen. But it didn't. He sighed, hefted the brown paper bag he was carrying, turned the key in the lock, and entered the building.

The first thing that greeted him was the stink; not of one thing in particular, just the accumulated aroma of the kind of people who lived here. It smelt like despair. He made his way to the lift, past graffiti on the stained walls proclaiming everything from "Carol Luvz Tony" to "For a Good Time Ring..." complete with mobile number. He jabbed at the button and waited for the lift to come. Nothing happened. The blessed thing was broken yet again, and the chances of anyone coming out to see to it this late on Christmas Eve were slim to negligible.

Sighing again, Eric made his way to the stairs, ready to climb the thirteen floors to his small flat. On the way, he had to walk past a gang of youths who were quite blatantly dealing drugs. He kept his head down and left them to it—it was the best way to avoid getting a kicking, he'd found. Eric also had to negotiate a section of stairway which was in total darkness—the lights above having been smashed a couple of weeks ago (again, there was no sign that anyone was coming out to fix them in a hurry).

As Eric wearily climbed the steps, he thought again about the face. It was hardly surprising, the more he dwelled on it. For one thing he was shattered—even before the refuge, he'd worked a full day at the office, catching up with work that had been piled on his desk by his boss, Mr Fitzgerald, so the man could take a long break over the holidays. Not that Eric minded: it was good, steady work, even if he did only get paid a pittance to virtually run that place.

Then there was the timing of the "vision". The anniversary of Jared Marlowe's murder. *Of course* the man would be on his mind, because while everyone else was celebrating there was still a part of Eric that was in mourning for the best mate he'd ever had in his life. The man he'd worked alongside, who'd inspired him to get into the whole charity scene in the first place. You could never hope to meet a more kindly, generous soul than Jared. Taken well before his time.

Eric reached the front door of his flat, and was about to insert another key to let himself in when he noticed the lock had been busted. Hanging his head, he nudged the door open with trembling fingers, aware that whoever had broken in might still be around (and was also probably one of his neighbours, looking for things they could sell to get high—possibly even some of the guys he'd seen on the stairs). Eric snapped on the light, readying himself, though he had no idea what he'd be able to do if he caught them in the act.

Fortunately, there was no-one inside anymore. His small bed-sit had been turned over all right—his chairs tipped up, sofa-bed in disarray, his bare Christmas tree kicked across the room—but the culprits had left empty-handed, mainly because there hadn't been anything in there to steal. Kitchen cupboards had been flung open, but what little food he had for the Xmas period he was carrying with him right now. Eric didn't own any electrical items like a TV, stereo or a Blu-ray player. He didn't have that much free time to watch shows or movies—preferring instead, when he could, to kick back with a good—

Dropping his bag on the floor, he ran to the shelves where he kept the books he read at night. The well-thumbed paperbacks were still there, if strewn all over the place, but what had been taken were the leather-bound editions of classics his sister had given him all those years ago.

If Eric had been a swearing man, he would have done so right then. As it was he settled for a very strong "Bugger!"

He thought about ringing the police but A) He didn't have a phone, mobile or otherwise, and B) the police weren't likely to do much about it anyway. He'd heard many of the residents complaining about thefts and not one of them, to his knowledge, had ever gotten any joy from chasing things up... or indeed got their belongings back. Eric supposed he should be grateful he didn't have that much to take, but the books had meant a great deal to him. The only real reminders of Faye he had.

You still have a living reminder, he told himself, *in the form of Fraser, her only son.* He'd heard from the young man only that afternoon, seeing if his uncle wanted to get together for a drink over Christmas.

"You know I don't drink, Fraser," Eric had told him, keeping his voice low as he wasn't supposed to take personal calls at work. "I've seen too much of what it can do to people on the streets."

"God, you really need to chillax, Unc," Fraser had said to him. "Have a few laughs."

Going out and getting wasted wasn't the kind of thing that brought Eric pleasure. His work at the refuge, and tomorrow down at the soup kitchen—not to mention the charity fun run he was doing on Boxing Day—those were the kinds of things that brought him joy.

But Fraser was just Fraser, a whizz-kid computer expert with money to burn and the hedonistic lifestyle to match. Many's the time Eric had tried to get him to donate to some of the worthy causes he was involved in, but Fraser always told him he could put his cash to better use. It made Eric sad.

Though not as sad as the loss of those books. He sighed again, knowing nothing could be done and that he really should get some sleep before his early start the next morning. Eric touched the shelf where the tomes had once rested, then turned and retrieved his bag, taking it into the kitchen and unloading it. Inside was a pack of processed turkey slices, a few potatoes and some other vegetables: his Christmas dinner. He stowed them away in his larder (Eric didn't bother with a fridge as it was so cold inside the flat—especially at this time of year—that food was unlikely to spoil). The bread and cheese he left out as a snack before bedtime as he hadn't eaten since his usual lunch in the canteen.

Next he set to work trying to fix the door lock, tying string around the handle in an effort to make do for the night. Not the most secure of barriers, but what other choice did he have? He righted one of his chairs, then sat and looked at the door as he ate his bread and cheese—drinking a glass of water from the tap.

The meter ran out before he was quite ready for bed, so he had to light a couple of candles. They provided not only illumination, but a bit of heat as well. He picked up his Christmas tree, such as it was, and pulled out the sofa-bed, getting under the covers with his clothes still on.

In spite of everything that had happened—Jared and the break-in—Eric still felt happy when he thought of the good he'd done tonight, and all he *would* do over the next couple of days while he was off work (all the time Fitzgerald would allow him). It left a glow inside as warm as those from the candles, and it wasn't long before his eyelids began to droop.

*   *   *

It was a rumbling sound that made them snap open again. At first he thought it might be his stomach, as that often made strange sounds at night, especially if he hadn't had enough to eat. But no. This was outside his door, something—or some*one*—making their way

71

towards it. Eric sat up on the sofa-bed, the noise growing louder: a heavy thudding now, like boots on the floorboards.

The burglars, he thought, *they've come back!*

Eric pulled up the covers, staring at the front door in the light from the waning candles. He jumped when the first bang came, thudding against the door's surface so hard it rattled the hinges. That was followed by another, then another, each one louder than the last.

"Go... Go away," Eric managed, finding his voice, but only just. It sounded like a mouse trying to shoo away a lion. "There's nothing left. You've taken everything I have."

There was another thud on the door, this one threatening to splinter the wood like Jack Nicholson on an axe-wielding spree.

What do they want? There was no way he was going to let them in.

Thud! Thud!

"Look, just go away!" Eric repeated, his voice rising a bit higher; it was the best he could muster in the circumstances.

They didn't go away, though. Instead the people outside his door seemed to redouble their efforts, slamming harder on it until the string holding the knob began to unravel. Eric leaned back on his bed, pulling the covers up. If they got in here, he didn't stand a chance. He was a wiry individual, but not built for fighting: he had neither the frame nor the stomach for it. They'd pulverise him. Maybe even do to him what they did to—

Jared.

Eric stared, open-mouthed, at the doorway. The door itself had been knocked down, landing with a bump and sending dust flying in every direction. In its place stood a lone figure, rather than the gang he'd imagined. Its shape was indistinct, made worse by the flickering of the candles, but regardless of this Eric was able to make out its face quite clearly. It was the face he'd seen downstairs at the front door, the face of the man he'd had to identify in the morgue after the stabbing.

"Jared?" he said out loud.

"Hiya Eric, how's things?" asked his former best friend as he made his way further into the bed-sit.

As he'd done before, Eric blinked, only this time the image didn't go away. *I must be asleep*, he thought. That was it; he'd been drifting off when the banging noise started. It was some kind of nightmare brought on from seeing what he thought he'd seen as he'd been turning the front door key. That being the case, he saw no harm in replying.

"Things are... They're... I'm...". He completely lost the thread of what he was saying. "How have you been keeping, yourself?"

"How have I been...?" Jared laughed; it was a hollow sound. Then he didn't so much walk into the room, as float. "How does it bloody well look like I've been keeping?"

Eric screwed up his eyes this time, but all that did was bring the rest of Jared into sharper focus. Now he could see the man's tatty suit and raincoat—it was the one he'd been wearing the evening of the attack—and he could see the red stains where the knife had slid into him, at the chest and torso. Jared touched one of the wounds and his fingers came away crimson.

"I'm dead, Eric. It isn't a whole lot of fun, I can tell you. Now, I know exactly what you're thinking, mate," said Jared, "but you're not dreaming this. It's real. I'm here. That was me before with the buzzers, too. Neat trick, eh?"

Eric looked past Jared, wondering why his neighbours hadn't reacted to the ruckus, come out to at least see what was happening. Perhaps they'd decided they didn't want to get involved.

"Don't worry about them, they can't hear me. It's you I've come to talk to." Jared smiled, but it was a chilling sight—his face was blue-white, his teeth stained where he'd coughed up blood.

"It's the cheese, then," murmured Eric. If he wasn't asleep, it had to be what he'd eaten before bed.

"What's that? Cheese? Hardly. Since when was cheese used to call forth ghosts from beyond the veil?"

"I meant it'd affected me," explained Eric. "Poisoned me somehow."

"Oh," said Jared, "I see. No, it's not down to any kind of dairy products, I'm afraid. I wish it was that simple." Jared frowned, then pulled up the chair Eric had been sitting on earlier, keeping vigil at the door. He glanced around at the flat. "So, this is where you've ended up. Onwards and upwards, eh? The place I was in when I was alive looked like a palace compared to this, and that's saying something."

Eric tentatively leaned forward on the sofa-bed. "And where..."

73

He swallowed dryly. "Where did *you* end up?"

"I'd have thought that was bloody well obvious."

Eric shook his head. It wasn't to him.

"All right," said Jared, also leaning forwards. "Now listen. What I'm going to tell you, what I've come here to say tonight before it's too late, it might not go down very well with you."

"I don't understand," said Eric.

"No, and that's the whole thing. You really don't understand how things work. How could you? You're still... Well, you're still *alive*, not to put too fine a point on it." Jared looked him right in the eye. "But that's a good thing. Much better than the alternative, I assure you. It's just what you're doing with the time you've got left that's the problem."

Eric still wasn't following him.

"All right." Jared clapped his hands together. "Where to begin? Okay, you remember what I used to be like in life, don't you?"

Eric nodded. Of course he did, he'd just been thinking about it tonight, when all this happened (which gave even more credence to the notion that he was either dreaming or whacked out on dodgy stilton).

"Always giving, always doing something for someone. Working my fingers to the bone to earn money to give away. Mankind was my business, Eric. Just like it's yours now."

Eric gave another nod. "You were the one who taught me that."

"Not intentionally, I have to add. But, okay, let me teach you another lesson, before you have to learn it the hard way, my friend." There was a bitterness to Jared's voice which hadn't been there when Eric had known him. Then again, maybe that's what being stabbed to death did for you. "Everything I ever did, all the people I helped, and what did it get me? I was knobbled taking the charity money we'd raised standing on freezing street corners to the bank."

Eric's eyes fell. "I know. And I'm sorry. Maybe if I'd gone with you—"

"Then you'd be just as dead as me, mate. Don't you get it? Regardless of everything we did, no-one had our back."

"What do you mean?"

"I mean I could have been cut some slack, you know? You fight the good fight, then you expect a few favours along the way."

74

Eric saw what he was getting at now, and was very surprised to hear it. "That isn't how it works."

"Fucking tell me about it!" spat Jared, taking Eric aback once more, especially with his bad language.

"That wasn't why we did what we did."

Jared leaned even further forwards, wagging his finger. "Maybe not, but perhaps, when I tell you this, you might see things a little differently."

Eric doubted he would. He wasn't the person he was because he wanted something in return, even if it was protection against the horrors of the world. What happened to Jared had a certain kind of warped irony to it, but that didn't mean he had a right to be saved that night, no matter how much he or Eric wanted it.

"No-one intervened because nobody was there to, pal. I didn't go on to get any stars in my crown because there's nothing... afterwards. Nothing at all."

"What?" gasped Eric.

"Why do you think I'm still hanging around here instead of there? Why do you think I still look like this? I'm stuck in the form I had when I died. Took me all this time to even appear corporeally. It's a lot harder than all those films make it look. And as for Clarence and his mob..." He swivelled on the seat. "Do you see any wings? Well, do ya? No, didn't think so."

"Maybe you're working for the other side, then?" Eric ventured.

"There *are* no sides! That's what I've been trying to tell you." Jared looked genuinely hurt by this, and Eric did feel guilty for suggesting it. Jared had done a lot of good in his time, more so even than him. Would he really have gone over to the dark side? "Look, believe what you like, but I'm telling you there's blackness, Eric. You die and there's nothing. No white light. No warm fuzzy feeling. No gates. Nada."

Eric thought for a moment about this. If Jared *was* right, then that would alter a fair few people's opinions about how to conduct themselves in *this* world. But that didn't include him. Eric wasn't doing what he was doing for any kind of reward, in this world or the next.

"I thought you might feel that way," Jared told him, reading his thoughts again. "That's why I brought a little back-up. I don't want

75

you wasting what's left of your life, like I did mine. Now that really *would* be a sin."

"I'm not wasting—"

Jared held up his bloodied hand. "Shut up, Eric. Whether you like it or not, you're going to be visited by three ghosts... and Yvette Fielding." Jared grinned when he saw the terrified look on Eric's face. "All right, I was only joking about her. I wouldn't wish that on anyone. But you are going to meet three of my lot: those who make it their business to show mortals the truth—before it's too late."

"Then I'll refuse to see them."

"Expect the first at one o'clock," said Jared, ignoring him and getting up.

"Wait a second," Eric said, rising too. "How will I know him?"

Jared, who was fading out even as he began walking away from Eric, looked over his shoulder and, grinning again, said: "He'll be wearing a pink carnation."

Then the spectre of Eric's late best friend vanished from sight, leaving the room the way it had been before he appeared (door and string intact), and leaving Eric wondering if the encounter had even happened at all.

The First of the Three Spirits

Eric spent the next thirty minutes or so looking at his watch, hoping either it had all been a hallucination or he was still snoring away to himself on the sofa-bed rather than checking the time.

When one o'clock came and went, he breathed a huge sigh of relief. Regardless of whether he was awake or asleep, the ghost Jared had talked about hadn't shown up.

No sooner had he thought this than the room began to shake. Eric tapped his watch. "Bugger," he said, remembering now that he always set it fast so he'd never be late for anything. Eric held on to the bed as it rattled beneath him, a terrible wind building up, swirling around and putting out the candles—yet the room was still well lit, swelling with a preternatural glow. Eric felt a presence behind him, and turned to see a figure standing in his kitchen. It was sepia in colour, and from certain angles looked to be an old man, but from others it had the face of a young boy, even a baby.

"Hello Eric," said the apparition in a shrill voice.

"Wh-Wh-Who are you?" spluttered Eric, teeth chattering at the sight.

The thing floated through into what Eric laughably called his living room, tutting. As it did so, Eric saw that its body was made up of old photographs, layered on top of one another. "Show a little backbone, man! It's no wonder Angela did what she did."

Angela. Eric hadn't thought about her in so long. Now, thanks to this... thing he saw her face again, saw her as she *used* to be. He shut his eyes, shaking his head. "That's what you're trying to do, isn't it? To change my mind? Make me think about the past?"

"Well, I wasn't going to, but what a great idea!" said the ghost. It grabbed a photo from its chest and threw it at Eric. "Here, take a look at this."

Eric couldn't help himself. He picked up the old photo and stared at it, recognising a twelve-year-old him, outside, playing in the snow with a bunch of other kids: hiding behind cars and lampposts, throwing snowballs at each other, at passers-by. One old woman shuddered when a cold projectile struck her back and the young Eric giggled.

"At least you knew how to have fun back then," the ghost said to

77

him, and Eric suddenly realised they were actually *in* the photograph, the edges still clearly defined.

Eric stood transfixed, watching his younger self. He'd forgotten all about this, about the Christmases he'd spent playing with pals from school.

"Eric! Eric? Where are you? It's time for tea! It's your favourite, chips, fish-fingers and mushy peas."

He recognised his mother's voice immediately, turning to look for her even as the boy Eric started to snigger with his friends and ran off down the road.

"Where's he... Where am *I* going?" he asked, setting off after the boys. But the ghost held him back, shaking its head. "They can't see or hear us. How can they, when this is just a snapshot from long ago?"

But there was more to this "snapshot", much more. Eric wanted to go back and see his mother, the woman who'd single-handedly brought up both him and his sister. But the ghost had other ideas.

"Not that way—up here," it said, pointing.

And suddenly they'd caught up with the Eric of the past. He was hassling some other kid who was wearing glasses, down one of the alleyways. "I lent you that comic for four days, Baker. You've had it over a week now, where is it?"

"It's at home. I'm sorry. I keep forgetting to bring it back to school," answered the other kid, obviously frightened.

Eric couldn't remember any of this, or perhaps he'd blocked it out of his memory? But why? He soon saw when the younger *him* spoke again.

"Four days, fifty pence a day we said. That means you now owe me four quid, plus interest."

The kid with the glasses just gaped at him. "What?"

"You heard me," said Eric. "Pay up!"

"B-But I haven't got it. After Christmas I might have a little money but—"

"Not good enough. A deal's a deal and we shook on it. Alan, Sam." The younger Eric stepped aside and let his mates come forward. What the present day Eric saw next made him balk. His friends started to beat up the kid with glasses who couldn't pay.

"No, stop!" shouted the older Eric, moving forward again; then he remembered what the ghost had said. He couldn't affect things here because they'd already happened. The beating had already played itself out: at *his* behest. Eric watched his younger self enjoying the spectacle. How could he have been so cold?

"Pretty good little racket you had going, I'd say," the ghost told him. "Pity you didn't keep it up. You had a bit of an edge back then."

"No, I... this can't be right," said Eric.

"Oh, I promise you it is. You were always the troublemaker growing up, Eric. Your mum and Faye were constantly getting you out of scrapes. Don't you remember? Must have been something to do with not having a father figure."

Eric covered his face with his hands, but the ghost pulled them down, simultaneously handing him another photo from its body. Eric took it reluctantly, and felt compelled again to look at the scene: this time a nightclub with flashing lights and disco music. He frowned, then saw himself at the bar with a pint of lager. He was in his late teens maybe, still hanging around with a couple of mates, having a laugh, getting increasingly drunk.

("You know I don't drink, Fraser. I've seen too much of what it can do to people.")

Eric turned to the ghost, who was at the side of him again—this time jiving to the music. "*Yeah*, this is more like it," the thing, that was both old and young at the same time, said. "Can't beat the '80s for dance tracks, can you?"

Eric ignored him, focussing instead on his past self. He was being egged on by his pals to approach a young woman with blonde hair, who was also with a couple of friends. The trio of women kept turning around and pointing: laughing. Then the blonde one turned and looked at him.

"Angela," whispered the present-day Eric.

The ghost stopped dancing for a second and nodded. "Bit of all right, isn't she?"

She was more than that—she was stunning! Eric watched as his teenage self plucked up the courage to swagger across to her. All false bravado, he stumbled over a few corny chat-up lines which Angela's companions laughed at, then just asked if they wanted a drink. If *Angela* wanted a drink. He could see the hesitation in her

79

eyes, but she nodded.

"Rum and coke," she told him.

Then later they'd danced, and he'd somehow persuaded her to give him a kiss under the mistletoe hanging from the glitter ball above the dance floor.

"So, one thing led to another and..." the ghost began. "What am I telling you for, you already know this story."

Eric did, but strangely enough he'd forgotten *how* exactly they'd met and how it had gone from there. It hurt too much to think about Angela at all these days.

The ghost danced around him, peeling off another photo—from its leg this time—and placed it in front of his nose. Here, Eric and Angela were in a flat, not that much bigger than the one he was currently occupying, but much more homely. Decorations were up, the tree was covered in tinsel and lights. Angela turned towards him and the ghost, the slight swelling of her pregnant belly clearly visible.

"Don't," said Eric, tears welling in his eyes. "Please don't show me this."

The ghost ignored him and let the scene unfold. Young Eric and Angela were talking about a job opportunity that he should take. After all, they were going to be a *proper* family soon.

"Mr Fitzgerald really seems like someone I could learn from," Eric was saying as he came up behind Angela, placing his arms around her and stroking her stomach.

"You should go for it," Angela told him. "Work your way up and in a few years, who knows where you'll be at that company?"

"But we both know where you ended up, don't we?" said the ghost, switching again between young and old. "You didn't learn from Fitzgerald at all. You learned instead from..."

Another photo, ripped from the ghost's arm, was shoved in front of Eric. It was of him and Jared meeting in the office. God, they both looked *soooo* young. Jared had clapped his hand, the grip firm. Here was a good man—unlike Fitzgerald, as Eric had discovered, with his underhand dealings and dodgy book-keeping. The more time Eric spent with Jared, the more he realised he could actually do something with his life. The amount of money Jared raised for various charities was something to aspire to, the amount of his time he set aside to spend with the poor, the needy, the sick.

It opened Eric's eyes. And once that had happened, they couldn't be closed again.

"But at what cost?" asked the ghost.

A further photo now, which Eric refused to even acknowledge— so the ghost forced him to see, sucking them both inside the picture of a hospital ward. Angela was crying, head pushed into the pillow. Eric rushed through a set of double doors, having only just made it there, once everything was over.

"There were... complications," the doctor told him before he went in. "We did our best."

"Thank you," Eric told him. "I'm sure you did."

When Angela saw him, she sniffed back the tears. "Where have you *been*, Eric? Where were you?"

"I'm so sorry. The orphanage—"

"The orphanage!" Angela let out a wail. "You were with those... those... When your own child..." She couldn't speak anymore, turning away again and crying into the pillow. The Eric of yesteryear reached out his hand to place it on her shoulder, but then withdrew it.

The Eric from the present was crying freely, but the spirit wasn't about to let him off that easily. "It didn't end there, though, did it? In spite of this, you carried on, spending more and more time away from home. Away from Angela."

"No!"

"Oh yes," argued the ghost, showing him the photo he'd dreaded most. The one of Angela sitting alone on Christmas Day, still in the same flat they'd owned years before, two plates of dinner on the table in front of her. And where had Eric been?

"I was... I needed to—"

"You were helping those who couldn't help themselves. I know."

As Eric continued to watch, Angela rose and picked up the phone, dialling a number. "It's me," she said down the line. "Can I come over? I need you. I need to be with you."

Eric was crying again, the anger welling in him. "You..." he almost said "bastard", changing it at the last second to, "Bugger."

The ghost spared him the sight of Angela in the arms of another man, thankfully ("He was everything *you* showed the promise of being: exciting, going places. He wasn't the first, and wouldn't be the last, of course. But they all shared that common trait, Eric. While you tried to save the world, staying stock still at the same time."). But what he did show Eric was so much worse.

A final photograph, and this one had Eric serving some ragged men at the soup kitchens as he did every year. He watched himself doling out the hot broth and the kind words in equal measures, then looked over at the ghost as if to ask why he was showing him this. How could it possibly change his mind—this was what he was meant to do, what Jared had inspired him to do.

Jared. This was all connected to him. Because, as they watched, those same men left the kitchens and walked the streets. Eric and the ghost saw them notice a man strolling down the road wearing a suit and raincoat, carrying a holdall. Eric watched in horror as the men he'd just helped nudged each other, nodding across at the guy, then following until they spotted a good place to jump him.

But Jared was reluctant to part with the holdall, and they saw why when they yanked it from his hand and got a look inside at all the cash.

"No, you leave that alone. It belongs to—" The man's cries were silenced with a knife to the stomach, but one blow obviously wasn't enough, because they kept on ramming the blade into him, over and over. Leaving him bleeding red against the slushy white snow.

Then they ran off, abandoning Jared Marlowe in the gutter to die.

Eric fell backwards, a hand to his mouth. Fell back out of the photograph and into his flat. He was trembling, in shock from the knowledge that the people he'd been trying to help, to feed at this special time of year, had thrown it back in his face—murdering his best friend in the whole world.

"Jared," said Eric, not able to take the information in.

And he was still reeling when the next supernatural visitor arrived in his home.

The Second of the Three Spirits

It took Eric a moment or so to realise that the thing had appeared under the tree.

But it was big, so big in fact it dwarfed the tree itself and he almost fell backwards over it, stumbling to bat away the visions that the sepia-toned ghost had exposed him to.

Eric wiped his eyes and stared at the box.

It was brightly coloured, all reds and golds and greens, wrapped up with the greatest of care and tied with a bow on the top. As with the buzzer downstairs, the last thing Eric had been expecting it to do was talk.

"Don't just stand there lookin' at me, then," said the box, jiggling. The voice this time was fairly gruff, in direct opposition to the one from before. "Open me up!"

"What... who...?" Eric began.

The box let out a groan. "Isn't it *obvious* who I am?"

"Erm, not really."

"I'm a bleedin' Christmas Present," said the box, jiggling again. "Think about it."

Eric frowned. He had no idea what this had to do with what Jared had told him at the start. He didn't need any presents, especially one that was *telling* him he needed it.

"Well, come on then. What's wrong with you? Most people like to open Christmas Presents."

To be honest, it had been so long since anyone had given Eric a gift at this time of year, he'd forgotten the procedure. His usually came in the form of a smile from someone he'd helped.

"Don't be so bloody wet," the present sniped. "Get your arse down here and get openin' me. *Right now!*" The voice sounded so much like his boss, Mr Fitzgerald, that Eric instinctively did as he was told, getting on his hands and knees and pulling at the bow. It came away easily, as did the paper on top—like it was helping Eric itself to get it open; which, in all likelihood, it was. Eric opened up the box, curious—having come this far—to see what was inside.

It was a box, wrapped just as intricately as the last one. Eric heard gruff laughter.

"What is this?"

"It's another present," came the reply. "So go on, open it."

Eric felt stupid, and he felt duped. But that curiosity hadn't left him, plus this game was at least taking his mind off the things he'd just witnessed thanks to the sepia-coloured spirit. He undid this parcel too, only to find... another box.

"Heh-heh-heh," came the laughter again.

"You've got to be kidding."

"I am and I'm not," said the Present. "Half the fun of opening me is the expectation, so I like to tease it out a little. Don't worry, it'll be worth it."

Eric's head lolled. "I doubt that very much."

"What if I said you could sell what's in me, raise some money for charity. If you must."

That got Eric's attention. Not that he fully trusted what this or the other ghosts had told him tonight. But it was worth having a peek inside the present just to make sure. If there was a way of making some money here—to feed and clothe the needy, of course—then he owed it to them to continue.

"All right," Eric said, diving in again, ignoring the laughter.

This went on for some time, a smaller present inside each of the presents he was opening. Like Russian dolls, he placed them in a row on the floor of his flat. There were ten in total, and when Eric finally came to the last of them, he looked over to see that they'd formed themselves into a rough figure beside him, held together with the wrapping and bows, which also created the illusion of a face. This only fazed him momentarily (after all it was no more strange than a person made of photographs) and then Eric undid the final present.

"Aha!" he said, taking out his reward. "Paydirt!"

The Present hadn't lied after all, because in here was a top of the line, compact Handycam. Had to be worth at least a couple of hundred pounds, if not more. Eric was just glad this hadn't been here when he'd been robbed.

As he took it out, he saw a red light flashing on the side of it. The blessed thing had been accidentally turned on before being wrapped up. Eric turned it over and over in his hands, looking for the way to switch it off again. He opened up the viewing screen on the side, hopeful that the button might be concealed in there. But as his eyes caught the screen, he was surprised to see that the image being recorded didn't match the scene in front of him. The camera should have been picking up the tree, the edge of the window, the cracked plaster of the walls. Instead there was another room entirely: a much bigger, finer room. Eric waved his hand in front of the lens, but the camera failed to pick it up.

"What's going on here?" he asked.

"Why don't you have a closer look and see?" replied the Present in that rough voice, and in spite of himself Eric did, putting the viewfinder up to his eye. It was like looking through one of those magic tubes when he was a kid, seeing a picture that he knew shouldn't be there at the other end. Only this one was moving. Someone came into shot and Eric's eyes trailed them: a woman, wearing a long, flowing silken gown. She was beautiful, hair expertly coiffured, face perfectly made up—red lipstick covering her pouting mouth. She had the kind of lashes that could blow a man away... in more ways than one.

As she moved around the enormous room, Eric took more of it in. There were paintings on the wall, and though he was no expert he suspected these were the real deal: a Constable, a Landseer, even a Monet. Any one of them would be able to fund the refuge for months, maybe even years. There was a roaring fire under one of the paintings, the mantel covered in cards, with a clock in the middle. There was a grand piano situated in the far corner of the room, next to a set of marble steps, and two bookcases along the back wall, full of the kind of tomes he'd lost tonight (though Eric suspected the owners hardly touched them; like everything else here, they were for show—to show *how* incredibly rich and powerful these people were). In the other corner was a Christmas tree so tall it reached the high ceiling, covered in lights and baubles, with a gigantic fairy planted on the top.

As the woman drifted across the space, feet covered by the robe so that she herself resembled a ghost, Eric felt a sudden pang of jealousy. *No*, he said to himself. *They're just things. Material goods that you can do without. It's* people *who are important.*

"Why are you showing me this?" Eric asked the new ghost. It didn't make any sense. He didn't even know this woman, didn't recognise this place. He felt seedy, like some kind of voyeur.

85

"Keep watching," replied the spirit. "You'll see."

Eric did as he was told and as he watched, he saw a man come into view. A portly fellow he knew all too well. It was his boss, Mr Fitzgerald. The man waddled down the steps, holding onto the rail for support, passing the piano and joining the woman on the massive couch in the centre of the room. Two of the biggest, comfiest chairs Eric had ever seen flanked this, and all of them were covered in the most expensive dark leather—waxed so much that it was a wonder people didn't just slide off the seats.

So that's it, all this belongs to him*, paid for by his cutthroat and underhand work dealings.*

Fitzgerald kissed the woman on the cheek, slobbering over her and squeezing into the gap—his huge girth initially proving a stumbling block to sitting comfortably. Eric realised this must be Fitzgerald's wife, Vanora. He'd heard some of the other office workers talking about her every now and again: about how she was Fitzgerald's fifth spouse; about how she was a former model and beauty queen (he could believe that now); about how it had been the money rather than Fitzgerald's other "charms" that had attracted her. Nevertheless, Eric also knew that there had been a product of this union, as mind judderingly disturbing as that was to imagine (so Eric chose not to). A young boy about the same age as his own child would have—

Eric mentally shook his head, telling himself not to go there again.

As if on cue, and preventing Fitzgerald from becoming any more amorous with this wife—which nobody needed to see—a small boy in pyjamas came down the steps, laughing.

"Now, Timmy, you know it's way past your bedtime," said Vanora. "Santa won't come and leave you any presents if you're not a good little boy."

Timmy looked at her sideways, as if about to question whether Santa existed at all, but decided not to chance it and came over to give his parents a hug and kiss before heading back off to bed. When he walked across, Eric noticed the boy had a slight limp.

"What's wrong with him?" he asked the Present.

"There were... complications at his birth," replied the gruff voice. "But he pulled through. He's a tough little cookie. Plus, he had the finest doctors money could buy helping him through it."

86

Eric was silent. He watched Timmy jump up on Fitzgerald's lap, wondering what that feeling might have been like. To have been a Dad to such a lovely little tyke. Fitzgerald, however, looked like he couldn't wait to get rid of his son—probably so he could get his hands on Vanora again.

Vanora gave her son a kiss and then told him to get off back to bed and go straight to sleep. "There's a good boy," she added.

As soon as Timmy was gone, Fitzgerald was slobbering over his wife again, this time his hand riding up her gown. He muttered something about giving her an early present, and that's when Eric pulled the viewfinder back down from his eye.

"Ugh," he said. But the image of the house, of the life his boss was living, remained with him. Surely Fitzgerald didn't deserve such happiness, did he? After all the dishonest things he'd done, the people he'd screwed over? Though Eric felt bad for thinking it, there was also a part of him that resented Fitzgerald for having Timmy at all; that felt like the boy should have been his.

"He played the game," said the Present. "Built up his business—through whatever means—and now he's reaping the benefits."

"I didn't say a thing," Eric replied, but then he didn't need to. With these guys it was enough to just think it. He looked down and saw that the image on the viewscreen had changed, thankfully. It now showed his nephew, Fraser, with a couple of other youths his age, hitting the town on Christmas Eve.

Curiosity got the better of him again, and Eric pressed his eye to the viewfinder. He watched as the lads entered a club, a techno beat throbbing in the background. They ordered at the bar and began drinking their lagers.

"Look familiar?" asked the Present. "This was how *you* used to have a good time before you became such a stiff."

Eric ignored him, concentrating on what Fraser was up to. He and his mates had already spotted some girls in the corner wearing skimpy green elf outfits and had gone over to begin chatting them up. Fraser was much cooler and much better at it than Eric had ever been, and within minutes he was up and dancing with one of the women: a very attractive brunette whose hat flopped from side to side as she gyrated around Fraser. It wasn't long before she had her arms wrapped round him, and he was whispering in her ear. Next thing her tongue was down his throat, so far it looked like she was trying to clean his Adam's Apple. Eric pulled a face, feigning disgust—but in reality he wondered what it would be like to be kissed again, to have someone pay him attention in that way again. It got very lonely inside his flat all on his own.

"It's your choice," the Present reminded him. "This is Fraser most weekends, out on the town—and on the pull."

"I'm not sure I want to know."

"Aww, leave him alone. He's young, free and single. He's also seriously loaded. He could have any woman he wanted. And he frequently does!" As the Present was talking, and as if to demonstrate, Fraser was leading the elf outside where they climbed into a taxi—and promptly began snogging again on the backseat as it transported them to his place.

Eric raised an eyebrow when he saw Fraser's pad. He knew the lad was doing all right, but this was something else. An exclusive top floor apartment with balcony, the place was kitted out with all the latest mod cons and an interior that looked like the inside of a spaceship: all white walls and chrome. Fraser's TV alone covered most of one wall, a digital flatscreen which he flicked on to one of the music channels as he fixed the elf another drink from his well-stocked bar.

"Wow!" Eric exclaimed.

"I know," said the Present.

Not long after, Fraser took the dark-haired elf off by the hand and into the bedroom. Again, Eric moved the camera down before he could see any more. He hadn't wanted to see Fitzgerald at it, let alone his own nephew. The young man's lifestyle, though, had made Eric think. He'd always maintained that Fraser was wasting his life away: the clubs, the drinking, the casual sex. But wasn't he only making the most of his time on this planet? If Jared was right—and Eric still wasn't convinced of that—then which one of the two of them was actually using this gift called life to the greatest advantage?

"That's easy," said the Present, answering the rhetorical question. "*Him.*"

Eric shook his head, he'd had enough of this. He was just about to put down the camera for good when his eyes caught the viewing screen again. It was no longer throwing back an image of Fraser and the girl. Now it was showing him something altogether different.

"Angela?" he said.

"Angela," confirmed the Present.

She was sitting alone at a table again, in a place that looked not dissimilar to the flat they'd once shared together. But instead of a turkey dinner in front of her there was a half-empty bottle of gin. Eric pressed his eye up to the viewfinder, just as she opened her clenched right hand. She was holding a selection of different coloured pills, sitting there staring at them through tear-stained eyes.

"No..." breathed Eric. "Don't show me this."

"It's my final present to you. She's all alone again, Eric. Those other guys never stuck around for very long." The Present's voice grew even deeper. "She could be yours again. You could save her. All you'd have to do would be to become the man you always should have been. The man she *thought* she was marrying in the first place."

Oh, that was low. Eric gritted his teeth, shook his head again. No, he wouldn't be blackmailed, not even when he wanted Angela back as much as he did. He threw the camera across the room. It smashed to pieces on the already cracked wall.

"There's just no pleasing some people, is there?" grumbled the Christmas Present Ghost. "I wish I'd bought you socks instead now."

And before Eric's eyes, the wrapping paper and bows separated, causing the box figure to fall apart and collapse right there in front of him.

The Third of the Three Spirits

Eric remained on his knees for some time; he felt like a broken man.

He'd discovered that not only was there nothing whatsoever on the other side—not even if you'd devoted yourself to helping your fellow man—but if he'd taken a different route in the past he might still have a wife, and probably a child as well (once again, the image of little Timmy coming down those steps flashed across his mind). What's more, he'd been shown that his best friend had died at the hands of people he himself had been kind to, plus his ex was about to top herself because of the car wreck her life had become...

All because of him.

So engrossed in his misery was Eric that he hadn't noticed he was in almost complete darkness now that the ghosts had departed. It was appropriate somehow, reflected how he felt inside. But this was no ordinary gloom, as he soon discovered when it reached out and touched him on the shoulder. Eric started, rising and spinning around to try and catch sight of whatever was out there. He saw nothing, couldn't even see the hand in front of his face.

"Who's there?"

No reply. If it was the third and final ghost of the evening, then he'd at least expected it to give some smart arse reply like the others. He asked once more, and again there was no answer.

The darkness tapped him on the other shoulder and he spun around in a different direction. If he'd been thinking straight he would have wondered how he hadn't fallen over something, or hit a wall by now. "This is not funny," Eric complained. "If you're here for me, then just get on with it, will you?"

An outline revealed itself, faint yet still part of the blackness. Eric squinted; it looked very much to him like a cloak and hood, but he couldn't see any hint of a face. Still without saying anything, the third ghost did as it was instructed and "got on with it".

Ironically, the whole thing started off as a faint light this time—bright against the darkness. Then a series of lights, like lasers, shooting out of the black and projecting an image. An image that soon became 3D, wrapping itself around Eric like something out of a futuristic SF movie by James Cameron.

Eric found himself looking at an office. An empty chair in an office, to be precise. *His* empty chair at the office. But that was all right, this was Christmas Day, had to be—he could tell from the sparse decorations Fitzgerald allowed. And nobody worked there on Christmas Day... Except today they were. Wendy from accounts, Roy manning the phones, Mal walking around with a piece of paper in his hand as always, trying to look busy but actually not doing very much. All acquaintances rather than actual friends; they simply couldn't understand any of Eric's obsessions.

They looked thoroughly miserable, and as Eric listened in he discovered why. All his work colleagues were moaning about the fact that Fitzgerald had made them come in. "'There are plenty more people who'd be glad of the job if you're not'," said Wendy, doing a pretty decent imitation of her boss—who was no doubt at home enjoying his day with his wife and kid.

"But where am *I*?" asked Eric.

Once again, the ghost who was there but not really there gave no reply. Eric heard his name and tuned back in to the conversation.

"He's better off," Mal said. "Least he's not slaving away."

Eric frowned. There was something about the way they were talking about him, something so very final. He swallowed hard. "So that's it. I'm dead, right? Is that what you're trying to tell me? I haven't got long so make the most of it?"

The hologram show blurred then and created another image. It was Eric, though he had to look really closely to recognise himself. He was sitting in a shop doorway, huddling against the cold. He had a long, matted and greying beard, to match his long, matted and greying hair. His clothes were virtually rags, held together with bits of string, and his shoes had more holes in them than a piece of Swiss cheese. *Right*, thought Eric, s*o I lose my job. And it looks like my flat as well. How?*

"Spare us some change," the older Eric pleaded, holding out his hand. But people were walking by, ignoring him. He hung his head in despair.

Eric watched as the version of him from the future got up, heading to the refuge where he'd once given so much of his time. Except he was stopped at the door by someone he didn't recognise—a volunteer who must have come along since his time there—and told that they were full.

"But I used to help out here," future Eric argued. "I gave all my money to places like this, to causes like this one. It's Christmas, for Heaven's sake! Have some pity."

The man just told him to get lost because he was stinking up the entrance.

Shaking his head, Eric shambled away.

So that was it: he was destined to become one of the people he'd helped, destitute and unloved. Where the hell was Fraser? That's what he wanted to know. His only family left in the world?

He watched as the hologram shimmered again and showed Eric a picture of himself hiding behind a wall, near a cash machine. Waiting for a lone man with a bunch of flowers in his hand to finish withdrawing some money. When he got close enough, the future Eric jumped out and attempted to snatch his wallet. The man resisted and Eric didn't appear to have the strength to fight him. More bystanders rushed towards the struggling pair so Eric cut his losses and ran. The present-day Eric next saw him hiding behind some bins, breathing hard and crying.

He wanted to as well.

The hologram shifted its perspective again and showed Eric his older self staggering along a train station platform. He watched as the ragged man he would become took out a photo from his pocket. Eric walked around himself, to see who was in it. He might have guessed. It was Angela, probably dead some years by now.

"Don't do it," he told himself, but he knew by now the man couldn't hear. "*Please*," he continued anyway.

A train was coming, too fast to be stopping at the station. Eric reached out to try and stop his future self from jumping in front of it, but of course it did no good.

Eric closed his eyes, refusing to look. But then he heard the sound of Fraser's voice. He looked again to see the hologram had settled on one final scene: Fraser, a few years older judging by the lines on his face and receding hairline, standing over a grave, tears in his eyes.

"Oh Uncle, why didn't you call me? Why did we drift apart like this?" said Fraser. "I wish you'd stayed in touch."

So that was it, *he'd* been the one who'd shunned Fraser—just like he'd blown him off that very day. His only relation.

Eric came round and stood beside Fraser, looking down at the gravestone his nephew must have bought. He'd been an idiot, a fool for all these years. But what could he do to prevent all this?

"I *have* to know, are these the events of what will be or what might be?" he asked.

Predictably, there was no answer.

But, seconds later, the hologram lightshow folded in on itself, and blackness returned. He couldn't tell for sure but he suspected the ghost had gone, if it had even been here at all. Perhaps it had been his own subconscious, and if it really had been a dream then that was trying to tell him something as well.

Eric sat up on his sofa-bed—where he'd begun this adventure—a changed man.

He was determined to do something about his life, about his attitude. He was going to get back his edge, get back Angela, and somehow make his mark. Eric hadn't figured it all out yet, but it would somehow involve Fraser dishing up the dirt on Fitzgerald (when he was in charge of that company, Eric would make sure the employees got their Christmas Day off at least, though not a second more. He would also throw his ex-boss a bone of a lowly office job; well, he didn't want to see poor Timmy out on the streets).

All thoughts of getting up to help at the soup kitchen vanquished from his mind, Eric plotted and planned and schemed: not least of which how he was going to get his leatherbound books back, with the help of either a few of his less savoury neighbours or some of the folk he'd come into contact with helping the homeless (he could think of a couple of excellent replacements for the "muscle" of his childhood friends).

The spirits had taught him much, and all in one night. He would put it to good use, and make the most of the time he had left...

*   *   *

Jared Marlowe observed his old friend from the safety of the otherworld.

His plan had worked beautifully, even if he did say so himself. He'd done what so many others had failed to do in the past, putting right a wrong that had taken place all those years ago, to Eric's ancestor. If the "powers that be" hadn't interfered back then, Eric's

93

line would have carried on being the cruelty and misery poster boys for evil that had been intended. But oh no, *They* couldn't have that—so They'd brainwashed old Ebenezer into being good, and kind. That's the version of the story Jared had been told, anyhow.

Told by his new master. The one he'd done the deal with.

Jared had been lying, of course, when he said there was nothing after death. There were sides, obviously, and he—after a lifetime of stealing, cheating and conning people—had found himself on the wrong one. Or the right one, as it now happened. Did he feel guilty about the way he'd manipulated his old mate, Eric? No more than he did about deceiving him in the first place—about letting him believe that he'd been murdered by homeless people Eric had helped, when in actual fact it had been the mob he'd been on his way to give the charity money to; paying off some of his own gambling debts (though he hadn't had quite enough to stop them from doing what they did).

He'd actually done Eric a favour in the long run, if he thought about it. All that do-gooding was fine, but he'd have much more fun this way (not as much fun as Jared had been promised if he could pull this off, however). Eric might also be happier, or so Jared told himself. He chose not to think about the many people Eric had helped—inspired by his own supposedly good deeds, which were nothing of the sort (he'd never bloody well asked Eric to emulate him, had he)—or *would have* helped in the future. It just meant that there was more chance they'd see each other again when his old buddy did eventually shuffle off his mortal coil. Oh, how they'd laugh about this.

Eric had finally been allowed to keep Christmas in his own way, just as his ancestor wanted to. Jared grinned, knowing he had escaped his fate because of all that he'd achieved—the thought of those flames, those chains and hooks made him shudder—and that his stunt here would be the stuff of legend in the years to come. Who knows, maybe they'd even write about it one day?

Jared wondered what they might call the tale if they ever did.

Perhaps a variation of what Eric's ancestor had once used as his catchphrase, something to emphasise how the Scrooge family had been well and truly screwed by those kiss-ass spirits before (he preferred his own versions much better).

94

Yes, that seems appropriate, thought Jared Marlowe, whistling merrily as he returned to the hot realm below that he now called home.

Rubbing his hands in anticipation of his own Christmas futures to come.

THE GREATEST MYSTERY

My dear and faithful reader. It is only now that I am able to recount the truly shocking events of what I firmly believe to be my dearest friend and colleague Sherlock Holmes' greatest ever mystery. Upon first reading these words, you may feel my claim is somewhat of an exaggeration. What about the case of the Baskerville Hound, you might ask, quite possibly his most famous adventure to date? What about his entanglements with the evil Professor Moriarty (the merest mention of which will later have great significance, I can assure you)? But I have faithfully chronicled the master detective's cases over the years and I can categorically attest to the validity of my statement. I alone was witness to its eventual outcome and, once you have finished this offering, I feel certain that you too will agree about the choice of its title. I can also promise that while I have been taken to task in the past for what Holmes called my embellishment of these accounts—the addition of, to quote the man himself, "colour and... life" (the latter an irony, as you will soon see)—there isn't a word of this that is not the whole truth. Whether you believe me or not is, in the end, your choice—all I can do is report the facts of this most singular case as I experienced them, no matter how strange they might seem.

The matter in question began with a simple case—although you might recall the air of strangeness and tension against which it was set, in the months approaching the turn of the last century. Indeed, these very events were thought by some to be interlinked, though you will soon realise that this was not in fact so. The real explanation goes beyond that, beyond anything you might have thought possible. But I am getting ahead of myself once more... The case in hand was an apparently straightforward crime, yet as Holmes is often at great pains to teach me, things are seldom what they appear at first glance.

And so, to the details. A lady by the name of Miss Georgia Cartwright called upon us one afternoon in late September, begging that we pay a visit to her cousin Anthony.

"In jail," Holmes said, motioning for Miss Cartwright to sit down. When he noticed her look of confusion, he waved a hand and explained: "The faint marks on your dress and your arms, a distinctive pattern showing you have recently been pressed up against a set of iron bars. Pray tell us of what your cousin is accused, Miss Cartwright?"

"I am sad to say Anthony stands accused of... of... murdering his fiancée, and *my* best friend, Miss Judith Hatten," she told us, gratefully accepting both the seat and the handkerchief I'd produced to dry her eyes with. "But he cannot have, he simply *cannot*."

Holmes sat down opposite her, steepling his fingers. "If you would furnish me with the facts, Miss Cartwright—and please do not leave anything out. Even the smallest detail might be of significance."

Sadly, it soon became clear, as she related what she knew, that the culprit could be *none other* than her relation. The night before last Anthony had visited Judith to discuss their forthcoming wedding. Upon hearing a disturbance in the living room, where Anthony had been escorted just minutes beforehand, the girl's only living parent—her father—discovered the young man standing over the body of Judith. His daughter had suffered a tremendous head wound. In Anthony's hand was a poker, the end of which was dripping with blood. Mr Hatten flew into a rage and had to be held back by his staff from attacking Anthony himself, while Miss Cartwright's cousin was held down until the authorities arrived.

Holmes frowned, obviously reaching the same conclusion as I.

"He swears it was not him, says that he cannot remember what happened, Mr Holmes. And I believe him. Anthony is the gentlest man in the world and he did so love Judith. I know he did. He would never have raised a finger to hurt her."

Holmes raised an eyebrow. "It is so often the case, however, that we do not *truly* know our friends and loved ones, Miss Cartwright.'"

"We grew up together and were as close as brother and sister. I *do* know him, Mr Holmes. Please, I implore you," she said, clasping her hands together. "Visit him yourself."

Holmes glanced sideways, attempting not to let this sway his judgement. But in spite of his somewhat cool exterior, my friend has never been able to turn away anyone in such distress. Yet I have seen him reject far more intriguing investigations, so something about this particular case must have piqued his interest. I wish to God now, looking back, that he'd had the courage to simply inform Miss Cartwright he could not help. If that sounds harsh, believe me it will not by the time I have finished relating this tale.

So it was that we found ourselves in a coach on our way to see her cousin at Scotland Yard's "charming" prison. The journey at least afforded me some time to glean Holmes' thoughts about the case.

"Surely it would be wrong to get the young woman's hopes up," I told him. "The man's destined for the noose. There might not have been witnesses to the actual deed, but being caught with the murder weapon in one's possession implies just as much guilt."

Holmes steadfastly refused to be drawn on the subject until we'd seen the prisoner for ourselves. Inspector Lestrade similarly conveyed the opinion that my friend was wasting his time, when we arrived and asked to see the man.

"I cannot understand why Miss Cartwright has brought you into such an affair," said the sly-looking policeman. "There was nothing untoward in the investigation, I can assure you, Mr Holmes." His tone was accusatory, as if he thought we were criticising his procedure. Nevertheless, he granted us full access to the man, in part because of all the help Holmes has been to the police in his career— often without due credit—but I think also because he was confident enough that nothing we discovered would make him look inferior in front of his own men. "The father is baying for the man's blood," Lestrade called after us, as if he thought that might change our minds.

When we arrived, the young prisoner had a haunted look about him. He was staring at the stone wall opposite, and from time to time just shook his head as if he could not comprehend how he had arrived in that dark, dank place.

"Your cousin Georgia has asked that we speak with you," Holmes said after making our introductions, but could elicit no response.

"She tells us that you deny any wrongdoing in the murder of Miss Judith Hatten," said I, and did notice a twitch. Then, suddenly, he was holding his head in his hands, tearing at his hair.

"I did not murder her," he whispered, almost inaudibly, then screamed: "I did not murder her!" Anthony looked across at us, eyes as tearful as his cousin's were but an hour earlier. "P-Please... Please, you have to believe me."

Holmes stepped closer to the bars. "Then tell us who did."

Anthony shook his head again, but it wasn't a refusal; it was simply that he had no idea what to say. What *could* he say, when all the evidence pointed towards him? He would utter nothing more, even when pressed, and we left not long afterwards—Holmes informing the guard on duty that his charge should be watched.

"I believe he may try to take his own life," Holmes explained to him.

The guard snorted. "It'd save us the trouble."

My friend flashed the guard a threatening look, then turned. "Watson, let us take our leave of this place," said he.

As we walked out of the prison, and as I was attempting to match Holmes' stride, I commented, "You cannot blame the guard. Miss Cartwright's cousin offers no defence."

"Watson," Holmes said, suddenly rounding on me, "did you not see it in the man's eyes? Credit me with having looked enough murderers in the face to recognise one. That man is indeed innocent of this crime."

"But how *can* he be?" I argued. "You've heard all the—"

He held up his finger. "And still he is innocent. I cannot explain it yet, but that is what I believe. He does not remember committing these acts, but I feel certain he saw them being committed."

I rubbed my chin. "He's definitely a troubled man, but guilt can block out memories. Or are you perhaps suggesting a split personality?"

Holmes pursed his lips. "You are the one with the medical knowledge, Watson."

"Well, I'd need to study him more to—" I was interrupted this second time by the blowing of whistles and policemen running past us. There was something afoot, a crime in progress, and even though we were already committed to this first investigation Holmes has never been one to let an opportunity to observe an offense—or to lend assistance with the same—pass him by.

We followed the police to a residence but a few streets away.

Holmes completely ignored Lestrade's warnings to stay back until they could ascertain what had happened and, dashing after my friend, I too witnessed the tail end of what had occurred.

Later, we would discover that the house belonged to Mr and Mrs William Thorpe, an ordinary couple in every single way—Mr Thorpe being a retired schoolteacher.

Screams had been heard emanating from their home; a woman's screams. As we entered the dining room, Lestrade still attempting to keep us back, we saw that these had indeed originated from Mrs Thorpe, but not because she was being assaulted in any way. No, these were the screams of a woman holding a dinner-knife in her hand, standing staring at the body of her husband, who was lying sprawled out over the dining table. From what I could see, and from later examinations, I can tell you that he was stabbed repeatedly with that instrument. It had been a frenzied attack, redness covering the table and dripping from the tablecloth. However, it would not be the final such scene we would witness during the course of this investigation.

As the police moved in closer, Mrs Thorpe stopped screaming and looked over in our direction. She had that selfsame expression on her face that Miss Cartwright's cousin had back in his jail cell.

One of disbelief.

"Lestrade!" cried Holmes, but his warnings came too late. Mrs Thorpe looked at the body of her husband a final time, looked down at the bloodied knife in her hand, then drew the blade across her own throat. A thick jet of blood sprayed across the room.

The police let me through then, but there was nothing that could be done for the poor woman; she had made a very thorough job of cutting through both the jugular and carotid arteries. My attempts to stem the bleeding were in vain, and as Holmes joined me we both heard her final gurgling gasps.

"I... ack... I didn't..." she breathed before dying.

*   *   *

Though we were fresh to the scene of this incident—able to examine it before Lestrade and his men could contaminate it, as Holmes would say—we found nothing amiss, save for the obvious brutal murder of Mr Thorpe himself.

As you know, I have long been a student of Holmes and his methods, so it was with a heavy heart that I watched him pace the room, sniffing the air, taking out his glass to pay closer scrutiny to a piece of carpet here, the edge of a table there, only for him to concede that—as she must have done—Mrs Thorpe had plunged the knife into her husband during the meal. Holmes pressed a gloved finger to his lips. "Ah, but it is the way it happened that is the most curious aspect, Watson," said he. "Note the way the plates are scattered on the table. The look of shock and surprise on Mr Thorpe's face. This occurred quickly. As if something unimaginable came over the woman. One moment sat eating dinner together, the next..." There was no need to finish that sentence, we both knew how that dinner had ended.

I nodded. "But what *could* have come over her?"

"Once again: you are the physician, Watson. I would suggest that you examine the body of not only Mr Thorpe," he encouraged, "but his wife as well. We shall also be needing access to the body of Miss Judith Hatten." Holmes looked over at Lestrade as he said this.

"I beg your pardon? What has the one thing to do with the other?" the policeman asked.

"Oh, come now, Inspector. Surely you can see the connection here?" The man could not, but I could. Two people murdered by their partners, both surviving halves—though Mrs Thorpe did not survive for long, I grant you—claiming that they did not commit the crime, flying in the face of all evidence to the contrary. This was turning out to be a case for Holmes, after all, and I could see the recognisable glint in his eye whenever there was a fresh mystery to be solved. Particularly one which would challenge his skills like this.

Lestrade allowed us to examine the body of Miss Hatten anyway, along with the others. But even as Holmes watched my explorations from a distance down in the icy morgue—not far away, yet not too close, either for his comfort or mine—I could offer him no new leads.

"The causes of death are accurate," said I, "a head injury in the case of Miss Hatten and repeated stab wounds in the case of Mr Thorpe."

Holmes looked past me to the grey bodies on the tables, and breathed in deeply—something I would not readily advise in such a situation. "But what of *Mrs* Thorpe?"

I shook my head. "Nothing that I could see, at any rate. Perhaps an examination of her blood..."

However not even that afforded us an explanation; no abnormalities which might have accounted for sudden changes in personality. Nor did Holmes' trip to the Hatten residence uncover anything, largely because Judith's father would not grant us permission to view the crime scene once he learned who had enlisted our help.

"No matter," Holmes said as we climbed back into the cab, heading towards Baker Street once more. "After so long, I doubt whether it would have yielded anything of interest."

While Holmes attempted to make some kind of sense of the incidents thus far—littering his room with everything from articles on insanity to reports alleging bodily possession by demons ("You cannot seriously be considering that?" I said to him when I discovered his notes, and he just batted me away with his hand), playing his violin into the small hours of the morning—more incidents took place.

In Kentish Town an antiques dealer named Falconbridge used an ornamental sword to disembowel his housekeeper (a woman he'd employed for many years and—it was rumoured—he also had a strong admiration for) then turned the weapon on himself. At Westminster Hospital a middle-aged builders merchant called Roberson took it upon himself to secrete a hypodermic needle about his person and inject his elderly mother with an overdose of morphine: a mercy killing, you might assume, but the woman was actually recovering from her malaise and was expected to be discharged within the month. Colleagues of mine who were present informed me that the relative, in a state of confusion and remorse, ran away. His body was later found in the Thames. Finally, passengers on a train bound for Waterloo described hearing piercing screams, only to witness a woman backing out of a carriage covered in blood and holding a fire axe. Her hands were trembling, as she looked left and right, then she dropped the axe and fled, eventually hurling herself from the moving vehicle according to the ticket inspector. Inside the carriage were found the dismembered bodies of her husband and their 12 year-old daughter.

It was the latter, I fear, that had the most telling effect upon Holmes. As we stepped onto that train, Lestrade now very glad of any assistance we could offer, my friend wavered, almost turning back. But he forced himself to look upon those remains. And I swear to you now, that in all my years serving in Afghanistan I had never seen the likes of it before—nor would I care to again.

"I should have been able to prevent this," Holmes said, under his breath, his gaze fixed upon the contents of that carriage.

"How?" I asked him, my own mouth dry as sandpaper.

"There *is* a pattern to these events. I simply cannot see it yet."

When we returned to Baker Street that evening, silence prevailing in the cab on the way, Miss Cartwright was waiting for us. She said nothing as Holmes stepped into his chambers, Mrs Hudson having informed us that the lady was waiting upstairs; Miss Cartwright merely strode towards him and slapped his face. Then she departed.

We discovered not long afterwards that Anthony had committed suicide in his cell by swallowing his own tongue. Lestrade said there was nothing that could have been done, but I knew Holmes disagreed.

I did not see him for some time after that. On the single occasion I did knock and enter his chambers, I found the room empty apart from the usual detritus of the case. However, on the table I also spied the means by which he was administering his seven percent solution; a habit I never did manage to free him from.

Holmes staggered from his bedroom then, still in his robe in the middle of the day—which, I have to say, was not that uncommon. He looked drawn and pale, like a ghost of his former self.

"Holmes, I really must—" But before I could get out another word, he flew at me, enraged. I thought for a moment he might attack, like the people we had been investigating, but instead he simply shouted:

"Get out! Get out! *Get out!*"

I did as instructed, retreating and allowing him to slam the door behind me. I heard a lock being drawn on the other side and considered it was for the best that I should leave him alone, in spite of how terribly worried I was.

An equally concerned Lestrade contacted me several times over the course of those next few weeks, informing me of yet more murders—drownings, beatings, stranglings—as well as suicides, asking if Holmes would be continuing his investigations. I lied and told him that the great detective was looking into several quite promising leads.

In reality, I feared that he had finally met his match. It is a conviction that I still hold to this day.

When I heard Holmes leave 221b Baker Street, it was the middle of the night. He told neither Mrs Hudson nor myself where he was going, but after his tirade I was not at all surprised. When Lestrade actually called at the house, protesting that he was no longer able to prevent the papers from reporting the insanity that seemed to have gripped London, I had to admit that Holmes was not present.

"Then where is he, Dr Watson? And why aren't *you* with him?"

I said again that he was chasing a line of enquiry, but the Inspector's words struck a nerve with me. It wasn't the first time Holmes had retreated into himself, nor the first occasion he had vanished without warning—and Heaven knows he had justification this time—but Lestrade was right; I should have been with him. I was deeply distressed about his condition, and if there was a connection between all of these bizarre events then I should be working *with* Holmes to try and resolve the issue.

I set out to look for my friend, searching all the places I could think of that he might go. I even tried some of the opium dens that he has been known to frequent from time to time, especially if he was looking for someone from the underworld of the crime community. During this pursuit, I discovered that he had indeed been spotted in that area of town—and spotted enjoying some of the more questionable vices it provided—but had departed some considerable time ago.

It was not until I had exhausted every single possibility that it struck me where I might find him. My years observing Holmes' methods has left me with not an inconsiderable degree of aptitude for deduction myself.

When I arrived at my destination, he was indeed present. Standing, staring out into space just as the "victims", those left behind after the murders, were wont to do. He looked no better for his absence— worse in fact than he had in his chambers. I approached cautiously, after my last encounter with him, not knowing what kind of reception I would receive.

"Ah, Watson," said he in a quiet voice. "My faithful friend and companion. I knew that you would find me here eventually." Holmes gazed down at the grave he was standing next to, the one containing the bodies of the family who'd died on the Waterloo train. "I am so sorry for my behaviour when last we saw each other. I was... not myself." He gave a slight laugh, perhaps realising the significance of his words, but there was no humour to it.

Not far away, I knew, were some of the other final resting places of those who had suffered during these past troubling weeks.

I joined him. "What happened was not your fault, you know."

He shook his head and turned to me. "I could not see it until now, but we have been facing my greatest enemy all along."

"Not... the Professor?" I said, struggling to hide the alarm in my voice.

"I *have* seen Moriarty, Watson, I will not deny it. My own punishment, perhaps. But no, my efforts at the falls were entirely successful. He remains among the deceased. Although through this experience, I have discovered why the murderers—if one can refer to them as such—are so quick to throw away their lives. I know now what they see... afterwards."

I frowned, conceding that I had no idea what he was talking about. If Moriarty had not returned from the grave—and the dark humour of my own musings was not lost on me, in light of where we were standing—then who exactly were we up against? I ventured my question out loud.

"I've been a fool, Watson. It has been right in front of my nose all along. Literally! The stench is so distinctive. But, you see, I've seen *Him* before as well, if only briefly. You recall the case of the Devil's Foot, which you so expertly set down?"

Good Lord, I thought to myself, *is Holmes making some kind of veiled reference?* Surely we were not facing the Fallen One himself; such a thing would have been even more preposterous than Holmes' theory about demonic possession. As it transpired, our foe was so much more terrifying, and less discriminating, than that. I nodded, remembering the case all too well.

"It happened when I subjected us to the burning powder that was used to induce both madness and... death."

"Are you saying a similar poison has been employed here to drive

105

people to such acts?"

He shook his head. "No, no, Watson. The *Radix pedis diaboli* has nothing to do with this affair, save for the fact that the one we must stop was present during that investigation also."

"I do not follow you."

"I have never spoken about what I witnessed under the influence of that powder, nor have I asked you what you saw."

"My dose appeared to be notably smaller than yours," I told him, remembering how I shook Holmes out of his hallucinogenic trance.

"Indeed." He looked again at the headstone before him, then cast his eye over the entire graveyard. "Consequently, I saw our enemy, Watson. A brief... suggestion, you might call it. But nevertheless it was *Him*, of that I am certain." Was my friend speaking of prophecy now? "It was a state I have been attempting to recreate during my absence from Baker Street."

"And were you successful in your endeavours?" asked I, when all I really wanted to do was voice my concern. The state Holmes was talking about almost cost him his sanity, if not his *own* life.

"I was indeed. I saw that which I was seeking, and more besides. I finally know what I must do. Actually what *you* must do, Watson." I still wasn't following his line of reasoning and I told him so. He placed a hand on my shoulder. "Right now, I have more need of your skills as a physician than a detective. Do you trust me, old friend?"

"Of course, Holmes. Implicitly.'

"Then I would ask you to visit your surgery, with the express intention of collecting the items we shall require for our task, and meet me back here tomorrow at sundown."

"Task, Holmes?" said I, still puzzled.

"Yes." He fixed me with a stare that I have never forgotten from that day to this. Then he said, more serious than I have ever heard him sound, "Watson, tomorrow evening I would ask that you kill me."

* * *

The logistics of Holmes' plan will soon become apparent, but you can appreciate my asking him to elaborate on his exclamation. However, he would not, merely stating that the following night he

106

would require me to end his life by stopping his heart.

"I simply refuse!" I told him.

"Then more innocent people will die before this is all over," Holmes said to me. "The killer has a taste for this now. He is using more and more 'hands on' methods, from what I can ascertain. He is taking pleasure in the tactile aspect of ending lives. If you will not do this for me, Watson, then do it for the victims yet to be claimed."

Reluctantly, I agreed, returning to my surgery to gather what I would require. The safest way I could think of to stop Holmes' heart temporarily was by way of administering an injection; a lethal concoction of my own devising, for which I also had the antidote. For Holmes had explained that he only required me to impede the beating of his heart muscle for a short amount of time. "Long enough to lure our prey out into the open," Holmes informed me.

Quite how "killing" my friend would achieve this, I did not know, apart from the obvious parallel it had with friends and loved ones suddenly doing the same thing across our city. Did he wish to recreate the madness of extinguishing life in such a way? If so, he could scarcely have chosen a more apt person to perform this action; Holmes has always been, and will forever remain, my best friend.

The wait of a day passed slowly, as I contemplated what I was about to do. In a few hours I would achieve what every single one of Holmes' adversaries had failed to do. Even Moriarty. I would murder the great detective, and he was going to let me—had *asked* me to do the very deed! The merest thought of it boggles the mind, does it not?

Nevertheless, I found myself once more travelling back to that cemetery as another thick fog descended upon London. The sky was darkening and the overall effect succeeded in chilling me to the bone. As I walked through that graveyard, knowing full well the people contained therein could not harm me, I still found myself shivering. When Holmes stepped out from the depths of a bank of fog and tapped me on the shoulder, it was very nearly I who found his heart stopping that night.

"You gave me an awful fright," I told him.

"My dear Watson, please forgive me." Regardless of the circumstances, and by the light of the lamp he was holding, I detected the hint of a smile playing on his lips. "Did you bring the required items?"

I nodded, showing him my medical bag.

"Splendid, then we shall begin." Holmes took me over to where a flat slab of stone was located, somewhere for him to lay as I carried out his request. He placed the lamp beside him so that I could see.

"Holmes, are you quite sure about this? I still do not understand why—"

He silenced me with a finger. "Please proceed. I know that I am in the most capable of hands."

Sighing, I took out the hypodermic and a vial, siphoning off a massive dose of my poison. Holmes, for his part, rolled up his sleeve and I saw exactly what the cost of his experimentations were; red welts on his arm, digging into the lines along his vein. I frowned, but said nothing, instead taking up his limb to give him the injection: quite possibly the last I might ever administer to my friend.

As the needle went in, Holmes reached over and patted my hand gently. Neither of us said a thing as he shut his eyes and waited for the drug to take effect. I sat there and noted the look of complete peace on Holmes' face. It was the first and only time I had seen him so content.

I took his wrist and felt for a pulse. It was still there, but faint.

"I never got the chance to tell you this before, Holmes," I whispered, still keeping hold of his wrist as the beats slowed. "But thank you. Thank you for everything."

Then, suddenly, the beating ceased.

I bowed my head, choking back the wave of emotion I felt at seeing my companion as dead as those corpses I had examined after the murders. Then I experienced it, a sudden jolt—so fierce I almost let go of Holmes' arm. I wonder now if I would have seen what followed had I done so, for I firmly believe it was the physical connection to Holmes at the time his spirit departed his body that allowed me to bear witness to what transpired. Yes, that is correct— you did not read wrongly. I can finally unburden myself of the knowledge of what happened in those ensuing moments. It is a memory I have carried with me now for so long.

A shape began to coalesce beside the slab, indistinct at first and shimmering—but as I blinked, refocusing on it, a familiarity began to reveal itself. A head, shoulders, arms, legs... it was a body, glowing white in appearance, and transparent. But eventually it took its true form. It turned to stare at me, and it was then that I saw the unmistakable visage of none other than Holmes himself. He mouthed something upon seeing me, but I could not hear him at that point and was too much in shock to reply anyway. I wondered whether Holmes had somehow infected me with his madness, for this must surely be what it felt like to experience insanity.

There had hardly been enough time to adjust to this new development when something else happened. The fog parted, close by, and at the same time began swirling round, taking on a form itself. It was difficult to separate the darkness beyond our lamp and the glow of Holmes' spirit from that which was bending the mist to its will. I soon realised my mistake, however, because again this was not a thing of our world. It was nebulous in appearance itself, mist-like though not *of* the mist enveloping us. The only reason I could see it at all was because of my physical connection to Holmes.

Like the latter, it too settled on a form eventually: tall and black, wearing what looked like robes but were not made from any kind of material known to man; rather fashioned from the same miasma as the rest of it. Its hands, when it reached out, were in contrast white and thin, almost bone-like but lacking substance. A finger whipped out, pointing at my companion's shade.

And its voice, when it spoke, sounded like thousands of voices speaking at once in my mind. "*Sherlock Holmes,*" it stated simply. "*I have come for you.*"

All the times he had cheated Death, in particular that celebrated occasion at the Reichenbach Falls, and now I feared that it had sought Holmes out—all because I had ended his life. But Holmes was right, there was a distinctive smell; it was one I recognised all too readily from my time serving abroad, and my career as a doctor on these shores.

"*No,*" I heard my friend say then, in a voice that was his but not his. "*I have come for you!*"

There was silence then, as if the creature in front of Holmes did not quite know how to reply. That silence was filled eventually by an explanation of sorts.

"*It wasn't quite enough for you, was it?*" Holmes continued abruptly. "*Taking lives like this. It wasn't... satisfying.*" He uttered the last word with all the contempt it deserved. "*You have watched for so long as we found new ways to kill each other. Watched and come for us when needed. All the while wondering what it might be like to actually kill, to tighten a cord until the last gasp of air emerged from a mouth, to plunge a knife through someone's heart until it beats no longer, to hack a child to...*" Holmes paused. "*I saw your pattern, you see. This isn't the first time you have slipped inside; you've worked your way through battlefields, have you not, choosing those who would not readily be missed. The poor, the destitute. I have seen them all. They told me what you have done. Yet that was not enough for you. The sweetest sensation, the longest and strongest high of all, comes from the murder of a loved one. To feel the connection severed at your hands.* Your very hands!"

Listening to Holmes' explanation, something I have done on many occasions at the conclusion of a case, everything fell into place. The reason why Miss Cartwright's cousin, Anthony, had done what he did—the reason those others did the same. It was a disturbing revelation to say the least.

"*You dare to pass judgement on me?*" came the voice that was a thousand voices, almost screeching the reply. It was filled with indignation that Holmes was even talking to it.

"*When your actions result in...*" Holmes' spirit looked over again at where the family from the train had their plot. "*Yes. Yes, I do.*"

There was a snarl from the black, mist-like shape, and it flung itself forward, just as Holmes had done back in Baker Street after wallowing in depression and indulging too much in his seven percent solution (or more?). The intent was different here, however, and we could both see it.

The shape raised both hands, in an effort to grab Holmes, to take him back with it, to drag him away and undo his very existence. I wished there was something I could do... But there was! I could bring Holmes back as he had instructed. We knew the identity of the killer, we just could not do anything about it—and never would be able to, I feared.

It was time to administer the antidote and restart Holmes' heart.

He looked to his side and could see what I was about to do. "*Not yet, Watson!*" he cried, then those hands grabbed him and Holmes was grappling with Death itself. Not in any figurative sense this time, but as he would have done any other criminal he was tangling with. Though how would he be able to defeat such a creation?

"*You... have been... with me... every step of the way,*" Holmes grunted as he struggled with his enemy. "*But even... you should know... there are consequences... to one's actions.*"

Something was happening behind me. I took my eyes off the spectral pair, to glance around. More shapes in the mist, breaking through in fact: one after the other. It did not take them as long as Holmes or Death to form. They had been waiting for this moment and were eager to strike. Not only were there the victims of Death's atrocious crimes, such as Judith Hatten, Mr Thorpe, the husband and child murdered on the Waterloo Train, but also those who had been so tormented by their spectral appearances that they had taken their own lives—and, I had to wonder, given a helpful push by Death itself? So there followed Anthony, Mrs Thorpe, the mother who'd turned that fire axe on her beloved husband and child, and more besides. I watched as those Holmes had spoken about, the earlier victims, both the murderers and the suicides that had gone unnoticed, unreported—the ones who had told Holmes their tales—all came marching through the mist. But they were also joined by those who'd been lost during the last few weeks, while Holmes had been attempting to get to the bottom of this very mystery: the ones Lestrade had not been able to keep from the morning editions. They surged through that graveyard as one, a phantom army heading towards Death, all craving revenge.

The black figure—whose face was still unclear to me, and I would imagine to Holmes—turned towards them, letting go of my friend. The horde encircled Death, crowding in and raining down blows that I did not think would have any effect, but evidently did. They were backed up by the power of those trapped between life and... whatever was on the other side. It suddenly dawned on me then exactly why Holmes had wanted to wait a day. It was October 31st, All Hallows' Eve—the time of year when these spirits would be at their most powerful.

"*Now, Watson!*" shouted Holmes, limping away from the scene. "*Bring me back now!*"

I snapped out of my daze, not wanting to let go of Holmes' hand because I wished to witness the last of this, wanted to see Death's end. But, of course, I should have known that Death is never, ever truly gone. How could it be? It is the other side of the coin to life. I saw the dark figure being smothered by ghosts, then let go and watched as the vision faded. While I worked—injecting Holmes with the antidote then pounding on his chest to get his heart beating again—I heard a faint voice. A voice made up of so many more. "*We will meet again*," Death promised Holmes, "*and not even your friend will be able to save you then*."

The words filled me with dread.

I couldn't see the "spirit Holmes" anymore, couldn't see any evidence of the battle that had taken place, but it did not matter to me at that point. I beat on Holmes' chest one final time, and he sat bolt upright, taking in a lungful of night air. He began to cough, though whether it was the result of coming back or the fog still surrounding us, I had no clue. But I held on to him anyway, until he was strong enough to sit up on his own. "Rest a little, Holmes," I warned him.

"I'm... I'm fine," he told me. "Thank you, Watson." Then he clasped my arm.

I nevertheless had to half-carry my friend through the graveyard and through the fog, into a more public place where we could hail the cab that would take us back to the relative safety of Baker Street.

Holmes spent the next few days recuperating, enjoying the ministrations of both myself and Mrs Hudson. When Lestrade called on us once more, I was able to inform him of the conclusion to the case. "You should not see any more deaths like those," I assured the policeman. I could not promise him the madness of the population would not continue, as indeed it did in the final stages of the 19th century until everyone was certain the world would not end. But of the murders committed by loved ones and subsequent suicides, there was no more sign. Due note had obviously been taken of the repercussions. As I already mentioned, the matter was put down to the singular time of the year and our calendar. I would not be pressed further on what had been amiss with those people, however much Lestrade demanded answers from both myself and later Holmes—for one thing, I did not know where to start; for another I was positive he would have us both committed if we spoke of what we'd uncovered. Nor did Holmes and I talk about what had happened and

112

what we had seen that day. To do so seemed somehow to invite the premature return of the culprit.

So you see, it is only now, with my friend passed on and myself nearing the end of my years, that I am committing this to paper. Even then, I doubt very much whether it shall see the light of day. Instead it will probably be dismissed, I fancy, as a work of fiction less credible even than some of those by Mr Stoker or Mr Verne. The final ramblings of an aged adventurer.

But I know the truth.

Holmes once spoke about his greatest foe without realising it, before he ever encountered the thing, during a case a long time ago. "The Adventure of the Six Napoleons" I believe it was, though my memory is waning, I must confess. He was in the mortuary then, not the graveyard, but he mused: "I am just contemplating the one mystery I cannot solve. Death itself." How prophetic those words should turn out to be.

Because although he may have prevented more innocents from going the way of Judith Hatten and the others, spared future "murderers" from the blame and guilt of something they had not done, Holmes had far from solved the mystery of exactly what Death was—nor what happens when we take our final breath.

The voice had been right, of course. It *had* seen Holmes again, and I had not been able to save him. But that is a story for another time.

For now, I have entrusted my recollections to the page and all that remains is for me, myself, to await the hand of that monster on my own shoulder.

Perhaps then, at least, I will discover the mystery of what Holmes already knows himself.

DRACULA IN LOVE

"The course of true love never did run smooth."
William Shakespeare
A Midsummer Night's Dream.

When Dr Jan Früber asked his receptionist to send in the next patient, the last thing he'd been expecting her to do was wheel in a coffin. He had a hard enough time sorting out the problems of the living, never mind the dead. Still, a patient was a patient, he guessed, no matter what state they arrived here in.

"This is Mr Drake," his receptionist said.

"I see. Thank you, Helga."

Helga sashayed out and closed the door behind her.

The psychiatrist walked around the wooden casket, made from the finest varnished oak. The handles looked to be brass, but on closer inspection Früber became almost entirely convinced that they were gold. He was just about to tap on the exterior when he heard a voice inside say:

"Would you mind closing the blinds." It wasn't a request.

There was a pronounced accent which made it sound more like, "Vud du mind klosink de blinds" but Früber understood and did as he was told, trotting over to the window to shut out the bright sunlight. Upon returning to the coffin, Früber switched on a tiny desk-lamp so he could see.

"I've closed them, Mr Drake. Now would you please come out of there. I find face to face contact essential in my line of work."

The trolley on which the coffin lay seemed to buckle and tilt, tipping the casket on end until it stood bolt upright. The lid swung open on its hinges, revealing a man surrounded by crushed red velvet. His face was ashen, slicked back hair drawing attention to prominent

114

eyebrows and a pair of full titian lips. His arms were folded over his chest, wrapping a black satin cape around himself. His eyes opened suddenly, he extended his cloak, and then seemed to float out of the box on a cushion of air.

When he spoke, twin fangs were just about visible on either side of his mouth. "My name is not Drake," he said in that same hammish tone. "It's—"

"Dracula," finished Früber. "Yes, I recognise you now."

"Drake is a convenient nom de plume I use from time to time when I want to travel incognito." Früber's attention shifted from Dracula to his oh-so-inconspicuous coffin. "I hate signing all those autographs, you see," Dracula explained.

Früber considered shaking hands with the "man" but on second thoughts sat down in his leather armchair instead. He motioned for Dracula to do the same in the opposite chair. Dracula settled down gracefully, crossing his legs and resting his hands on the raised knee.

Früber cleared his throat. "Might I say to start with what an honour it is to have someone of your stature visiting me. You're the first celebrity I've ever treated. I mean, assuming you're here for treatment and not to..." Früber quit while he was ahead.

"As I mentioned before, Doctor, I would rather all this business was conducted on the quiet. I do not want my private life splashed all over the morning papers. That is why I came here. You are both discrete and trustworthy... or so I have been led to believe."

Früber put his mind at ease on that score. "I quite understand how you feel, and let me assure you that whatever is said to me will go no further than these four walls."

"Good."

"So," said Früber, steepling his fingers as they'd taught him to do in training, "what can I do for you, Mr Dracula?"

"Please, Doctor. Call me Vlad."

"Very well, *Vlad*. What brings you to my humble little practice?"

Dracula folded his arms. His body language said a lot to the keen observer. Defensive, embarrassed. Quite obviously this was a vampire with things on his mind.

"Just try to relax, Vlad. Take a few deep breaths and begin when you're ready."

"Well," said Dracula, "the truth is I have not been feeling quite

115

myself lately, Doctor."

"How so?"

"I seem to find comfort in the strangest of pastimes nowadays. I have started reading poetry for one thing, and am addicted to the Sunday early morning 'matinee' on television. Last week it was *Now Voyager*. Have you ever seen it?"

Früber shook his head. "I don't believe I have."

"It stars Bette Davis. A wonderful piece of melodrama. It brought tears to my eyes, I can tell you."

"I'm more of a Bergman fellow myself."

"Ah, Ingrid!"

"Er, Ingmar actually. All that deep psychological conjecture. Simply can't get enough, I'm afraid. But do forgive me, you were saying..."

Dracula unfolded his arms and gripped the sides of the chair. "I have been behaving in a bizarre way, also. If I hear a song on the radio by The Carpenters I have to stop whatever I am doing and listen. And only the other night Igor—Igor is my home help, Doctor; I poached him from the Baron some years ago—well, he forgot to wake me up at the usual hour. Half-past four in the morning when he crept into the crypt. I ask you, what good is that to me? Barely enough time to get up, do my exercises and catch the news. I detest overlaying, it throws me right out. And yet..." Dracula stared at the wall behind Früber. "I could not bring myself to even shout at him. Normally the punishment meted out would have been quite severe. Quite severe..."

His voice trailed off as if he couldn't believe what he'd done; an opportunity missed. Dracula clapped his hands to his face. "Doctor, what on earth is happening to me?" he spluttered.

This was not good. Not good at all. Früber could sum it up for him in one sentence: "You're going soft." But there had to be a reason for this. After countless orgies of bloodletting and blood-*drinking* Dracula, Vlad to his friends, was losing it.

"And is that all you have to tell me?"

Dracula looked up, his eyes now as red as his mouth. "No. I have been experiencing... other problems as well."

"Work or pleasure?"

"To me they are one and the same, Doctor. I take great pleasure in

116

my work and my work gives me great pleasure! But recently I have not been able to, ah, *function* as well as I used to do. In all departments. Simply put, Doctor, I have not had a bite in ages!"

Früber raised his left eyebrow. "Ah, well it happens to us all as we get older. How old are you by the way, if you don't mind me asking?"

"Five hundred and seventy. Still in my prime."

"Yes. Okay, so I think the best thing is probably to start at the beginning." Früber made himself comfortable in the chair, the leather making faintly flatulent-like noises. "Now then, Vlad," he said, "tell me all about your mother..."

They had a fairly productive session. Dracula opened up about his early days in the Transylvanian town of Schassburg ("The other children were frightened of me. I cannot imagine why!"), the harsh imprisonment he endured at the hands of the Turks when he was but 18 years old ("There I developed a taste for torment and unspeakable acts of cruelty. I will never be able to thank them enough."), his life as the notorious Impaler ("Ah, the good old days. I miss them so much. Upside down, right way up. Even sideways. I never did tire of impaling.") and his initiation into the world of the undead.

To be brutally frank, though, everything after this was a bit samey: biting; necks; more biting; Van Helsing ("My old adversary. No one even comes close today, not even that meddlesome high-school girl..."); biting; book and movie deals; necks; merchandising; more biting... Nothing that could explain his sudden bouts of sentimentalism, the way he longed to see the sun rise again or walk barefoot along the banks of the Danube listening to the birdsong.

Their hour was almost at an end when it struck Früber like a bolt from the blue. Of course, that was it! Why hadn't he spotted it sooner? All the signs were there.

"Tell me, Vlad," he started, "can you pinpoint exactly when this change occurred? Has anything unusual happened to you of late? Have you met anyone new?"

"What do you mean, Doctor?" Dracula became evasive again. Früber knew instinctively that he'd touched a raw nerve. He pressed the issue.

"Anyone, I don't know, of the female persuasion?"

Dracula held his silence.

117

"I can't help you, Vlad, if you won't talk to me."

Dracula looked him straight in the eye—a pretty dangerous thing to do ordinarily—then said one name: "Cassandra."

Bingo! "And I take it you haven't..."

"No, no," said Dracula angrily, "nothing like that. I told you, I am off my food. We are just good friends."

"Good friends?"

"Acquaintances."

"And how often do you see this 'acquaintance'?"

"Look, Doctor, I do not want to discuss the subject. Our time together is almost at an end, and I wish to take my leave of you now." Dracula rose in a fury. Früber stood too, marching across the room.

"Vlad, the first step to getting better is admitting that you have a problem. I put it to you that you are in love with this Cassandra, whoever she is."

"Preposterous! I will not hear another word. Goodbye, Doctor Früber!" And with that he stepped back into his coffin and closed the lid with a bang. Früber tried to reason with him—through the wood—but could elicit no response. He had no choice but to let Igor, a hunchback with a slow gait and even slower eye, take him away when he arrived on the hour.

Früber had failed in his job. He'd let his most prestigious client, his *only* prestigious client, slip through his fingers. A once in a lifetime case—imagine what it would've looked like on his résumé!

But that was that. Nothing he could do about it. He would never see the Count again.

Or would he?

* * *

The very next weekend Früber received a phone call at home in the early hours of Saturday morning. It was Dracula in an extremely agitated state. He had to see the therapist as soon as was *humanly* possible. Would he consider opening up his practice that night? He would prefer night this time. Dracula was willing to double the usual fee, even triple it. Früber agreed on the spot—the money not important, but definitely welcome. He was determined to cure

118

Dracula, and that's exactly what he was going to do.

* * *

Früber sat in his office at midnight, the window ajar as instructed. It wasn't long before he heard the snap-snap of beating wings, and a distressing screech permeated the room.

The bat flew in at an angle, veering off slightly as if drunk. It hovered shakily in the centre of the office, watching Früber. The metamorphosis was a lengthy and strained process. Dracula slumped down in the chair when he'd finished, panting like a dog in a desert.

"My apologies, Doctor," he gasped, "but I grow weaker with each passing day. I do not know how much longer I can go on."

"Then the sooner we get to the bottom of this, the better. Yes?"

Dracula concurred. "The words you spoke at our last meeting have been *preying* on my mind, Doctor Früber. I was a fool to doubt your judgement. I have denied my feelings for long enough. You were of course right. I am in... love. Hopelessly and unequivocally." It took a lot for him to admit this and Früber had to admire the chap for it. A man in his profession and everything.

"Now we're making progress, Vlad. Perhaps you could tell me how you and Cassandra met first of all."

His story was laced with flowery prose about cupid and bells ringing in his ears, but essentially what happened was this. Cassandra, lovely, sweet, innocent Cassandra—the chaste kind of maiden vampires usually go for; a slight age gap, but that was nothing in today's society—had broken down on her way to see her parents in the local village. She had later explained that she was on a short reading break from the University of Transylvania where she studied Humanities.

Cassandra had had the misfortune to conk out in the middle of the forest and by the time she'd made it to Castle Dracula, seemingly the only building around for miles, the sky was grim and sunless. So it was with great relief that she stepped over the threshold, kissing Igor on the cheek for his act of kindness. The underling showed her to the phone but assured her that it wouldn't be working. Well, not since he'd disconnected it when he heard the knock at the door, standard practice at Castle Dracula when *dinner guests* arrive.

It was as she struggled to get an outside line that Dracula appeared at the top of the stairs, tall and lean, a dramatic figure with his cape unfurled. He'd been in this situation a million times before, and yet something happened when he clapped eyes on Cassandra's face.

"I was coming down the staircase, ready to swoop in for a nibble," he recounted, "when all of a sudden it was like someone had punched me in the stomach, Doctor. I cannot explain it."

Früber rested his chin on his hand, one finger reaching up towards his cheek—another stance he'd learnt at psychiatrists' school. "But what about all your other brides, Vlad? What about Winona? Haven't you ever felt the same about any of them?"

"There is no comparison! My brides have become bitter and twisted. All they do is nag me each night about the dust and cobwebs in my castle. They do not seem to realise that it gives the place character. Oh, sometimes I do not know why I bother! And as for Winny, well, she ran off with a fellow who looked suspiciously like that actor from *Speed*—you know, the first one; the good one— except his accent was a tad peculiar." Dracula snorted. "Not that I can talk. Anyway, I have not seen hide nor hair of her since."

"So what makes Cassandra so special?"

"I do not know. All I know is when I went to 'introduce' myself properly, I found I could not, you know... I simply could not! So we just talked. We chatted for hours, Doctor. About nothing. About everything. Do you know what that is like?"

Früber said that he did. Everyone has been there at some point in their lives. However for the Count, after more than half a millennium as a vampyr, this was all new territory.

"Then we held hands and sat by the light of the moon until almost dawn, when I had to make my excuses for obvious reasons. I do not think it would have made a very good impression, disintegrating on a first date."

"What happened next?" Früber was following the monologue closely. Trying to pick up clues that might help.

"Igor reconnected the telephone and she rang for a breakdown truck. Then she left."

"And...?"

"And I cannot stop thinking about her. All night I pace up and down in the castle, wondering what she is doing. My dear, gentle

Cassandra..."

He has got it bad, thought Früber. "You haven't seen her since?"

"Not since that night just over two weeks ago. Cassandra returned to the university shortly afterwards. She has been in touch, naturally. Wanted me to visit her, present me to her friends and, I suspect, eventually her family. But I cannot. She still has no idea who I am at all. I dread to think what will happen when she finds out!"

"And that matters to you?"

Dracula pulled a face. "*Of course* it does!"

"I am starting to see the enormity of your dilemma. The very crux of your problem. This is why you are unable to go about your business as usual, Vlad. For you fear that Cassandra will disapprove, and reject you. However, if you do not do what comes naturally, and soon, there will be no more Dracula and Cassandra will be mortified."

"What do you suggest, Doctor?"

Früber frowned. It was a tough one. He could tell him to forget all about Cassandra, but somehow Früber didn't think that would work. The man... creature... whatever... was besotted with her. Or Dracula could try to get her out of his system the other way. Bite the bullet— or the jugular in this instance. But then, the vamp had already stated that he couldn't do this, in spite of the fact he'd had ample opportunity. He just wasn't about to pounce on a girl who meant so much to him.

"Obviously you need to talk to Cassandra. I think you should come clean and explain what you do for a living, what you do in order to survive."

"You really think she will understand?" Dracula looked hopeful.

"If she feels the same way you do, I believe she will, yes. Quite honestly, Vlad, what other choice do you have?"

Dracula seemed resolved to the notion, gearing himself up for what he must do. But with it came the realisation that this might all work out for the best. If Cassandra could find it in her heart to condone his activities, then he could carry on as normal and still see her. An open relationship, that was the ticket! If, if, if...

"What I want you to do is go and see her tonight, tell her how you feel. Take it from there. You're both miserable apart, so perhaps you can come to some kind of arrangement."

"Yes, *yes!* I will do just that, Doctor."

"Then return here the following night and we'll talk about how it went."

Dracula thanked the psychiatrist for his sage advice and attempted to change back into a bat. In the end he had to do so in stages, screwing up his face. At one point he had the body of a bat but the head and limbs of a man. Eventually he got it right and flopped out through the window, plummeting several metres before catching the slipstream and flying on.

Früber came up to the glass and shouted after him: "Perhaps you should think about taking a cab tonight, Vlad!"

But his sentence was already lost to the empty stretches of darkness outside.

*   *   *

Cassandra was wide awake when she heard the sound of horses braying outside.

Her four poster bed in the dorms of the University of Transylvania was comfortable enough; actually it was rather luxurious as far as student accommodation went. But sleep had been an alien thing to her since she'd met Vlad the other week. A chance encounter with a tall, dark, handsome stranger, boasting a title, no less—just like in all those romantic novels. And what perfect teeth!

That night had been so magical for her she could still scarcely believe it. His company was so right and he was such a dreamboat. Sensitive, knowledgeable, caring. She'd thought the feeling was mutual, her love for him reciprocated. But after he dashed off that morning, like a rather masculine Cinderella from the ball, and then refused to see her again when she phoned... Well, now she didn't know what to think.

Cassandra pulled back the covers. She felt herself being lured to the window, her nightdress billowing around her. Looking down, she saw the coach below, an eccentric way to travel in this day and age—environmentally friendly, though. She hardly noticed the coloured gas seeping in through the air vents, coalescing next to her bed. Slowly taking on the contours of her would-be suitor.

"Cassandra, my little fluffy bunny." His greeting made her jump and she turned, a look of stupefaction on her face.

"How did you—"

"Come. Come and sit beside me." He appeared fatigued and unwell, a poor likeness of his former self. Cassandra crossed the room at his bidding.

"I thought..."

"No," Dracula said tenderly, "please, let me finish. Before you say anything else I have something I wish to tell you..."

*　*　*

The stroke of midnight on the following eve.

Dr Jan Früber paced up and down at the open window in his office. *How had it gone?* he wondered. *Good or bad?* Perhaps Cassandra had cast him out with a crucifix and Dracula, so disconcerted by the rebuff, had done away with himself. Could vampires commit suicide? He winced at the thought of trying to stake oneself in the heart. Or, looking on the bright side, maybe they were even now planning their future together—marriage, a honeymoon in Whitby mayhap? And Dracula was so wrapped up in it all he'd forgotten the appointment with his shrink.

But he wasn't waiting that much longer before a flapping of wings broke the silence. Dracula had risen from the grave again to discuss his love life.

This time, however, the bat zoomed past him and manoeuvred perfectly next to the chair. Dracula effortlessly morphed into his "human" guise, leaving Früber at a loss for words.

"Doctor, how pleasant to see you again," he said, the articulation strong and sure.

"Vlad, is that you?" *Who else, idiot?* Früber simply couldn't believe the marked change.

"The very same!"

"I take it things went well, then?"

Dracula started to whistle coyly, rocking back on his heels. "Erm, that all depends on how you look at it."

"Did you or did you not," said Früber, "sort things out with Cassandra?"

"I sorted things out, yes."

"And?"

"And, not to put too fine a point on it, Doctor... she is dead."

This he wasn't expecting. "*Dead?*"

"As a coffin nail, I am afraid."

"I-I don't understand. What happened?"

Dracula walked around and leant on the back of the chair. "I did as you said, talked things over with her, clarified who—what—I am, and how that could never change." He looked down, trying to remember every detail. "She took the news much better than I had hoped."

"She did?"

"Oh yes. Once I explained the benefits—eternal life, own transportation, ability to alter form at will, health insurance and dental plan—she wanted to give it a whirl herself. Could barely wait to get the bit between her teeth, so to speak. That way we would be together forever and could paint the town blood red each night. She practically insisted that I *do* her right there and then."

"So what went wrong?'

"Believe me, I only intended to take a pint or two, enough to convert her soul, to make her a child of the night. But I got a bit... carried away. It was not my fault, please understand that I had not eaten in so long. I stopped when I saw her body deflating, shrivelling up. But by that time it was too late."

"Oh my God, I'm so sorry."

Dracula waved a hand. "Do not be sorry, Doctor. The spell was broken last night. I am my old self again, snapping at Igor, chastising my brides, unencumbered by feelings of guilt, sorrow or... what was it you called it? Love—yes, that was it. Love." Dracula laughed, a hearty belly laugh like Santa Claus, only with a cape and fangs.

"I, er, I don't know what to say. Congratulations?"

"Yes, indeed. And thank you, Doctor. I do not know what I would have done without you. There will definitely be a little something extra for you when I come to settle up. Oh, and I fully intend to recommend you to all my friends. The Mummy, for instance. He's always getting himself wound up about one thing or the other. And as for the Wolfman, well he has this nasty habit of sniffing people's—"

"Thank you, thank you Vlad. It's much appreciated." Früber

didn't know how to feel. He'd done his job. This was a result. Okay, not the result he'd been expecting—usually there were no fatalities involved—but a result nonetheless. Dracula was back on top form and all was right with the world.

"Anyway, I cannot stand around here all night," said Dracula. "People to do, things to see. I thank you once again, Doctor."

Früber shrugged and stepped forward. He *would* shake the man's hand this time, he'd decided. It was how he saw off all his success stories. Dracula jerked the appendage up and down with glee.

He could feel the pulse in the therapist's wrist, the hot blood circulating round his veins. Dracula drew him closer, clapping him on the arm as all good friends do. Perhaps even an embrace...

Yes, it had been so long since he'd eaten and one virgin meal could hardly make up for that. The good Doctor wouldn't miss a little bit, surely. He'd understand if anybody would.

And Früber was oblivious to his intent, shaking his client's hand as the cape was hoisted up around him. As Dracula—Lord of the Nosferatu, Prince of Darkness and all-round archetypal villain—showed him just what a pain in the neck life, and love, could be.

HEARTLESS

Heartless.

That's what they were, pure and simple. Whoever did this and... She was surprised that joke hadn't been made already, black humour at the scene of crime; she'd heard it all before. Because if you didn't laugh, then you'd—

But nobody was making fun of this. They wouldn't dare. That would make them heartless, as well. Nobody ever made jokes where kids were involved. When they were the victims. Susie Ellis— Detective Inspector Susanne Ellis—stared down at the body. More than anything she wanted to look away, but found she couldn't. Couldn't help staring into those open, gaping eyes, the mouth a wet rictus of terror and pain. Couldn't help staring at the wound on the chest, that ragged gaping hole there.

A hole where this young girl's heart had once been. A hole...

"I'm afraid he had something called an atrial septal defect. We're really so very sorry."

"You okay?" The deep voice cut into her thoughts and made her start, but also broke the spell. She looked up and over at her sergeant of five years, Guy Parkes: six foot seven, who played rugby in his spare time, but also had the soul of a poet. Today he had tears in his own eyes as he joined her on the riverbank, though he was doing his best to hide the fact. Was probably thinking of his own kids that he barely saw, one of each now living with his ex and an accountant named Roger. Susie shook her head. "Yeah, me either."

"I just can't... I don't understand why someone would do something like this," she said to him. She'd seen too much of this over the years, too many people dead before their time. Susie was sick of it, if she was being honest. Tired of it; so tired.

"Is there any chance that it happened in the water itself?" Parkes

126

asked. "She fell in and... A rock or something, maybe a fish got at her?"

"Hell of a fish to do something like that," commented Susie. "No, this was done before she was dumped in the water, Parkes. I'd put money on it." She understood why he was looking for reasons other than the obvious, because it was just too hideous to contemplate. "The heart was cut—maybe even torn—out of that girl's chest. I'll wait for the pathologist to confirm it, though, obviously."

He glanced around at the CSI officers present, the people dressed in white suits. "I doubt we'll get anything forensics-wise," he told her. She'd already figured that out herself, a body in the water like that... It washed away any traces of who might be responsible. Nevertheless, the order had been given for divers to search the river just in case there was anything relating to this crime: a murder weapon would be nice. Well, not nice, but...

Susie studied the body again, crouching down, taking in other details. It was what she did, what she'd been trained to do. What she was good at, *when* she could detach herself, which was getting harder and harder these days.

Details, clues. Reasons.

The girl was no more than about 11 or 12 years of age, pretty, with long dark hair which clung to her face now that she had been washed up. She was wearing a floral dress, that looked like it had seen better days, and was still tangled up in the weeds which had caught her. Found that way by a passer-by walking her dog (weren't they always?) who'd called it in early that morning and set the whole circus in motion. The woman was currently being treated for shock in the back of a nearby ambulance. Susie would interview her in time, but doubted they'd get much. Just someone who happened to be in the wrong place at the wrong time.

"Dammit," she said, rising and shaking her head. There was nothing. No leads at all. Which meant they had a wait on their hands. Reacting instead of being proactive; Susie hated that. She looked around her, at the grassland on either side of the river, a wood in the distance. Usually, they'd be doing house to house, making enquiries as to whether anyone saw anything. But nobody lived round here, did they? Not even the walker, whose house was a couple of miles away apparently. It was the perfect spot to do something like this, either here or even further up this stretch of water. Totally isolated.

Except... Susie squinted, put her hand over her eyes to shield them from the morning sun. Yes, there—in the opposite direction to the woods, something beyond the hillock she was focused on. Smoke rising from somewhere.

"What's that?" she asked no-one in particular.

Parkes joined her, following her gaze. "Dunno," he said.

It wasn't the kind of smoke you'd see coming from a chimney, it was too thin, too small. "I do," she replied, having been dragged along on backpacking trips so many times when she was little. "That's a campfire."

She glanced at Parkes now, who raised an eyebrow. "Worth checking out?" he asked.

"Definitely," she replied. *Nobody lived round here, did they?* Maybe not permanently, but...

"Yes," said Susie again, thinking proactively. "Definitely."

"Then what are we waiting for?"

*   *   *

They'd taken a couple of uniforms with them, trailing behind in a squad car.

And when they arrived no-one seemed surprised to see them. Indeed, a few people were laughing and pointing as if they'd expected this turn of events eventually. Not that it meant anything; didn't necessarily mean they were involved in what had happened. But the very proximity of this encampment—consisting of camper vans, a few tents and small, touring caravans—meant there might be a possible connection.

It was something at least, thought Susie as she climbed out of her silver BMW. And something was always better than nothing. Parkes clambered out of the passenger seat and the car rose a good couple of inches off the ground with relief when he was free.

One man, who'd been sitting next to the campfire they'd spotted from afar, poking at a frying pan resting over the top of it with a fork, also rose at the same time. He wore a beanie hat—his long hair escaping from either side to fall chaotically about his shoulders—a long green jacket over a tatty jumper with holes in it, a pair of jeans which didn't really fit and looked in danger of falling down at any moment, and muddy, untied boots. He moved closer and Susie saw a golden earring glinting in his left ear as he walked; heard the stubble rasp on cheeks as he rubbed his face.

"Hey, look at that," he called out. "Some bacon to go with my eggs this morning."

Susie flashed him a grudging smile, then flashed him her warrant card—not that she apparently needed to. "DI Ellis, this is DS Parkes."

The man nodded. "Shephard," he replied. For a second she wasn't sure whether he was introducing himself or telling her his occupation. Then he jabbed the air with his fork, indicating a point past the two detectives; targeting the uniforms they'd arrived with, who were now out of their car too. "If you're planning to move us on, you're going to need more coppers than that." As if to emphasise his point, a number of men emerged from caravans behind him, one that was equal to the size of Parkes.

Who was bristling at her side. If there was one thing he couldn't stand, it was being threatened. Or someone laying down a challenge. Didn't matter how big that man was, or how many guys were spoiling for a rumble at the encampment, Parkes wouldn't be the one being carted off to hospital, Susie knew that. It explained why they were expected though, these folk were always on the lookout for the old bill arriving to turf them off whatever land they'd settled on; a consequence of the NIMBY brigade, not that there were any backyards for miles around here that Susie could see.

"We're not here to move you on," she assured Shephard, attempting to defuse the situation.

He cocked his head. "Oh?"

"How long have you been here, Mr Shephard?"

The man shrugged. "Not that long."

"Long enough to know anything about a young girl? About 12, dark hair. Last seen wearing a floral dress." It wasn't a lie, that was the last thing Susie *had* seen her wearing. The last thing she had been wearing before—

Shephard gaped at her, then cast a glance over his shoulder at a woman; middle-aged in a long, plain dress, waiting behind in the doorway of yet another caravan. She was watching what was transpiring but keeping well out of it in case anything kicked off. He faced front again. "Don't know a thing, Inspector. Why?"

"Just carrying out routine enquires," she told them. "Thought maybe she might have some connection to you guys out here?"

Shephard shook his head. "She in some kind of trouble?" he asked her.

"You could say that," answered Susie. Big trouble, the worst kind actually.

The man in the beanie's eyes flickered, as if he'd just remembered something and she wondered then if she'd get some kind of admission from him. Instead he came out with: "You said 'last seen wearing'?"

Susie nodded, had been wondering when he'd pick up on that. It was a certain kind of terminology and she'd used it on purpose. "Yeah, that's right. You see, she went missing." Again, she deliberately used that word rather than telling Shephard she was dead, or even murdered. Apart from the fact she didn't want that getting out just yet, Susie also needed to gauge his reaction to it. Also, not a lie: the girl had definitely gone missing from somewhere, before that happened to her. And something, a soul if you believed in all that, was definitely missing from her body now.

"Missing...?" Another look over his shoulder at the woman, who'd ventured down the steps finally. Was it Susie's imagination, or did she give a slight shake of the head. They were close then, those two: it was the kind of short-hand signal she and Parkes used all the time. Often all it would take would be a look.

"Uh-huh," said Susie.

Once again, Shephard turned back to face her. "Well, that's a... But no, we don't know anything about any girl. Missing or otherwise."

"Right," said Susie, looking around at the crowd gathering. "Okay. Hope you didn't mind the ask, though. Just doing our jobs. But if you do think of something..." She took out her card and covered the distance between them, knew Parkes was watching her like a hawk—not that she couldn't handle herself if anything happened. It didn't, thankfully; she just offered the card, and the man took it with the hand not currently holding the fork. He looked down at it, and when he looked up again Susie made sure she caught his gaze and held it. "We'll leave you in peace, then. You have a nice rest of the day."

She walked back to Parkes, motioning for them to get back in the car and for the uniformed officers to do the same. "You know they're just going to pack up now and get out of here, don't you? Now they're spooked."

Susie said nothing for a moment, then: "Perhaps. Perhaps not. We'll leave someone to keep an eye on what happens. But there's one thing I do know."

"What's that?" asked Parkes.

"That guy, Shephard, he was lying. Lying through his teeth—and lying right to my face."

* * *

Nothing came of dragging the river, and—as Parkes had predicted—forensics turned up sod all too.

The most they could tell them was that the body of the poor, unfortunate girl—aged 12—had been in the water for a few days before she'd washed up. Before she'd been found by the lady (one Karen Woodcoate, retired teacher) and her dog (Max).

The PM, which both Susie and Parkes attended, had shown that the heart had indeed been cut from the girl's body—and almost certainly when she was still alive. Minute traces of a drug, as yet unidentified but definitely opium-based, were found in the girl's system: imbibed rather than injected, as no needle marks could be found. More than likely the substance that she'd been given to keep her pliable and quiet while the deed was done. She wouldn't have had a clue what was happening to her, even as the muscle in her chest had been removed. But she'd probably felt it, if only going by the look on her face.

Parkes' own face had been stony as this news was delivered, the way his fists were opening and closing telling Susie that if the person responsible had been in that room he'd have torn them limb from limb.

He would have had to get in the queue.

From there on in, though, it had absolutely been a waiting game. And their search for the truth hadn't been helped by the fact that at some point, right under the noses of the officers tasked with watching them, the travellers' encampment disappeared without a trace.

Susie and Parkes had been about ready to go back, in larger numbers as Shephard suggested, to question every single person there—especially the woman that man kept looking back at. The officers in question, who later admitted they'd been distracted by a girl in her 20s bringing them hot drinks—probably laced with something—had been suspended, pending a disciplinary hearing, and would be lucky to ever work on the force again. "She was very friendly," was one of the copper's argument. "I'll bet she was," Susie had snapped, gearing up to go for the young idiot herself.

Not that any of this would do them much good now moving forwards. And she could've kicked herself for not taking down some of the license plates while they were there, because at least then they might have stood a chance of tracking them. "Wasn't really the time, or the opportunity," Parkes had reminded her, trying to make her feel better—and failing miserably.

They'd fucked up, all of them. Fucked up to such an extent that they might never get justice for the girl who'd died... who'd been killed. A girl who wasn't on their system, so they couldn't even name.

A girl that Susie dreamed about night after night, especially after a drink to take the edge off (just one, maybe two, not like before... she told herself). Dreamed about as she tossed and turned in bed. Sometimes she wasn't even sure she *was* dreaming. She'd wake, fuzzy, still a bit drunk, and think she could see the girl in the bedroom of her little flat, which she was living in alone since her last shitshow of a relationship ended so abruptly. Wake up and see her just standing there in the corner of the room, hair still wet and bedraggled from the river, floral dress still sticking to her, and that huge gaping hole in her chest where her heart should be. A couple of times she even swore she'd heard the girl giggling, and remembered thinking to herself: what have *you* got to laugh about? You're dead! Someone did this to you, someone killed you!

Of course, the girl would vanish as soon as Susie blinked a few times. The last remnants of the dream—the bad dream—disappearing when she was fully awake. At least it stopped her from dreaming about—

"We're really, sorry. There was nothing we could do."

"Can... can I just hold him? Just for a little while?"

"Sorry, but that's simply not possible."

"See him, then? Please?*"*

Simultaneously gave her something else to focus on, while reminding her all the time of her loss. A loss so long ago, which was still eating away at her. The child who'd be about the same age as that girl now. The one she'd never get justice for, because there was no justice to be had—another one of life's cruel jokes. A turn of events that was no-one's fault, like getting pregnant in the first place even after taking precautions.

The father had never known, she'd made that decision herself—and still believed it was the right one. They'd been kids themselves, having fun (and, yes, drunk it had to be noted). He'd been a mate but not husband material. Not even boyfriend material, really. With some people, a kid made them grow up fast. All it would have done with Ed was make him run a mile, probably off back to his own mummy.

No justice. None at all.

But she might be able to get some for the dead girl, Susie told herself. Or thought she could.

Then, of course, a few months later, came the call that she'd been dreading.

Another one. A second victim.

A second kid without a heart.

* * *

A boy this time.

A boy, just like the one that had been born without... Only in this instance it had been done to him, not by Mother Nature but by another human being. A human being so cruel they didn't deserve to be called that, because there was no humanity in them.

Left, down an alleyway in town next to the bins, as though he was just something to be discarded. No more than trash; a life, thrown away. Both Susie and Parkes were struggling not to cry at this crime scene, just about holding it together knowing that all eyes were on

133

them: other officers, CSIs, even journalists at the head of the alley being kept back. It would only take one photo of either of them looking upset, God forbid showing emotion, to appear in the local rags for questions to be asked by the higher ups.

"Good Christ," was all she could think of to say.

"Yeah," was Parkes' reply, with a hitch in his voice.

It was déjà vu, Groundhog Day, whatever you wanted to call it. Happy fucking Death Day might be more appropriate. The same thing, but in a different setting, with a different victim. The one thing connecting this to the girl from the river: the same method of execution. Susie was even willing to bet that there'd be traces of that opium-based drug in this lad's system.

This lad, who she couldn't take her eyes off. Looked about the same age, 12, with short hair and lightly tanned skin. He was dressed in clothes that looked like they hadn't been changed or washed in months, the jacket frayed at the sleeves and the jeans torn in a way that had nothing at all to do with fashion. The bottom of one trainer was coming off too, the rubber sole, making it look like some kind of animal with a gaping maw. The uniform of a boy who lived on the streets. Who was used to surviving on them.

Or not.

Someone had made sure he didn't survive, certainly. That heartless person, who'd ripped out this kid's—

No. Try not to think about that, she told herself yet again. It wouldn't do her any good, and wouldn't help this unnamed boy. Wouldn't help catch whoever did this, or bring them to justice for not one, but two murders. That's what Susie needed to focus on right now. Here, in this alleyway, as the sun was setting. But again, she was so, so tired.

"Didn't have any ID on him," Parkes informed her, his voice interrupting her thoughts. "Not that we were expecting him to, really. Just this." He held up the object in his gloved hand, and it caught the remnants of the light that were left in the day, reflecting off its metallic surface. The way they moved hypnotised her for a moment, just like the body, the wound had done. Then she snapped herself out of it, taking the proffered piece of evidence. Turning the thing over, examining it from every angle.

It was a small mouth organ.

"He had some change on him too, a handful of coins. Probably used that thing to busk and make a few quid," Parkes continued.

Susie nodded. "If he did, then someone around here will have seen him doing it. Will know him. Maybe even the person who called this in." That had been an anonymous 999 call, from a phone box just up the road. A panicked recording Susie had already listened to.

"Unless it was just someone who stumbled on the body, didn't want to stick around for obvious reasons," Parkes suggested, leaving that hanging in the air. "So, what're we thinking? Get uniform to canvas the area?"

Susie pursed her lips, motioning for one of the forensic people to pass her a clear plastic bag, into which she slid the tiny instrument that had belonged to the boy. "I'm not sure that's the right approach, we'll probably get as much out of the folk around here as we did at that encampment before." Susie was pretty damned sure none of the homeless people in the area would open up to coppers in or out of uniform—they could smell plain clothes police from a mile away—regardless of whether one of their own had been murdered or not. There just wasn't the trust, and she couldn't really say she blamed them. "But we go by the book again." Or *be seen* to go by the book at any rate. So she gave the order, ticked that particular box. Needed to be seen to be doing something, rather than falling to pieces.

Then she wandered down the length of the alley and pulled out her mobile, made a phone call herself.

One that might actually get them some results.

*   *   *

The meeting with her CI, in an abandoned factory on the west side of town, in the middle of the night—alone, regardless of the fact Parkes had wanted to tag along—had at least given her a name.

"Giovanni," the stooped-over man called Birdie had informed her. Because that's what he did, Birdie, inform. She'd had the conversation about his own name with him so many times, trying to get him to change it, but he'd told her that nobody who was in his line of "work" would be stupid enough to call themselves that. Hiding in plain sight, he told her.

"Italian, then."

135

"Parents might have been," offered Birdie, shrugging, then coughed like he was trying to hack up a lung. He was not a well man, probably due to all those years sleeping under bridges and in alleyways himself. Keyed into the way of life here, it was one of the things that made him such a good snitch. "Who knows. But that's your kid. Used to play that harmonica of his near the entrance to the shopping precinct sometimes. Was good with it too, catchy tunes."

"Right," Susie replied, looking around her. The shadows in that place made her nervous, not helped by more sleepless nights of late. More hangovers, in every sense of the word.

"No-one's seen him around for a little while," Birdie had continued. "Guess nobody will now."

"Any particular reason he's been off his patch?" she'd asked.

Another shrug. "Sometimes people get better offers, you know what I mean? Maybe someone took pity on him."

Yeah, or maybe they'd pretended to before—

No pity in that, in what had been done to him.

"I can ask around a bit more, see if anyone talked to him recently. But it's risky, you don't want people thinking they're being accused of anything."

"Unless it's someone who actually did it," mused Susie.

"Yeah, I'm not sure I'd like to run into them anyway," Birdie admitted.

I would, she'd thought. So would Parkes. "Do what you can," Susie had said.

"One thing in your favour was he was well liked. Don't know if he knew it, though. But he was a good kid, y'know? Pleasant-natured."

A good kid. What a waste.

Susie had paid the man, giving him a little extra on the understanding that he spent it on the right things—like maybe a night or two in a hotel, some square meals. But she was all too aware of Birdie's addictions and habits; not that she could talk. Not that she had a leg to stand on in that department. Besides, she had other things to think about at the moment.

Like the fact that despite their best efforts, the press had got wind of this all. That they were putting two and two together and coming up with a pattern. A potential serial killer in the making who was preying on kids. Headline heaven.

"Didn't even give us a chance to try and control the narrative. I mean, how are they getting hold of this kind of information?" Susie's own boss, Chief Superintendent Gillian Robson demanded to know when she hauled her into her office. "There's stuff in these articles that... Here, for instance," said the woman from behind her desk, streaks of grey running through her black hair like the Bride of Frankenstein—and just as terrifying when riled. "This stuff about the boy being taken somewhere to... because of the lack of blood in that alleyway. How are they finding out about that, Inspector?"

"I have no idea, sir," Susie admitted. She hadn't been best pleased about the articles herself. All it did was interfere with the investigation, slow things up and muddy the waters (bad choice of phrase given what had happened to the girl). It just put more pressure on Robson, and subsequently on her.

"Well, you bloody should have some idea," snapped her boss. "Helicopter views, Ellis! This is *your* investigation, after all."

"I'm aware of that, sir." Fucking narratives, helicopters. More bullshit buzzword talk from meetings.

"It's bad enough that our only suspects got away!"

"That really wasn't my—"

Robson held up her hand. "And we're still nowhere trying to trace those gypsies."

"They're called travellers these days, sir."

The woman ignored her. "Nowhere with identifying the little girl?"

Susie reluctantly shook her head. She was nowhere with any of this, sadly.

"And just look at yourself, you look like you haven't had a kip in a year," Robson carried on with her rant.

There was no arguing with that, Susie was beyond exhausted; and, actually, talking about it just made her want to yawn, which she had to stifle. But she wasn't the only one.

"Your man, Parkes, too. Looks like he's rolled out of a skip." And it was true, neither of them had been getting much in the way of downtime lately; bags under both sets of eyes, grabbing the first thing to hand when getting dressed in the morning for fear of being late. Or not even bothering to get changed at all, falling asleep on the couch after a few too many wines, beers, spirits (in her case anyway). But then what did Robson expect, when all this was going on? When that bitch was breathing down their necks?

Then there were the dreams, the nightmares. Parkes had been having a few of those as well, he'd eventually admitted. That was hardly surprising either, given the things they'd both seen.

"I mean, I'm beginning to wonder if you're up to the job, Ellis. The last vic being a boy and all."

Susie gritted her teeth, wanted so much to rant and rave back at the super but knew she had to hold it all in. Knew what she was driving at. What Susie had once been through, though not common knowledge, was definitely in her file. In her psych evaluations. Including how she'd dealt with the grief—or hadn't. "I'm more than capable, sir."

"Are you. *Are* you, though? Because from where I'm sitting this has been one catastrophe after another. It's a lot to unpack." Robson gave a deep sigh. "Children, Ellis. These were children."

"I'm well aware." She couldn't be *more* aware of that.

"So, we need results and we need them soon! Or you know what will happen."

Susie had a fair idea, she and Parkes would be taken off the case for starters. They could unpack that! Then it would follow them around like a bad smell the rest of their careers, get used anytime anything went wrong in future cases (again). More importantly, it would mean that they wouldn't *ever* get justice for the unnamed girl, for Giovanni. The good kid, the pleasant-natured kid.

The one who was the same age as the boy who never got the chance to—

She looked into who the leak might be, but didn't get very far. Could have been anyone in the bullpen, or even the pathology department? In the end it had done them a favour, however. They might have had countless phone calls about it, many of them nutters claiming to have information that just turned out to be more dead ends, but there was that one call she'd taken herself. The person who'd phoned her number directly.

"You never said that she was dead," was how he'd started the conversion.

"Shephard?" asked Susie, recognising the voice.

"You said missing. We knew she was missing, but you never said..." She could hear the crying down the line. "That you'd... you'd found her body."

Susie said nothing, didn't want to scare him off again.

"Oh God, Phoebe. Poor Phoebe... Maggie's in bits."

"Shephard, if you have any information about all this..." And he did. Quite a bit of information, as it turned out. The young girl's name was Phoebe Stanley, she'd been with them for a few years now since her own parents buggered off and left her with Shephard and his partner Maggie. They'd done their best for her, but had been rowing with the girl more and more of late. She'd become a bit of a handful, stealing and such. It was what he thought the police were visiting about that morning. She'd often talked about finding a better life, somewhere away from them.

Sometimes people get better offers, you know what I mean?

"Said her own parents hadn't wanted her, that we didn't either really. That wasn't true, Inspector. We did. We... we loved her. She was like a daughter to us." Then one day she just left, and they hadn't seen her again. Never would see her alive again now. "We stayed in the area in case she returned," Shephard told her.

Well, she had—after a fashion. Just not in the way any of them would have preferred. Susie had no luck getting the man to come in and make an official statement, though; there was just too much bad blood between him and the boys in blue for that. "If I come in, I might never get back out again," he told her. But she had a name to fit the face now, and some kind of idea what had happened in the run-up.

Phoebe had wanted a better life, maybe Giovanni as well. Where had they gone, though? How had they ended up there? Birdie had eventually got back to her with a clue about that after asking around. Some place the boy had talked of where a warm bed and food was potentially on offer. Someplace safe.

"You mean like a hostel or something?" she asked her informant.

"No idea. None that I'm aware of around here, apart from the Sally Army. Hey, you're the detective, Ellis."

It was something to look into, definitely. And something was always better than nothing. A place to start. Not that she'd *had* to look into it when all was said and done, because Susie doubted she'd have found the place anyway just by searching. No, the answer came that weekend when—shattered—she'd gone home and crashed, helped along by a bit too much JD.

The music had woken her this time, rather than the giggling. Or the sense that someone was in her bedroom, carried over from her dream. A catchy tune, distinctive... played on a harmonica. In spite of the drink, Susie had sat bolt upright—and there they were. The boy now standing next to the girl, playing his instrument. Giovanni and Phoebe, both with pale faces—almost blue, clearly dead—complete with matching wounds on their chests.

Susie's breath caught in the back of her throat. "Is... is this... are you—"

Phoebe had giggled once more, hand to her mouth. Seconds later, Giovanni stopped playing and walked over to Susie. She was trembling, didn't dare move or say anything else. Which was good, because she needed to listen. Hear what the boy had to say as he leaned in and whispered.

The next thing she knew, her phone was going off and sunlight was flooding into her room. She'd gone back to sleep, or passed out—one or the other. Crawling over her bed, bleary-eyed, she snatched up the mobile from the bedside table.

"Boss?" Parkes asked, probably worried because all he'd got were mumbles when she'd answered. There was a lead on who might have blabbed to the press, a DC on the team who was passing on information in exchange for certain... favours from a female journalist.

Batting it away with her hand, even though Parkes couldn't see it, Susie said to him: "I don't care about that right now... I mean, good, that's good. But I think I might have something." She paused then. *Did* she? Did she really have something? Was she really going to go by something she'd been told by a dead boy in a dream? A nightmare? A nightmare brought on by drink, more than likely (no, she drank *because* of the bad dreams, right?). Then suddenly she was telling him anyway. "I may have an address, the name of a place actually. A place to start looking." Something, which was better than—

"Oh. Right," was his response. So she told him. "Worth checking out?"

"Definitely," she replied. Being proactive again.

"Then what are we waiting for?" came his reply.

*　　*　　*

To his credit, Parkes had said nothing when he'd picked her up in his blue Mondeo to drive there.

Nothing about what he could so obviously smell on her breath from the night before, knew well enough by now how she coped with the stress. So what? There was a lot of it about on the force (and Parkes himself wasn't averse to knocking a few back after work). Nothing about how rough she clearly looked, either. He hadn't even asked how she'd come by this new information, not that she would have told him. Susie might have gone as far as saying it was "another informant", no further.

But she had said to him: "One thing, Parkes. I'd appreciate it if we could keep this visit between you and me for now, until we know more."

He'd nodded. "Sure. So we're under the radar on this one, then?"

"Pretty much. We're on thin ice with Robson as it is." She went on to tell him about meeting with her recently, about how they were a whisker away from getting pulled off this. She also told him what she'd found out about the place they were making for, about the person who owned it.

"Friends in high places, eh?" Parkes said.

"Yeah, shitloads of money buys you those kinds of friends."

Especially inherited money. Inherited, like the building they were driving to right now. Huge, with wings on its left and right, originally from the 1700s and built in the classical style: but with scaffolding on one side now, showing it needed repairs. Equally massive white-framed windows ran along its length, and columns stood guard at the front door. They'd had to drive along country roads to get there, out in the middle of nowhere as it was. Away from prying eyes, Susie thought to herself. Away from the usual systems of checks and control.

Aswarby Hall.

They pulled up in the driveway, which itself was in the shadow of various tall trees; oaks and firs predominantly. The pair climbed out

141

and made their way to the front door, Susie knocking on it with a brass knocker in the shape of a lion, but with wings on either side. Moments later, the door was opened by a woman who looked to be in her late 50s or early 60s, wearing an apron. Her hair was the opposite of Robson's, completely grey apart from a few streaks of black here and there. "Y-Yes?" she asked.

Susie held up her warrant card, informing the woman who they were. "Would it be possible to come in and have a word."

"What's all this about?" she queried, frowning.

"Perhaps inside?" Susie pushed, and the woman finally relented—letting them in. "And you are...?"

"Oh, I'm Mrs Bunch, dear."

"You run this place, do you?" asked Parkes next. "This... what exactly is this anyway, if you don't mind me asking."

The woman smiled. "Of course not. Well, I don't really know what you'd call it. But we help young people who are down on their luck."

"Right," said Susie. "That's kind of what we'd heard."

Mrs Bunch's brow creased again, perhaps wondering who they'd heard that from.

"Only... only you don't seem to be officially registered anywhere."

"No, well, we... It's all a bit complicated," she told them.

I'll bet, thought Susie. And dodgy as all hell, too. But that didn't matter when you could buy off the right people, did it.

"The youngsters we help, they don't... Well, they come and go, you see. Don't like people knowing where they are."

"Okay. And how many are actually... How many 'youngsters' are you helping right now?"

"At the moment, none," Mrs Bunch admitted. "We scaled down in recent years. But we're having a bit of work done on the place, getting it up to scratch now for even greater numbers in the future when we officially launch... relaunch." She laughed at that for some reason.

Susie nodded. "I see. But no work going on today?"

"Not on a Saturday, no."

"So, you and Mr Abney—"

"Professor Abney, you mean."

"Of course, of course." Former Professor Abney, that was. Professor of Ancient Mythology at Cambridge—until he wasn't. "Is he around, by the way? I'd quite like to have a quick chat with him."

"He's— Look, you still haven't told me what this is about, Inspector."

"Just routine enquiries."

"Yes, but enquiries about *what*?" asked the woman, slightly annoyed. "Have there been any complaints?"

"No, no. That's not it." There hadn't been any complaints because nobody really knew about this orphanage, halfway house... whatever the hell it was. No complaints from the children who allegedly had stayed here either, because—as the woman said—they very often didn't want to poke their heads above the parapet. Didn't want to go on record as being *anywhere*. "We're looking into a couple of suspicious deaths," Susie said finally. It was one way of putting it. A way that wouldn't just immediately get them thrown out, or flag what they were doing to Robson—with absolutely nothing to back it up.

"Oh my." Mrs Bunch's fingers went to her mouth. "Suspicious deaths, you say. I can't think what that might have to do with our—"

"Probably nothing," Parkes cut in, glancing sideways at Susie. "But we have to follow up every lead."

The grey-haired woman nodded, but looked like she didn't know what he was talking about. "We have nothing to hide here," she told them.

"Then you won't mind if we have a little look around?" Susie said.

Mrs Bunch opened her mouth as if to say something, then simply nodded again. "Of course, anything we can do to help the police. I'll give you the guided tour."

They started with the downstairs, which included popping into the Games Room—complete with huge snooker table, screens for playing computer games on and also lots of board games. Then they were shown the extensive library, all kinds of books in case the kids staying there wanted to read ("Reading is actively encouraged here, in fact!" Mrs Bunch told them. "And the professor is more than willing to lecture, teach a lesson or two..."). Next came the recreational areas where kids could just hang out and sit, or chat. Relax a bit, which was more than they'd probably been able to do in

143

their previous situations. Here and there were photos scattered about, on the walls, propped up on tables, of the place when it was full of those youngsters Mrs Bunch had talked about. They certainly seemed to be having fun, happy, laughing. The old lady was in some of them, being kissed on the cheek in one shot. And there was a man who looked of a similar age to her in a couple of others, with wild white hair and glasses, wearing a bowtie; presumably Professor Abney (Susie couldn't help thinking they made a nice couple, like they should be running a Mom & Pop store in the States or something). Abney had his arm around a youth with spiky hair in the picture she caught sight of; certainly no animosity, whatever was the case.

"And there's just the two of you here, looking after things?" asked Parkes.

"At the moment, yes. No need for more staff right now," Mrs Bunch told him.

There were kitchens, too, which were extensive—as well as a big dining area. "Some of the poor mites we deal with are used to just eating scraps," Mrs Bunch informed them. "So sad. We always do our best for them. As Professor Abney says, what's the use of money if you can't do something with it."

"Quite," said Susie. It was all pretty convincing she had to admit, even the evidence that work was going on inside and out: tools lying around, ladders and paint and such. "And where did you say he was at the moment?"

Mrs Bunch gaped at her, looked like she wasn't going to reply at all, but then said: "There's been a bereavement in the family, his uncle sadly passed away. The professor has been making arrangements to look after his cousin, Stephen."

"Cousin?"

"Much younger cousin," explained Mrs Bunch, "his uncle's son. As you can imagine, it's been taking up a lot of his time so it's probably a good job we're not as busy as we once were here."

It was Susie's turn to nod. That was fair enough, she supposed. As they came back to the foyer, about to head upstairs, she noticed a door nearby—not far from the telephone table. "What's in there?" she asked.

"Oh, that's just the wine cellar," Mrs Bunch clarified. "We keep it locked because, obviously, we don't want the kids getting in, helping themselves, making a mess." She gave another titter. "There are things of value down there."

"I don't suppose we could—" Susie began, but already the woman was heading upstairs to continue on with the tour. Which included lots of bedrooms, again some in the process of being renovated. It reminded her a little of that movie with all the mutant people and the jet underneath the house. And that bald guy who could read minds, he was a professor as well. It would be a pretty damned handy talent to have right now, she thought to herself. Because on the face of it, there was nothing suspicious about this place at all—and she had to concede, she was starting to question why they were even here. Told of its location, what, by drunken hallucinations, by ghosts? It was absolutely ridiculous!

Then again, it *had* been where the boy with the mouth organ had said it would be, out in the countryside. Or maybe Susie had read about this place somewhere, heard about it and forgotten? Was all this just down to her subconscious, a vivid imagination? That was no way to run a police investigation, was it? No way to get a helicopter view or whatever, unpack things. Control the narrative...

As they passed another closed door, Mrs Bunch waved towards it and told them it was Professor Abney's private office. Again, locked for obvious reasons and he was the only one who had a key. Then they were being led back down the stairs again, but Susie paused halfway.

She and Parkes exchanged a look then, and she said, "Mrs Bunch, is there any chance I could use your facilities? Back there?" Susie thumbed up the stairs.

"Oh, yes. Certainly," said the woman.

"Mrs Bunch, maybe you could tell me more about the day-to-day running of the place," Parkes said to her, holding out his hand for them to carry on down the stairs. He'd got exactly what she was trying to say to him: keep her busy for a while.

As Susie retreated back to the upper floor, heading not for the toilet but that office. By the time they came back with a search warrant—and what grounds would she give anyway—they'd have cleared out anything that might be incriminating, if indeed there was anything. She tried the door, just to check, and found it locked like

145

Mrs Bunch had said. Not that it was going to stop her. Susie took out the small pick she always carried with her, attached to her keyring, that she'd been shown how to use by a thief she'd once known called Grant. It took just seconds to gain entry when you knew what you were doing, and quietly she opened and closed the door again.

There were more books inside here, covering the walls. Tomes about religious beliefs, paganism, the Orphic poems, the worship of Mithras, Neo-Platonism, the superstitions of the Romans of the Lower Empire... Nothing really that surprising given what the man had once taught. She only had time to scan the spines, flip through a few of them—and a lot of it went over her head—before heading for the desk at the far end, a big oak affair with a leather armchair tucked underneath it.

Resting on this was a laptop, which she opened. It came on, but was password protected. Susie gave it a few goes, picking things like Roman gods or words from those book titles—she even tried "griffin" in honour of that door knocker—but it was never going to be that easy. They'd need the techies to crack that thing open, and again they'd need a warrant. Next she tried the drawers on either side of the desk, found those locked as well. She was just taking out her pick once more when she caught sight of something that stopped her in her tracks.

On her left, pinned to the wall, was a calendar. She rose, moving towards it. Some little voice at the back of her head was reminding her that she'd spent too long up here as it was, that she should get out of the office before she was discovered—Parkes' conversational skills would only stall Mrs Bunch for so long—but she was mesmerised by what she saw.

Nothing else was marked off this year, only one date. March 24th: today. And it was marked with one note, in what she assumed was the professor's own handwriting. It simply said: "Stephen's 12th Birthday."

Again, not really proof of anything on its own—but something inside her clicked. The cousin he was looking after, his uncle's young son, 12 tomorrow. The same age as Phoebe and Giovanni. The same age they'd been when they died... for all she knew, on their birthdays as well.

She might have gazed at that calendar all day, had it not been for the noise. The sudden and loud bang that made her jump. That shook her into racing towards the door, stamping down those stairs.

It was obvious what had happened even before she reached the bottom. For one thing, Mrs Bunch was still holding the smoking revolver that had done the damage, pulled from somewhere deep in the folds of her apron. For another, there was Parkes, on his back, lifeless eyes rolled up into his head. His hands, those hands she'd seen clenching and unclenching whenever he was mad, were like upturned spiders now, rigid from the pain. And at his chest was a gaping chasm, black and red at the same time, blood still pouring from it, pooling on the floor. Parkes' own heart, with a hole in it, just like—

"I'm afraid he had something called an atrial septal defect. We're really so very sorry."

Susie felt like screaming, but nothing would come out. She'd done this. She'd dragged them out here to this place in the middle of nowhere, knowing that there was some connection to the murders. But never once, since that door had been opened, thinking Mrs Bunch was capable of—

Ironic. All those big, tough guys Parkes had taken on over the years... But there'd be no carting off to the hospital, it was too late for that. His stalling days were over.

"I couldn't let this go on," she explained to the police officer now joining them on the ground floor. "This... this façade. I know why you're here, *of course* I know. I'm not sure how you found out but... But the good work must be allowed to continue. Do you understand?"

"Good... *Good work*..." Susie's mind was racing. Was she talking about looking after the kids there—all those photos, the happy, smiling faces—thinking maybe that was all over now? Didn't matter, because: "He's dead, you bloody psycho. You've just killed my partner!" It wasn't until she saw him just now that Susie realised how much weight that word carried. How much she actually did care about this man. *Had cared* about him. A person who knew just what she wanted and when, who could read her like one of those books in the library here. She might not ever have had a romantic relationship with someone worth a damn in this life, but she had Parkes. She'd *had* Parkes, until—

Speeding up towards the foot of the stairs, Susie was readying to attack this woman, a lady who looked like butter wouldn't melt in her mouth. Except when she got nearer, the woman trained that old-fashioned pistol on Susie. "Please don't," she told her. "I had no choice with your sergeant, he was asking too many awkward questions."

"Questions..." Susie just couldn't wrap her head around this. Questions were an excuse to shoot someone dead in cold blood? "He had kids," she said then.

Children...

Mrs Bunch had the good grace to look a little bit upset at that. "Then I'm truly sorry. But he was just so *big*! Too much potential for things to go wrong. For things to get out of control."

This woman, this murderer—had she killed those two children as well? Susie wondered; she was more than capable of it—she obviously thought Susie was less of a threat. Well, if she thought that, she was wrong. But let her think it, let her think it for now, because that was the only thing keeping Susie alive. It was the only thing giving her time to work out what to do, how to maybe wrench that gun from Mrs Bunch, put her down.

But she never got the chance to do any of that. By the time she noticed, was able to tear her eyes away from the horrific scene before her... by the time she spotted the door that had been locked before was open—the door to the wine cellar, Mrs Bunch had told them—it was already too late.

She felt the blow to the back of the head, and briefly there was pain. Nothing like the pain Parkes had obviously felt, but pain nonetheless.

Then there was nothing at all.

*　*　*

When Susie woke up, she had trouble realising she was even awake at all.

It was so black where she was, very similar to being unconscious. Only there was light coming from somewhere; faint, but it was there. Then came the ache, the thudding in her skull. Much worse than a hangover, but her vision was blurred all the same. She blinked once, twice. Nothing was coming into focus this time, not yet.

Next the coldness hit her. Might just be the shock, she thought; might even be because she was dead herself? But no, it was because of where she was, not her condition. Susie was shivering, that meant she was still alive... didn't it?

And then there was the smell. The distinct smell of damp. Of rot and decay. She lifted her head and wished she hadn't bothered, the thudding turning into a sharp pain that ran up the back of her head and down her neck simultaneously. Before she could stop herself, Susie let out a howl. It echoed, coming back to her from several different directions at once. But there was no other noise, no reaction to her cry. She was alone wherever she was.

Now she tried to lever herself up, squeezing her eyes shut tight then opening them again. Shapes were starting to make themselves apparent. Strips of something in front of her, blackness cutting through the weak light, which at first she took for gaps in her vision, were in fact—as she now saw—bars. Iron bars.

She was in some sort of cell.

Nothing like the ones they had back at her nick, those were cosy compared to this. The exact opposite of this, actually, with white walls and a cot, a mattress, rather than darkness and a stone floor. It was the same difference, though: she was a prisoner.

Memories rushed back at her then, of why. Mrs Bunch, Parkes, what had happened while she'd been twatting about upstairs in the office. If she'd stayed with them, maybe... No, they might both have been shot. Parkes would almost certainly have thrown himself in front of her to take the bullet anyway. No point thinking about that now, she was here. In here, alone. Hadn't done a very good job of controlling the narrative, had she? Totally out of control! Fucked everything up, like always.

Susie used the bars to pull herself up, clocking the huge padlock on the door of that cell. She fell though, her legs like jelly, landing further back inside. Hands out and touching something... lots of somethings. Susie's face soured, the smell even worse now. Using her hands she felt around, and some of what her fingertips encountered was soft, some of it hard.

She checked her pockets, nothing had been taken. She still had her phone, so she flicked it on—and wasn't surprised that she couldn't get a signal. Couldn't get on the net. They would have relieved her of it if they thought she could call for help. But the light it was providing did at least show her what she'd landed amongst.

Some of it was flesh, some of it bone.

Bodies. There were bodies in this place with her, stretching back towards the far wall. Some old, some from not that long ago. All of them small, none adult-sized. The children who'd come to this place, those kids seeking a safe sanctuary—or had been told there was one at Aswarby—were all dead now. None of them had moved on, as such. None of them had *survived*, then. Susie blinked, couldn't help contrasting the photos from upstairs with these lifeless things surrounding her. They'd trusted Mrs Bunch, and she'd—

Don't want the kids getting inside... making a mess...

Poor mites we deal with...

Things of great value...

Susie scrabbled around, ignoring the pain, shuffling towards the door of the cell. Pulling herself up fully, reaching round for that lock, she took out her keys and her pick. She was fumbling with it, however, her coordination not quite there. And when there came a noise off to her left, she dropped the keys on the floor—on the other side of the bars, just out of reach.

The sound was a door squeaking open, letting in more light from above. It illuminated not only a set of steps downwards, but the area in front of Susie. Confirming her suspicions, telling her exactly where she was. The rows of bottles in racks, sticking out like missiles waiting to be fired. She was in the cellar, the wine cellar. No jets, no helicopters though—nothing but death down here.

Not too far away was another desk, but more functional than the one upstairs in that office. This was a simple wooden affair, like a workbench or something. On it was a small tray, what looked like a small can of lighter fluid and two glasses, one of which still had a yellowish liquid in it. Next to these was a cake with candles on top, and something she couldn't quite make out, covered over with a tea-towel. Beside the desk was an equally basic chair, but it wasn't empty. Far from it.

Slumped on the thing was another body, that of a boy with blond hair, dressed in jeans and a shirt. On top of his head, which was lolling to one side, was a paper party hat; the kind you got in

150

crackers. *Please don't be dead, please don't be dead*, Susie said to herself, but then she heard a small moan come from the lad, could see he was still breathing.

This was soon eclipsed by footsteps, heavy on the steps. Susie looked up and over, seeing Mrs Bunch descend. She saw her captive watching and smiled. "Ah, you're awake then."

"Let me out of here!" shouted Susie.

"I'm afraid I can't do that, dear," came her reply. Everything she said was in such a reasonable tone, like it was the most normal thing in the world to lock people up with the corpses of dozens of children you'd butchered. "It wouldn't be wise. Not in our best interests, you see."

Our, not *my*. But then, someone had to have been behind Susie to whack her on the head. Someone who'd crept out of the cellar, leaving the boy behind. And she saw who that was next, following Mrs Bunch down.

Professor Abney. Both these looneys in it together. Abney— complete with mad white hair, spectacles and bow tie, same as he'd appeared in the photos—looked over at Susie as well, grinning, before nodding towards the boy on the chair. "I see you've met Stephen, then. You interrupted our little party down here, Inspector! We were celebrating you see, for different reasons I grant you."

The pair reached the bottom of the steps, moving into the cellar proper—and Abney turned up the lights in there, so they could see where they were going. Mrs Bunch dawdled near the stairs, while the professor went over to the bench, holding out his hand. "There was music, cake." And now Susie could see, 12 candles on that cake. For Stephen's twelfth birthday. "I even let the young tyke here have some champagne." He picked up the glass that still had liquid in it, to illustrate. "Oh, he didn't want it at first but I... insisted. It seems to have gone straight to his head, though."

"Probably the opium you put in it," replied Susie bitterly, ignoring Abney's laughter. "Stephen! Stephen, wake up! You're in so much danger!" she shouted then, not really believing for a second it would rouse him; he was too doped up for that.

Abney rounded the table, making sure he had everything he needed. Then he looked to one side, at the racks of bottles, and headed towards one. "Ah yes, that's more like it. Quinta do Noval,

151

vintage port. Do you partake, Inspector?" he called across to Susie.

What was this now, the bastard was going to have a tipple before he... And was he offering her one too? "Are you for real?" she spluttered, still hanging on to the bars for support.

"Oh, very much so. I'm *very* for real. Couldn't be more real."

"If you hurt him, I swear to God—"

"God?" said Abney. "*God?* What do you know of God? Nothing, that's what! Nothing of the power of *a* god, that's for certain."

"You're insane," Susie told him, then looked at Mrs Bunch. "You're *both* insane. All these children in here, you... You killed them, didn't you?"

"They did not die in vain, dear," Mrs Bunch answered in that oh-so rational voice of hers. "Stepping stones towards a miracle."

"A miracle you will soon witness," Abner chipped in.

So she hadn't been left alive merely because she wasn't deemed a threat. Since she was there anyway, they wanted her to witness whatever this madness was.

"How are you finding your lodgings, by the way? They're not quite up to the standards above, but they serve their purpose as all things do. A throwback to when my ancestors used to keep their enemies in here. Keep your enemies close, eh?"

"And your victims, apparently," spat Susie.

"Victims? Victims? There are no victims in all this, Inspector. You make it sound like we do this for sport, for fun."

"Don't you?"

"Of course not!" barked Abney. "They were part of my... experiments. Some early attempts, I'll grant you. But none wasted efforts; all steps along the road to one glorious final destination. It needed to be perfected though, you see, and until last year I didn't have access to the correct materials."

"Looks like you had access to all the materials you wanted, you just had to lure them here Professor."

"No, no, no. Not *ingredients*, materials. Writings—specifically the formula. I only had parts of the puzzle. Tantalising accounts of what was possible via certain rituals, practices. All granted certain boons, like being able to turn or hold back time, or the ability to hear thoughts, to influence the weaker minded." His eyes flicked across to Mrs Bunch then. "Or the young. Only for short periods, you understand." Susie couldn't help thinking about that other professor again, the bald one in the wheelchair. What he could do in those movies, in those comics. But that was fiction... "Some might call such practices barbaric, I suppose, but—"

"Barbaric! *Barbaric!* What you've done here..." Susie cast a brief look over her shoulder for effect, then wished she hadn't when she caught a glimpse of those corpses again. "What you've done is monstrous! Inhuman!"

There was no humanity in them...

"Inhuman, you say. Inhuman practices to become... *more than* human, Inspector. Is that not worth the sacrifice?"

More than human? What the fuck was he talking about? "Whatever you were trying to do, these weren't your sacrifices to make! Either of you!"

"A means to an end," Mrs Bunch countered.

Abney's eyes dipped. "There wouldn't have been quite so many if I'd uncovered the formula earlier. It was the writings of Hermes, you understand. Hermes Trismegistus lit the way."

"I don't care if it was Jeffrey fucking Archer, you're—"

"You keep interrupting me, Inspector!" The professor jabbed a finger in her direction. "How can you ever possibly hope to understand if you..." He sighed. "Perhaps it doesn't matter. You'll see for yourself soon enough. See my ascension."

His... relaunch?

"The only thing I want to see is you going down for this," Susie shouted back. "I just wish we still had the death penalty."

"That won't matter either, soon. I will be beyond Death's reach."

Susie shook her head. "Where's your compassion? Your love? Your heart?"

"Funny you should mention that particular organ, because in the end it held the key! So simple really, I only needed the three. But I didn't know that when I... Three, the magic number when all's said and done. A small price to pay for such a large reward: to be able to fly; to become invisible; or change one's appearance. To be invulnerable, immortal. A deity! Three hearts, 12 years of age. Three—"

"Three more dead children!" Susie bellowed at him. "What did you do with them, their hearts? Phoebe's, Giovanni's? What are you going to do with Stephen's? Eat it?"

Abney laughed even harder. "Why, of course not! I'm not a savage, Inspector. *Or* a cannibal! The heart must be turned to ash and mixed with..." He held the bottle of port up again, opening it and pouring some into the empty glass remaining, before setting it down again. "But taken from a living subject; that's the important part. Stephen will be my crowning glory." He plucked the party hat from the lad's head, as if to emphasize the point. "The one who'll activate my powers."

No humanity...

"Your powers? Have you even heard yourself?" Of course he had: more than willing to lecture, teach a lesson or two. Liked the sound of his own voice, Abney. Susie shook her head once more, wincing as she caught sight of the remains behind her. "But why leave them for us to find this time? Why not just put them in here?"

"All part of this specific sacrament, Inspector. In order for it to work, they must be returned to where I found them, and how I found them; clothes and so forth. Minus what I needed, naturally. The three, the trinity. I will do the same with Stephen, once I have finished my work." The professor pulled away the tea-towel, the cloth; revealing the blades beneath. He picked up one with a ragged edge, like a breadknife, holding it up to the light and testing the end with a fingertip, which he quickly withdrew. Razor sharp. He walked back around to the barely conscious Stephen, and began to unbutton the lad's shirt.

His *work*. Work which included murdering kids—cutting out their still-beating hearts and burning them with lighter fluid. Holy shit! Susie had to get out of there, stop this from happening again. At least save one, if she couldn't avenge the others. She thought again about the pick, trying to reach it; neither Bunch nor Abney had noticed her keys. But they were so far away, impossible to reach. The lock, maybe she could wrench it off or whatever. Had to try something, because it was better than—

"Definitely worth checking out..." Susie heard then. Might have been her own voice urging her on, but this was much deeper. A voice she recognised. Shaking herself, she grabbed at the lock again—and it fell open. Her mouth did too, in shock and surprise. Had she got further with picking it than she realised? Or...

154

"What are you waiting for?" came that deep voice again.

"Parkes?" she whispered, but there was no reply. Susie shook her head a final time. What *was* she waiting for? She'd been given a chance here, an opportunity to save Stephen. Susie tore the lock away, pulled on the bars now not for support but to open the door—which she did with a loud squeak.

Both Abney and Bunch looked over.

Susie stumbled through the gap, trying to will her legs to work properly. Aiming herself like one of those missiles she'd compared the wine bottles to.

"Mrs Bunch, if you'd be so kind," said Abney, nodding at the woman hurtling towards them. The old woman nodded her compliance, and Susie had to wonder whether he was still using that influence on her, or maybe he'd never needed to. Maybe she was just devoted to this monster? Didn't matter, the fact remained she was in Susie's path.

In her path and drawing that gun out of her apron. Aiming it just as Susie had aimed herself.

A shot rang out, echoing, but Susie somehow managed to dodge it. Getting closer, closer. Another bang, but this time she wasn't so lucky. The bullet hit her like a fist in the shoulder, spinning her and toppling her over. She landed hard on the cold floor again, trying to ignore the pain in both her head and at her shoulder.

Bunch was still coming, still holding that pistol out in front of her. About to pull the trigger and put Susie out of her considerable misery, while behind Abney was raising his own weapon: seconds away from bringing it down into his cousin's chest.

Suddenly she heard it, not a voice this time, but something else. The cries of the lost, so many from that cell behind. Unable to help her, she knew, but crying out in sympathy because they'd been there. They'd died down here at the hands of these crackpots, who seemed oblivious to their woe.

But then Susie heard something else. Something that even Abney and Bunch heard: giggling, at first; followed by a tune. Not the music from Stephen's birthday, whatever that had been. But music played on the harmonica.

The woman with the gun paused. The man with the knife paused.

Next thing Susie knew it was happening. Mrs Bunch was being

lifted off the ground, her finger twitching on the trigger, the revolver letting off a shot that went wide. But even the echo of that couldn't drown out the giggling, the tune being played.

A similar thing was happening with the professor, she saw. He too was being lifted by something, a force that was tearing into him, that caused him to drop his weapon. Susie winced at the blood—so much blood, spraying everywhere. Abney's own shirt had been shredded, then the flesh at his chest. Something burrowing inside...

Searching for his heart.

Meanwhile, Mrs Bunch was being flung repeatedly against the wall of the cellar—and it looked very much to Susie like she was exploding from the inside out. Again, that muscle in the centre of her chest was the goal, and finally she dropped her gun, which clattered uselessly to the ground.

As quickly as it had started, the carnage ended—and both cadavers, for neither of the pair were still alive surely, dropped to the ground at the same time. Abney fell across the workbench, while Mrs Bunch slumped down the wall.

All was quiet, and after the noise of the last few minutes—including the screams of the two people being attacked—the silence was deafening. Susie's vision swam, she was close to blacking out once more, but couldn't yet. Nobody even knew where they were, and she didn't want to just leave Stephen down here like this again—though at the same time wasn't sure she'd be able to get him upstairs.

Using the last of her strength, Susie managed to crawl across to where he was. "St-Stephen... can you hear me?"

The boy, head still resting on his chin, mumbled something.

"I'm... I'm going to go get help," she said, then took his hand. "E-Everything's... everything's going to be okay now... I promise."

She thought she saw him nod, but might have been mistaken. It was enough to spur her on, to crawl back across the floor and up those stairs. Out into the hall. She checked her phone again, and had been right—even above ground there was no signal.

Trying not to look at the body of Parkes, which hadn't been moved, she scrambled across to where the landline was, hauling herself up onto the table it was resting on. It took all of her last reserves, but she phoned 999, said her name and that she was in trouble, then left the phone dangling as she herself dropped to the ground unconscious.

At one point she was aware of someone being there with her, then lots of someones. Whether they were alive or dead, she couldn't tell.

But then she slipped back into the blackness and was aware of nothing more.

*   *   *

When she woke up in the hospital, Stephen was sitting beside her.

He'd been there when they found them, so the authorities said. Had made his way up the stairs himself and laid down with Susie, then hadn't left her side, apart from being checked over himself, the whole time she was in there.

Susie had managed a smile, and he'd smiled back. They hadn't even needed words.

Things moved quite quickly and yet at a snail's pace again after that. The police had found not only her and Stephen following their ordeal, but Parkes, the bodies in the cellar—of the children, of Bunch and Abney—plus plenty of incriminating evidence up in that office. Books, handwritten notes about what the professor had been up to, lots of stuff on his laptop, so the techies said. The builders hadn't been near that place for months, he'd dismissed them while he was cooking up the final stages of his plan; probably told Phoebe and Giovanni when he took them back to Aswarby Hall the same lies Bunch had spouted. And there had never been any other staff.

"The man was clearly deranged," Robson had told her when she visited. "Wanted to turn himself into some kind of superman or something, and had managed to convince the housekeeper there to help." Whether that had been possible because of those practise rituals he'd performed wasn't really important now. The same was true of how he'd managed to persuade both Phoebe and Giovanni to come with him. Perhaps he'd shown them pictures of the other children in happier times, perhaps he'd offered money? Maybe he hadn't needed to read their minds to know they wanted a safe place to just *be*. Ironically, they'd have been better off staying where they were.

The rest of the kids were still being identified—if they ever could be—but in the meantime a double funeral was held for Giovanni and

Phoebe when Susie was feeling better. Stephen insisted on attending with her, holding her free hand, the one not in the sling, the whole time. Shephard and Maggie had come too, along with the other travellers who'd known Phoebe—who'd loved her—and so had Birdie, bringing with him some of the homeless folk whose lives had been touched by Giovanni.

As for Bunch and Abney, not one person came to see them off.

Their bodies looked like wild animals had been at them, so the coroner had said. Looked like their hearts had been torn from their chests. Their blood was on those knives though, so it was assumed they'd turned on each other at the end and Susie didn't say anything to contradict that. Just like she refused to be drawn on how she and Parkes ended up there in the first place, just put it down to good policing and instinct. Helicopters and narratives.

To be fair, she wasn't quite sure herself that she'd seen what she'd seen. Could all have been down to the concussion. Then again...

She remembered getting free of the cell, trying to stop them, getting shot... and very little else. She'd tried to save Stephen, get justice not only for Phoebe and Giovanni, but all the kids down there. In the end, though, perhaps vengeance hadn't been hers to mete out. Abney had been right about one thing, the hearts were special, they were the one thing that enabled that revenge—and even now Susie wasn't sure whether it was the two children or Parkes who'd done for Bunch. Maybe he'd got some revenge of his own for the taking of *his* heart?

Susie had explained to Parkes' ex and his kids when it was time for the sergeant's funeral, with honours, how brave he'd been. How he'd been doing it to try and help some other kids. How they should always remember him, because he wasn't really gone.

Which, in a sense, was true. Susie still felt like he was around sometimes, even though she'd taken a desk job now where she didn't have to see death on a regular basis, and had cleaned up her act. But Parkes had a new job of his own, because she could have sworn that on the way back from her partner's funeral, looking out of the window through the fog that had descended, she'd seen him with Phoebe and Giovanni in tow, waving. Walking off together into the mist, holding hands.

Knew that he was looking after them, just as she'd eventually taken on the role of guardian for Stephen. She looked after him, and he did her. They'd saved each other, in more ways than one. He'd inherited Aswarby, of course, but had sold it—on the proviso that it was used to actually help struggling kids this time. That the renovations be finished and the place be staffed by qualified professionals. Everything above board.

Eventually, Susie told him about her own son, about how much she still missed him. And he opened up about his father; how much he missed the man. How much he would have liked Susie.

Had Abney been involved in that too, the death of his own uncle? Or had it just been another cruel twist of fate? Perfect timing for the professor to pounce, his third and final heart falling into his lap like that...

Susie was just glad that hadn't happened. Was thankful they had each other, that love and compassion had won out in the long run; making her feel sorry for those who lived without it. Proving one thing, if nothing else.

How powerful the human heart was.

How special it really could be.

MASQUES

From up here, no-one would ever suspect there was anything wrong at all.

He stood looking through the gigantic window out over the city, lights twinkling, mirroring the starry, moonlit sky. It was hard not to feel like he was above it all, not just because physically he was, but because that height brought a certain sense of detachment. Or at least it should.

If that were the case, then why was he awake at almost 2am? And why was there a cognac clenched in his fist? A cognac he'd just used to wash down another dose of Temazepam; the drug he had prescribed for himself, and not for the first time.

The problem was that Dr Stéphane Rollin, the youngest medical genius of his generation, had one major flaw. He let his work get to him: he cared to the point where he could see the faces of the handful of people he'd not been able to help over the years. It had always been this way, from when he was a lowly intern, right up to the lofty position of senior "in demand" consultant at St Auguste's teaching hospital. He could picture the face of the first patient he'd ever lost right now if he closed his eyes, a 52 year-old man called Pierre-Louis who'd come in complaining of a pain in his leg and had died of a blood clot before Stéphane had been able to even diagnose, let alone fix, what was wrong with him.

Pierre-Louis had definitely made him look more closely, to work faster, to *be* better, but that man had also been the first of those unfortunate patients he now carried with him forever.

He'd learned to cover this at work, rising in the ranks swiftly— with hardly anyone being able to spot this drawback under his cool, businesslike exterior. And he'd been able to handle the few cases he'd lost, the good he'd done far outweighing this. He was too hard on himself, deep down he knew that. But that's what came of being pushed from an early age, by a single mother who'd demanded nothing but complete dedication to his studies.

Now, though... well, now things were different. There were many more faces tonight. Dozens, hundreds, that he hadn't been able to save. And couldn't block out, not even in the arms of Camille, his former actress girlfriend who he'd met a little over two years ago when he diagnosed her rupturing appendix.

She was in the bedroom sleeping right now, didn't have a clue what was really going on inside his mind. He'd shielded her from it, everything he'd seen since his first-hand exposure eight months ago. How could he talk to her about the things he'd witnessed? How could he talk to *anyone*?

His first encounter had been in a rural part of the south, at an isolated farm in the middle of nowhere. Stéphane had been called in to consult on the case, receiving a phone call from the World Health Organisation after an "incident" had been brought to their attention. They'd sent a helicopter, which picked him up on the rooftop. When he arrived at the camp that had been set up just outside what was being called the "Isolation Zone", the amount of police there told Stéphane just how serious the situation was.

He was met by a Professor Lewisohn, whose work in the field of virology was well known to Stéphane. "What exactly is all this about?" he came right out and asked, as he was suiting up: putting on yellow HazMat gear, including self-contained breathing apparatus, clear plexiglass separating him from the world.

"We're dealing with something that could, potentially, become a Level 4 Biohazard," Lewisohn answered seriously, being equally blunt. Stéphane frowned, realising full well that the man was referring to a virus fatal to humans for which no treatments had yet been developed. Diseases such as Marburg and Lassa fever fell into that category. But this was new and Lewisohn would greatly value his opinion on the matter.

They were driven to the farmhouse in question, ground zero for the hazard. "The family inside were discovered by a visiting friend," Lewisohn explained. "That friend rang the emergency services, but had contracted the disease herself by the time they arrived."

"By touch, or inhalation?" asked Stéphane.

Lewisohn shrugged. "We're hoping just by touch, as the person in question let herself in. She might even have touched the..." He let his sentence tail off. "But who knows?"

"Wasn't the friend able to tell you anything more?" asked Stéphane.

Lewisohn didn't answer that. Stéphane found out why when they parked up and entered the farmhouse.

She had died with the phone still in her hand, the receiver now on the floor by the chair in which she lay slumped. "Christ almighty," said Stéphane when he saw her.

In all his years as a practising doctor, he'd never seen anything quite like this before. If he hadn't known it was a woman, and if she hadn't been wearing a skirt and top, he wouldn't have been able to tell. Because her face was featureless, completely red in appearance: not from some sort of rash; no, this was where the blood had pumped through her pores, covering every inch of skin as if someone had smeared thick tomato sauce all over it. Her hands were the same, a deep crimson in colour, and from the way her clothes were saturated, it was clear that the rest of her body had sweated blood as well. Her passing had not been an easy one: that much he could tell by the way her hands gripped the arms of the chair, scarlet fingers digging into the material.

But the family, oh God the family...

They'd obviously been getting ready for breakfast when this hit. The father had collapsed over the table, his blood turning the chequered tablecloth maroon. Mother had been coming in from the kitchen, perhaps hanging on to the doorjamb there for support before toppling headlong onto the floor.

Stéphane had walked around that table, hardly able to look at the final two victims: by their size children, one probably about five, the other little more than a baby in a high chair. He heard someone just behind him and blinked away the tear welling at the corner of his eye, before Lewisohn had a chance to spot it through the clear mask.

"You can see why we brought you here," said Lewisohn, still on the other side of the room. Stéphane gazed across, puzzled. He'd felt sure the man was closer than that. "We could definitely use someone of your diagnostic expertise to figure this out."

It was true, Stéphane could usually crack a case from whatever

162

symptoms presented—his colleagues often joked that he made House look like an amateur—but even he had to admit he was damned if he knew what had caused this. Whatever it was, it had struck the family fast: crippling them before they'd had time to get to a phone. It had overcome the friend just as quickly, barely giving her a chance to dial the emergency services and warn them. But were it not for that, this... this sickness might already have spread. As it was they had a chance to contain it and study the site.

Looking out now over the skyline, Stéphane had another swig of the brandy, draining the glass he was holding. His hand was shaking, *he* was shaking—the memories, as always, doing their worst.

They'd taken what samples they could back for analysis, but to date they hadn't revealed their secrets to him. Had the mystery disease been contracted from wildlife? A scratch from an animal? Some kind of weird variant of foot and mouth which had passed from cattle to humans—causing bleeding instead of blisters? Something from the Ebola family perhaps? Or a biological attack of some kind? Something man-made? But why use it all the way out here—unless it was some kind of dry run? The more he studied it, the less he was able to determine.

In the end, frustrated at his lack of progress, Stéphane had returned to St Auguste's, in the hopes that they wouldn't see any more "incidents" of this kind. But he hadn't forgotten, could never shake the images of how that family had met their end.

Then, a little over two months ago, Stéphane had seen the first reports on the TV. To begin with, a handful of cases: rarities all; anomalies. But soon, very quickly, people were dying in great numbers in the rundown parts of the city, *his* city. Their bodies— when discovered—were completely red, having sweated out most of their own blood. Sufferers complained of sharp pains and dizziness before the attacks, and the final stages came upon them swiftly. The authorities were informing people that there was nothing to worry about, that the disease was carried through direct bodily contact and had spread in these areas because of poor living conditions. The screen threw back images of the sick in local hospitals, lying in their beds, doctors and nurses running back and forth attempting to ease their suffering.

"That's awful," Camille had said, sitting beside him on the sofa,

163

but an hour later—and after watching some rubbish reality show—she'd dismissed it almost entirely from her mind. Which was more than Stéphane could. Those people were dying because he hadn't been able to figure this out; it had followed him here because he hadn't been able to find a way of stopping it.

The next day he got in touch with Lewisohn at the WHO. "All we can really do is monitor the situation," the Professor had told him. "Keep on looking for a cure. But if this escalates, Stéphane, it won't be long before the military take over completely and infected areas will have to be sealed off."

Neither of them said what they were both thinking: how long before this becomes airborne?

The clock in Stéphane's living room struck two, causing him to jump. When he turned, Camille was in the doorway, silky nightie clinging to her curves. "What are you doing up, my love?" she asked.

"Couldn't sleep," he said honestly.

"Come back to bed," she told him, "and we'll see what we can do about that."

Placing the glass down, Stéphane followed her back to the bedroom, but if he slept tonight he knew it would have more to do with the Temazepam and cognac than anything Camille could muster.

*   *   *

Again, the dream.

In it, he saw the rooms. The coloured rooms.

The first blue, the second purple. As he moved through them, he took in the green of the third space, the orange of the fourth, the white of the fifth. He was aware that behind him there was laughter, and when he turned he could trace a line back down through the rooms to the place he'd come from: the place he'd dreamed of before.

The party; some kind of ball. He'd been there only moments ago, hadn't he? Mixing with the guests, dancing. The visitors wore strange clothes, old fashioned, the women twisting and turning in beautiful gowns that must have cost a fortune. The men were no less regal in their attire, with chains hanging from their necks, complimenting the folds of their tunics. But all had one thing in common: their faces were obscured, each covered with odd-looking disguises.

Masques.

Some simple, painted affairs, others much more ornate—resembling animals, birds, fish. Some people were eating, others drinking wine. Everybody was obviously enjoying themselves. Except one person.

The person he'd followed into these rooms to begin with. The person who'd been mingling with the crowd as well, his red, blood-splattered robe mocking their pleasure.

Stéphane had tried to shout out, to get the interloper to stop, reveal himself: for, as it was, they had their back to him. Yet no words would issue from Stéphane's mouth.

How dare he! How dare this intruder come here and spoil their fun? Actually *make fun* at their expense?

At *his* expense.

These were his thoughts now, and they made him angry. That was why he was moving through the rooms, eager to grab hold of this villain, with the intention of hanging the swine. Or maybe...

The knife was out of its sheath even as he thought it. He'd teach the man a lesson he would not soon forget. As if this reminder of the plague was not enough, he'd had the nerve to enter these rooms set aside for guests only, which the servants had spent so long preparing.

How dare he! Just how dare he!

It spurred Stéphane on, even though he seemed to be moving so slowly—the figure ahead increasing in distance if anything. He contented himself with what he would do when he eventually caught up with the wretch, bathed in the light from those windows, which illuminated the colours: the blues, the purples, the greens... Shining on them as he passed.

Orange and white, then violet. So close now to the last room, the black room where the swine would find no escape. Where there were no doors but one.

The one he would be blocking off, knife in hand at the ready.

But he was actually gaining on the robed figure, time speeding up. He had his free hand stretched out, fingers just inches away. They brushed the material of that bloodied robe. Then, with a stretch, they found purchase. His hand came down on the man's shoulder,

165

simultaneously pulling him round.

And what he saw made him scream out loud at the top of his lungs.

* * *

"Baby? Baby, wake up!"

Camille was shouting, looming down on him—her face ashen in the moon's glow. Stéphane gasped and scrambled back on the bed.

"Sweetheart, it's all right. You were just having a nightmare," Camille said, reaching a hand up to brush the hair out of his face.

"What?" he said, confused. "No..."

"Ah-huh," said Camille. "Listen, I'm worried about you. I don't think you should go in to work tomorrow; take some time off. Maybe we could book a holiday."

Stéphane's breath was still coming in short bursts, his heart racing. The sheets pulled around his naked body felt damp.

Blood... was his first thought. *I've been sweating blood.*

"What?" he repeated, as he hadn't really heard Camille's words.

"A holiday, just you and me. I think you need to get away from that hospital for a while, maybe go down south."

He shook his head. "Out... out of the question! There's... I have too much work to do."

"You're working too hard, Stéphane. You know it and I know it."

Stéphane looked over at the clock by the bedside table, the digital numbers telling him it was 4:30. Hardly worth going back to sleep; he'd be getting up in an hour or so.

"I'm okay," he said, patting Camille's hand and removing it at the same time. "Really, I'm okay."

As he climbed out of bed he knew her eyes were trailing him. And he knew she was right. Maybe he *was* working too hard, but he had to do something to make sure there wouldn't be any more faces waiting for him when he got back home that evening.

* * *

He began the day by going over more test results for the virus, which now officially had a name thanks to the media. They were calling it "The Bloodbath". Not a bad moniker considering the amount of

166

people who were falling for it. All because Stéphane didn't *get it*. There had to be something he was missing.

For weeks now he'd not only been perusing the original samples again—running simulations in an effort to try and come up with some kind of treatment—he'd also been doing historical research. If there was even the slimmest chance this disease had been around before, then it might help in their quest to fight it.

The internet had proved a good starting point and turned up a few probable leads. The symptoms were close to those of tuberculosis, so Stéphane ran searches for any kinds of variants of this in written history. On a couple of occasions he thought he might have something, but they turned out to be nothing more than embellishments on the disease by fiction writers.

The Black Death was another avenue he was exploring, as some believed that might have been caused by a viral hemorrhagic fever— or VHF—rather than a bubonic plague.

A Red Death instead of Black, mused Stéphane as he sat back in his chair, tapping a pen against his lips.

He was about to continue his search, going through accounts one after the other, when a call came through to his office. A young man had been brought into the hospital after crashing his car nearby. The paramedics had delivered the injured fellow to St Auguste's for treatment, little realising that the blood on him wasn't solely due to the accident. "He's bleeding from his pores, Dr Rollin," the medic spluttered down the line, "just like on the news."

"Tell everyone to put surgical masks on, right now!" he said. "I'm on my way."

So they had one. Finally, a live sufferer in their hospital. Stéphane wasn't sure looking upon his face was a good idea, but he had to—it would spur him on more. Urge him to find a cure for this Red Death.

By the time he got down there, after donning gloves, scrubs and mask himself (by rights he should have some kind of air-purifying respirator as well), the victim was arresting: spasming and crying out in pain. Held down, he coughed up into the face of a nurse who was beside him, the blood hitting her forehead and eyes—she screamed and fell back against the wall.

Before Stéphane could order any kind of treatment, the man went rigid and collapsed back on the bed. Stéphane stepped closer, but again there were no features to see. Just a mask, like those first victims back at the farm: a mask of blood covering his face.

The nurse was still screaming as Stéphane ordered the area to be sterilised, for them all to immediately hit the showers and soap themselves clean while he called it in. As he looked up, though, he thought he saw one of the doctors at the man's bedside flicker and change: the scrubs becoming robes, the surgical mask becoming—

A hand fell on his shoulder, another nurse—male this time—asking if he was okay?

Okay? Were any of them? How could they be? How would they ever be again?

When he turned back again the doctor in front of him had returned to normal.

*   *   *

They all had to be tested and declared clean before they were allowed to leave that day, and only the nurse who'd been in contact with the blood was kept overnight for observation in the isolation ward.

He was not in the mood for what he found when he returned to his apartment. Camille and a bunch of her buddies—only a couple of whom he knew—were in their living room. They were all dressed smartly, the women in eveningwear, the men in suits. Some were seated, some standing admiring paintings on the wall or other ornaments, and they all had drinks in their hands. When she saw Stéphane come in, Camille got up and met him at the living room door.

"You're late, darling," she said.

"Something came up, a patient," he told her. "What's going on?"

"Dinner party, remember? You said this date would be okay."

Stéphane vaguely recalled Camille mentioning something the other week, but hadn't really been listening—he'd had a lot on his mind lately. "Look, could we do this another time? It's been a long day and—"

"They're all here now." Camille looked over her shoulder and waved back. "Come on, Stéphane. Go get changed and I'll fix you something to drink. You'll feel better once you've relaxed."

A dinner party with a room full of strangers wasn't his idea of relaxing, but he didn't feel like arguing either, or chasing them out. He was too tired for that. Stéphane went into the bedroom and took the pills out of his jacket pocket, popping one before tossing his raincoat onto the chair by the bed.

When he returned, the guests were already being ushered into the dining room by Camille, and the smell of some kind of chicken dish was wafting through from the kitchen. As she placed a glass of red wine in his hand, Stéphane was beginning to think this might not be a bad way of staving off the faces, the memories, after all.

The conversation over the first course of melon or soup revolved around either investments, politics or sport. As Camille took away the dishes and began serving up the coq au vin, the couple to Stéphane's left, Hélène and Jacques, were also keen to shoehorn holidays into the mix. "Your lovely lady tells us you might be going away soon?" Hélène said.

Stéphane attempted a smile, then took a long drink of his Merlot. "She's trying to persuade me, but things have been a bit... hectic lately."

"Count yourself lucky you're not involved in all that Bloodbath business," chirped up Gabrielle, a middle-aged singleton that Camille knew from the showbiz world, whose plastic surgery fetish had resulted in a permanently surprised expression.

"Lucky that's all been confined to the 'slums', you mean," added a guy called Philippe who Stéphane didn't know and didn't really want to. "Still, nasty."

Stéphane remained silent during these first ignorant remarks. But as they all tucked into their meal, they just couldn't leave this juicy topic of conversation alone.

"Best way to deal with it would be some sort of cull," spouted Pascal on the right, who had something to do with antiques, while his wife nodded vigorously.

Stéphane stared at him in disbelief. "Those are people you're talking about," he said. "Not animals."

"Not far off in some of the less discerning parts of town," joked Philippe in-between mouthfuls of chicken, but shut up when he saw Stéphane's stern expression.

Camille shot Stéphane a look that said "what are you playing at?"

He ignored it.

"You don't know what you're talking about. Those people are dying," said Stéphane.

"But they're..." began Pascal, then suddenly dropped his knife and fork on the table, the metal clattering against the crockery of his plate. His forehead furrowed and he let out a low moan. His wife stopped eating too, turning to see what was wrong, but by then Pascal was clutching his side.

"Stéphane..." said Camille, biting her lip, perhaps wondering if it was her cooking that had done it.

Now Pascal was bellowing with pain, grabbing his side again, attempting to stand but not being able to find his feet. He collapsed back into his chair. "Oh my God," said Pascal's wife, feeling his forehead. "He's burning up!" When she brought her hand away again, it was red.

To Stéphane's left, Hélène and Jacques were also attempting to stand, wobbling to their feet. Their faces were screwed up in agony and, as he watched, crimson began to ooze from the skin of their cheeks, making it look like they were crying tears of blood.

Gabrielle began to scream. Not because of what she was seeing, but because it was also happening to her. The permanently surprised expression became even more shocked as blooms of red flowered at her temples, her chin. When she looked down at her arms, she shrieked again because they too were weeping blood, the trails running down and dripping from her fingers.

Neither of them said what they were both thinking: how long before this becomes airborne?

"Stéphane," repeated Camille, "do something!"

But as she turned to him he saw her own face was awash with blood. She gritted her teeth and emitted a loud whine, doubling over with discomfort. There was a bang, as Philippe fell onto the table, then slid down over the edge, taking some of the tablecloth with him.

Stéphane's mouth fell open; he didn't know what to do next.

Then he felt a presence behind him, and he turned quickly, half-rising, knocking over his glass of wine. The redness ran like a river across the white cloth.

No-one should be there, but he saw a robed figure, turning, making its way out of the dining room.

No, you're not really here... You're from my dreams; an hallucination brought on by the Temazepam, mixed with the wine. You're not real, you hear me. Not—

Stéphane looked back at the people round the table, to Jacques gargling with his own juices as he reached out pleadingly for help, to Camille—oh Lord in Heaven no, not Camille; her face painted over, a flowing red canvas with no eyes, nose or mouth.

Stéphane twisted around—it was a blessed relief not to see any more of its effects—and just caught the edge of the robed figure's cloak as he exited the room. Stéphane went after him, leaving the screams and cries of terror behind.

Running through the doorway into what should have been the hall, he found himself in another room. A large room; a blue room.

You're still tripping out. Tripping when you should be helping the people back there, your... Camille's *friends.*

He looked back and through the doorway, saw the folk there, those still standing, faces covered in red masks. And somehow he knew it was that bastard's fault, the one who was ahead of him.

Looking down, Stéphane realised he still had his dinner knife in his hand.

He began after the robed figure, who had now stepped through into a second room, blue giving way to the purple in there. It was all frighteningly familiar from his dream. Stéphane knew that when he ran through the purple room, in pursuit of the figure, he would pass into... Yes, there it was, the green one, then orange and next white, followed by violet.

As before, although he was running, he was not even close to catching up with the figure—who seemed, if anything, to be moving incredibly slowly. Stéphane practically fell into the final room and blackness descended on him. Blackness tinged with red: the windows in here tinted scarlet.

The figure had halted and remained with his back to Stéphane. Suddenly nervous, the doctor gripped the knife and raised his free, trembling hand.

A large ebony clock up on the wall chimed the hour. Stéphane looked at it and when his eyes fell again, the figure was turning.

Its face was a skull, bleached and bare: and twin "eyes" shone red out of its hollow sockets.

171

Stéphane let out a shrill yell.

*　　*　　*

When he sat bolt upright in bed, drenched in sweat again, he was aware that the alarm on the clock beside him was beeping.

Air was hard to come by, but as he looked around, gauging his surroundings, recognising the familiar bedroom even in this half-light, his breathing slowed. There was a figure next to him, lying still. Camille. How the alarm and his restlessness hadn't woken her, he'd never know.

God, that had been intense, more so than any of the previous times. Stéphane had felt like he was really there, that the people at the dinner party had been dying. That *Camille* had been dying. That the robed figure was real.

The robed figure wearing the—

Rubbing his face, he turned on the bedside lamp and looked over at his girlfriend again. "Camille. Camille, are you awa—"

The sheets covering her were stained red.

Stéphane's heart almost stopped there and then. He reached out a hand and this time it was shaking more than it had done in the dream. Then he withdrew it, getting out of bed instead and walking round to the other side.

Her face was in shadow, but even he could see that it was no longer a face at all. It was a mask. A red *masque*. Stéphane's fist went to his mouth and he stepped back, nearly tumbling over the chair there.

No, this was not real. This could not *be real...* How could he have passed on the virus? He'd been tested, cleared! It didn't make any sense.

He could no longer stay in the room, in his apartment.

Pulling on his clothes, Stéphane raced from there and didn't look back.

*　　*　　*

When he arrived at the hospital, he was told the news that the nurse had died.

Not only that, but the disease had spread rapidly throughout St Auguste's. Patients and staff alike were taking up beds, the wards littered with victims who were haemorrhaging their lifeblood onto the crisp, folded sheets; the air filled with the screams of those in anguish.

Red on white; white on red. A portent of death, especially in a place like this.

Stéphane retreated to his office, only to find a message waiting for him on his answer machine. It was from Lewisohn. The first cases had been reported in England, in Germany, Russia—even the United States.

"I-I don't think there is much hope for containment now at all," he was saying. "The virus is disseminating too quickly."

Stéphane sat back in his chair and looked up at the ceiling. The "faces", the masks of the dead were too many, people he hadn't been able to save. He couldn't confine them to home, they were invading his mind here at work too—dammit, they were *here* in this very building today!

There had to be a way—something to put a stop to this. To save those yet to be infected, and at the same time avenge those already dead. Like Camille.

There was. And he knew what it was now.

Stéphane took a handful of his pills, then left his office again. He searched, moving from floor to floor, ward to ward, snatching up a scalpel from an abandoned trolley as he went. He searched for the one thing that could give him his answers.

Just when he was beginning to think he wouldn't find it, he saw the robed figure bending over one of the patients: up until recently a junior doctor herself at St Auguste's.

The Red Death. This plague, this disease given form which was now sweeping through his hospital, his city. His world. "Hey!" he shouted, and those who were still able-bodied, or were only in the early stages, looked over, no doubt thinking him insane—because none of them could see it. None of them had ever been able to. But it had been there on every occasion, right from the first bodies that they'd found at the farmhouse. Always at his shoulder.

The figure looked up, still wearing that skull mask—then turned its back on Stéphane.

No, not again. Not this time. This time you're going to face me in the flesh—this time I'm going to kill you!

Stéphane set off after the thing, ignoring the calls from his fellow doctors. The Red Death passed through into another ward, and Stéphane was not surprised at all to find that the colour in there had changed from the usual stark ivory to blue. Pushing on the double doors, the robed figure entered the next room, and Stéphane saw a hint of plush purple. Ignoring the cries of the dying in bed as he ran past, Stéphane stuck to its heels, through the purple and into the green, then orange, wards (there should not have been this many all in a row). The white one wasn't that much different to how it should be, except that it was more bleached, the people's faces in here—Jesus, their faces!—were in negative. It was with a sense of relief that Stéphane plunged through the doors into the violet ward, and then quickly on to his final destination.

Where he saw The Red Death waiting for him, back still turned.

Stéphane raised his hand, determined to once again spin the figure around—but he didn't need to. The Red Death turned of its own volition. And spoke:

So, finally, we meet.

The words jangled in Stéphane's head. "Why are you doing this? What do you want from me?" he asked, having now found the one person he could—he *must*—talk to.

I think you know that already, answered the figure, its skull mouth not moving at all. *You look so much like him, you know. The Prince.*

"Who? I don't understand."

After everything I did, he still found a way to escape me. A child, an illegitimate child born of one of the servants. One of the servants who survived.

Stéphane had no idea what the hell he was talking about: what Prince? What servant? Survived what? He was about to ask again what was going on, when he remembered the dream of the party... Not the dinner party, but the one from long ago, with people in old fashioned garb. Had that been him? No, not really—and some part of him knew that the man who'd thrown the affair hadn't cared about anything but himself and his own safety: celebrating the fact that he wasn't outside with those victims of the plague.

It has taken some manoeuvring, but you have finally come to me—

174

just as he did. A change of name over generations, just one more mask to hide behind. But his line could not escape me forever.

The voice sent shivers down Stéphane's spine. "He was my ancestor, wasn't he?"

The Red Death nodded. *He hid from me, but I found him. Just as I have found you.*

"But I'm not *him!*" argued Stéphane. "Whatever you think, whatever you want, it doesn't make sense. Why kill all those people just to get to me?"

The Red Death laughed then, long and hard. It was no less chilling. *Such an ego. I do this because it is what I am. Inevitability. This is, and always has been, your destiny.*

"But I'm not him," Stéphane said again. "I-I wanted to save those people, I care about them. I'm not hiding."

You hide from your true nature, The Red Death continued. *The faces haunt you because they represent something else. They conceal the fact that you failed. You like to win. It is not the souls themselves that you care for!*

This made Stéphane angry. "No!" he shouted and came at the robed figure with the scalpel. "I'll kill you and then all this will be over."

The Red Death swatted aside the weapon, gripping Stéphane by his neck. The gloved hand felt cold on his skin.

If you care so much for them, then the cure is still within your reach. Your life... for theirs.

Stéphane clawed at the hand but could not shift it. He'd been foolish to think that he could fight this creature. There had never been a cure, no man could ever have found it, because this disease wasn't like any other. But it was still offering him a way to... to win.

No, to *save* those people!

"Show me," said Stéphane. And it did. The Red Death's eye-sockets glowed, and he could see a future where the sick were healed, where the onslaught of the virus was at an end. Where it simply petered out, just as it had done before all those years—all those centuries—ago. In exchange for one thing. In exchange for his essence, which he had to give willingly: the sins of the father revisited on the "son". "Do it, then. If you're going to—just get on with it."

175

The Red Death nodded again, satisfied. Then Stéphane began to feel heat in the hand that gripped him. Or was it on the skin at his neck, burning up. And the pain, dear God, the pain! At different points inside him simultaneously, like his vital organs were exploding.

But that was nothing compared to the bleeding. The thick gouts of redness that were forcing their way up through his flesh, running down his face, covering him. Drenching his whole body, causing the clothes to stick to him.

He saw only one face now, felt sorry for just the one person: reflected in the glowing eyes of The Red Death. It was the face of Dr Stéphane Rollin.

As everything began to blur around him and he felt himself slipping into shock, Stéphane heard the sound of a clock chiming the hour from just beyond where The Red Death had been standing.

Then there was nothing but blackness.

Blackness tinged with just a hint of red.

PAW PEOPLE

Well, what would you do?

What would you ask for? Just think about it for a moment... That's how it gets you. That's how this works. The lives we lead are so— There's always something we need, something we want. Money, fame? Love? Even if we already have all the cash in the world, all the fame and fortune, people who love us, there'll be something.

It's just how human beings are, there's always a *lack*. A void in us waiting to be filled. Desire, longing. An unquenchable thirst for more. I guess that's what keeps us striving to do better, to keep chasing our dreams. Which is all well and good, but there's a baser side to it. A hunger for... whatever. And if an offer is on the table to fix things immediately, then why not? What's the harm in it?

Plenty, trust me. Things will get fixed all right, just not in the way you might imagine.

That immediacy has only grown worse over time, as the pace of life has sped up. We want things, and we want them right *now*. No waiting. Fast food, box sets of TV shows—rather than waiting for them to drop week by week, like when I was a kid—access to books that don't even have to be printed, access to information on our computers, tablets and our phones. None of that boring going to libraries and researching, hunting down information—like I had to do when I first started all this. No need for legwork. The very thought of craving something and then getting it straight away, how appealing, how tantalising is that?

I bet you're thinking about it right now, that question I asked. What do you *really* want? Running through all the possibilities, not just the usual: being stunningly handsome or beautiful, irresistible to the opposite sex. But also those which require at least some imagination. Things that seem impossible, out of reach to us mere mortals, but really aren't. Not given the correct set of circumstances, the right tool for the job. Nothing's out of the question.

You want to be invisible? Rob banks, right? See what really goes on behind closed doors in the seats of power? Sneak about in the men or women's showers at the gym? Or even creep around in their houses like in that movie with the guy who's in everything, you know the one I mean, from those phone commercials... Go into space? Explore the galaxy, find out if there really are Vulcans or Stormtroopers out there, or little green men from Mars? No problem. It's yours. Or, or, how about immortality—living forever? Without having to fight people with swords, either, cutting off their heads as you move through the ages. Just outlive everyone, go on indefinitely? How great does that sound? Teleportation, that's another one. Being able to will yourself somewhere and just appear—you don't even need to have blue skin or a tail. Cuts out all that driving or commuting on trains with sweaty people or drunken football hooligans singing their team's anthems on their way back from a match, usually out of tune but very loudly. Just *poof!* and you're there, visiting your kids in Australia and back home for dinner. Nice, eh? Nice in theory. Or even world peace, if you're feeling in a benevolent mood. No more wars, no more fighting—because, remember what the Terminator said, it's in our nature to destroy ourselves. You could end all that in seconds, in a heartbeat. Or just get rid of all the evil there is or ever was, like the woman in that story being tempted by the demon, Alice something or other. A Faustian pact that ended up getting turned on the one offering it.

Clichés, the lot of them! I guarantee there isn't anything you could come up with that I haven't already read about, or heard about, or come across on my travels. And let me tell you, I've travelled *a lot*. Devoted so much to this in terms of time and money and—

None of it ever works, that's what you need to know. There's always a catch, it was designed that way. Was never meant to help us, to make our lives easier. To fill that void. It was intended to punish us for ever wanting things in the first place, for not living with or accepting that void, and not being grateful for what we already have. I can understand it, truly I can. I get where all this was coming from, but still...

Okay, take the being irresistible thing. Sounds wonderful, doesn't it? Not so much when you're being chased by admirers down the street, all wanting a piece of you. When you can't get a second to yourself. Or when they're breaking down your door, smothering you with "love". You never seen *Buffy*? Come on!

Or the invisible thing? You forget for one second you're in stealth mode and try crossing the road: *bam!* That bus isn't going to see you, is it? And space? Hope you can survive with no atmosphere, then. You won't even get to see those other worlds or aliens if your lungs are collapsing. Or all the water in your skin and blood is vaporising, your body blowing up like a balloon. You could ask for a suit, or a ship, if you have any "asks" left—but even then you'll end up the same way. The suit has no oxygen tanks, for example, so you're still gasping for air; or you have the suit, you have air, and you're just floating around in the vastness of space, stranded... until you *run out* of that air. As for the spaceship, forget the Enterprise or the Falcon, it'll probably have no fuel, so you're stuck waiting to die once more. Tony Stark in *Endgame*. You see? Do you get it?

All right, let's take the living forever thing. That one's a no-brainer really, it was even mentioned in the film with all the decapitations. You'll outlive everyone you've ever cared about. Find the love of your—*very* long—life, or even the loves, plural, and they'll age, wither and die. You'll have to stand by and watch all that, powerless to help. You could make them immortal too, I suppose, but then watch them turn into nags or go off you over time, so that all you want is to make them disappear—and you're back to square one! You can't win, there's no prize at the end of the line here, no Quickening. Who wants to live forever? You fucking won't, trust me.

How about the teleporting? you enquire. Assuming you're not getting into any pods with insects, because that never ends well, you'll probably find yourself melding with a brick wall or something. Or miles above the ground so that you're suddenly plummeting, because you can't control where exactly you'll end up. Australia? But nobody said anything about being at ground level... Okay, world peace? Get ready to spend the rest of your life alone because everyone's disappeared. There aren't even any vampire creatures to keep you company, because you wanted *peace*, remember? You could ask for a partner, someone to take the edge off the loneliness, but then you're in the same boat as the person who wants to be

179

immortal. There'll be something wrong with your other half, believe me. You'll soon get on each other's nerves. Abolish all evil? You'll be bored out of your mind within a week. And it all depends on what your version of sin is, doesn't it. You might be banning everything from that tipple you like to a Saturday night bunk up, all the things you enjoy gone because they're now classified as "wrong".

So, where does that leave us? Nowhere, to be honest. Like I said, there's no way to win. It's like Vegas, you can't beat the house no matter how hard you try; not really. There are rules, it's just that we're not privy to the most important ones. But here's what I know. You get three tries. Usually. If you're still alive after the first. Three and three only... Why three? Dunno, haven't a clue. That's one of those things we'll never know. The number three's powerful, though. It's ancient. You see it all the time in those old fairy tales: the three pigs; three witches; three fairy godmothers; three bears and so on. Three. No more, no less. It's the magic number, after all, as the song tells us. You can't ask for an infinite amount, it doesn't work that way. Well, you can, but it'll just be a waste because you'll only get three... if you're lucky. Or unlucky, as the case may be. And it almost certainly will be.

Perhaps it's so the game doesn't go on indefinitely with just the one soul? So it can be passed on and mess with someone else? Share the fun around, give more folk a chance? Like I say, I don't know why. It just is. Has been since all this began, in its current form anyway.

Let me give you a case study from my considerable files and maybe then you might understand better. There was this one guy who used the... item in question. Let's call him Mathew. Not his real name, only I know that. I know *all* their names, but there's no reason to share them with you. It's enough to tell you what happened to Mathew and his wife, Lisa. Again, not her real name and you're not getting the surnames—there is such a thing as people being entitled to their privacy, you know. So, Mathew and Lisa. For a while Mathew—Matt—had begun to suspect that his wife might leave him, was getting bored. People fall in and out of love all the time, the shine wears off marriages doesn't it. Usually means those people weren't with the right partners in the first place, or they were right for a short time... But I'm getting off topic.

Matt didn't want to lose Lisa, you see. Was more into the marriage than she was, clearly. I'm not taking sides here, by the way, it was just a sad situation and Lisa wanted out. It was about to get even sadder, though, when Matt came by a certain object. Was offered it in a pub, by a friend of a friend. Told how to use it, not even warned about the consequences. The friend of a friend—we'll call him Dave—was done with it, glad to be rid of it, but didn't tell Matt that. It had already done the damage to Dave's life, but that's another story. Matt had one thing and one thing only on his mind, he wanted to force Lisa to stay. Against her will, obviously, but she wouldn't know anything about that once he was done. At least that's what Matt believed.

So he did the deed, asked that he and Lisa never be parted. That she couldn't leave him, just like he could never leave her. A few days later she was diagnosed. (Oh, that's another thing I forgot to mention, it doesn't always happen immediately—sometimes there's a time delay, like when you sign a contract and there's a grace period... only there isn't with this kind of deal, none that I'm aware of anyway. The waiting is probably just another form of suffering.) Lisa had a wasting disease, one that would see her lose the use of all her motor functions within weeks. That would force Matt to look after her, become her full-time carer. Couldn't even have breaks, holidays, because some minor crisis or another usually occurred to drag him back. He was happy to do it at first, because Lisa had always been his world—and now she'd literally become everything in his world. Until eventually it became too much and he tried to put it right again, used his second bite of the cherry to course correct—only waited that long because of what had happened the first time, how it had backfired, and the hatred he now saw in Lisa's eyes. Matt asked for her suffering to end. Poor choice of words, looking back, and you can probably guess what happened, can't you? End her suffering? Yeah, doesn't take much working out...

Ended hers, but only added to Matt's—which was probably the point. Which was when he opened door number three, asking this time for Lisa to come back again. Which she did, waking up in the hospital after they'd called it. A miracle of miracles, back from the dead! (Wasn't the first time that had happened.) Or a deep coma, they reasoned. What's more, she was beginning to recover from her disease—one that Matt had been told there was no cure for. A cause for celebration surely, that she'd only be in a wheelchair a few months, then was on track for a full recovery. At which point she would inevitably leave Matt, which she'd been planning on doing anyway. Mathew, for his part, drank himself to death not long after that—after the restraining order had been granted at any rate. A judge ruling that he couldn't come anywhere near Lisa ever again...

Not convinced? How about the sportswoman—Anne, this time, though you might be able to figure out who she is once I've told you—who came by our fabled object and asked for speed. To run faster than all her opponents on the track, which she did, rising in the ranks until she became a minor celebrity, with all that entails. Endorsements, sponsorship deals. Books ghostwritten about her life. Heading for the Olympics... where she bottled it, essentially. Was so worried that she wouldn't win the most important race of her career, as she saw it, she asked for even more speed, a guaranteed win. Which, in fairness, she got. Anne was a positive blur going round that track. She might not have asked for super-speed like something out of a comic book, but on that day was the closest thing to it in our reality. The fastest thing on two legs. And of course she won, like it had ever been in any doubt. But then came the bad news, the other foot falling—and falling fast—Anne going at such a click that she'd been unable to slow down and ended up tripping, falling. Breaking both of her legs.

The surgeons did their best, but informed her that she'd probably never walk again, let alone run. She'd go down in history as having won that race, having been clocked as the fastest person ever, but would never be able to do the thing she loved most in the world again. Not just competing, but even a simple jog in the park would be off limits. Anne's third ask, as you can imagine, was to be able to run again. Which she got. The surgeons went back in and operated, state of the art stuff which took all of her wealth, and got her up and running again... after a fashion. She could only make it to the end of her street, and even then at a snail's pace, and every single step she took was excruciating. It was the price she paid, the lesson she had to learn.

Now, I know what you're thinking, and yes—to some extent these people brought all this on themselves. If Matt had been content to let

Lisa go, he might have met someone else who felt the same way he felt; who would have been happy to stay with him until they were both old. Anne, if she'd trained hard enough, might have won those races without cheating. Without the... ha!... the inside track. Their needs, their desires... Their greed, I suppose. It's what attracts this thing like a magnet to metal.

It's helped politicians in the past win elections, helped people into positions of power. Ever wonder why on earth some of those world leaders ended up where they did, when they were nothing but incompetent fools? Chances are at least a couple of the ones that spring to mind had help. I can neither confirm nor deny that, and it won't matter anyway by the time I'm done. None of it ever ended well, their ambitions fulfilled but it made them the target of assassins, heaped more responsibility on them than they could ever cope with. Meaning that it wasn't just the people who made the ask that suffered, others did too as a by-product. Innocent people, if such a thing even exists. Innocent with regards to this whole affair anyway.

Look at how many casualties have lost their lives, just because some military dictator laid his hands on the item and put in their requests. Entire societies, tribes, those who follow certain religions, wiped out of existence because of—

But then, you probably wouldn't know. This is the universe you're familiar with, even if it has been adjusted, tinkered with at another's behest. Their whim. I only know from my research into all this, my notes. A record of everywhere that damned monstrosity has been, everyone who has at some point "owned" it. Or thought they did, because it doesn't really have an owner as such. Just a purpose. A mission. Instilled in it way back when, in a distant land, by a man who wanted nothing more than to show that fate ruled people's lives and those who interfered paid the price. I often wonder if he realised, that those who had nothing at all to do with it—who didn't interfere with anything—ended up paying that price as well. Not through choice, but by accident. Collateral damage in this... I'm not even sure what to call it. A game? It's not really a game. In classical times the gods took great pleasure in ruining human lives for sport. Look at Zeus, he put it about something chronic, and did he pay? No. Rather it was the poor unfortunates who got fucked—literally and figuratively, after the fact—who suffered. No doubt he would have argued that they didn't have to participate, but he was a god for Christ's sake! Try saying no to one of those... (I've just thought, the Three Furies—that's another!)

But again, I'm rambling. Perhaps it's time I told you a little about myself, maybe that will explain things a bit. Explain why I'm doing this, why I have been for so long now. I'm nobody special, let's get that straight from the get-go. Just someone who stumbled onto the truth, became obsessed with it. Though not until—

Okay, full disclosure, I lost my parents at an early age—and not in the way you'd probably expect. Wasn't illness, or a car accident or whatever. They were in the wrong place at the wrong time: building collapse. Collapsed right on top of them. The authorities were digging around in the rubble for days looking for survivors, but they only found a handful and my folks weren't among them. I remember feeling numb when I was told; I was only seven. Remember feeling like my whole world had ended, that if there was just something I could do, then... Of course there wasn't, and my world didn't end when theirs did. I went on without them, was shipped off to stay with my aunties who lived together at the time—still do actually, they were never really interested in partners or the like. I think it was a religious thing, because they were pretty strict. Didn't know quite what to make of me, especially when I was acting out in my teenage years. Only took me in, I suspect, out of a sense of duty, because it was the right thing to do. They used to describe what happened to mum and dad as an act of God. An act of God, I ask you! What fucking God would drop a building on someone?

Anyway, they did their best. Tried to put me on the right path, even though it was like wrestling with marmalade at times. I think they were glad to pack me off to uni eventually, their good deed done with and they could get on with their lives. I was lucky to get in actually, because I'd almost been chucked out of school a few times, but at the last minute I buckled down and studied. You might not think it to look at me or my life, but I've got quite a decent brain up there. It helped that I was applying for a course I'd quite enjoy, aiming for journalism at the end of it all.

It was while I was there that I stumbled upon the story. It was part of an optional unit, total accident, but when I read it I connected with it on a level that I couldn't possibly have dreamed of. You're probably aware of it yourself, it's quite a famous one. And like so many people you'll doubtless think it's made up. Fiction. The story just a story, end of... well, story. I mean, there are some people for whom it's passed into the territory of urban legend. Who do believe it, in the same way some think Klingon is a real language or Jedi is a religion. They're dismissed in the same breath as those guys.

The simple fact is, however, it's true. It's all true.

Obviously the names have been changed and certain details have been fudged, like the notion that it could only be used three times by three different people then it was done. That's rubbish, total and utter rubbish! It's been used so many more times than that, as I think you can tell from what I was saying before.

At first it was just a hobby, something to pass the time when I wasn't studying—and afterwards when I wasn't working for that tiny newspaper covering local fetes and the machinations of small-town politics. This secret subject was so much more interesting, I'm sure you'll agree. Fascinating, actually. Uncovering the inspirations, tracing the real life soldier who'd spent time in India, who'd come across the thing in question—the tale behind that. Of the fakir who'd given it this power to prove a point, or more likely to get his revenge on humanity. Or probably on the invaders who'd taken over his land, leading indirectly to the loss of his own family. More than likely taking his inspiration from even older legends about the djinn.

The first man who used it had killed himself, that much was true. Had asked to die at any rate, after two other failed attempts to get what he wanted—or *thought* he wanted. I've since found out what he asked for, and tried to reverse, but I won't share that with you here because like as not you'll never sleep again. It's enough to say that he deserved his fate, before the item was passed on to the soldier, the sergeant major who carried it away to these shores.

His requests were more understandable, the first simply to be happy. To lead a happy life specifically. After some of the horrors he'd seen in his time serving abroad, he felt that wasn't too much to hope for. The catch that time? He found he couldn't stop laughing, wasn't able to open his mouth without guffawing at everything—so much so that he was almost committed because folk thought him insane. His second ask was to get him out of that predicament at the asylum, then the third to reverse his original request—as you would.

185

Back to square one, and he counted himself lucky. It could have been a damned sight worse, as you can probably appreciate by now. Hence the warning he gave the family in question before it was passed on. That there are always consequences if the thing is used.

And boy were there consequences!

As you perhaps know, prompted by the wife of the fold, the husband eventually asked for money. A relatively meagre amount, enough to pay off what they owed on their house. How he came by that money was part of the trick, the way these things always backfire on the ones doing the requesting. Compensation for their son who said goodbye to them that morning and they never saw alive again. And he didn't just die, he died *horrifically*. Mangled up in the machinery where he worked. Jesus, the agony he must have been in!

Though probably nothing compared to the agony of coming back. The old couple, in their sorrow, used the item to restore their son's "life", if such a word could be used. Then waited for him to return, after he'd been buried—having to claw his way out of his grave and shamble back to the only home he'd ever known. There was no-one around to witness all this, obviously, so we only have the word of the parents to go by who—unlike in the story—say they did see the state of their boy. It was the thing that made his father undo what he'd done, letting his lad have his final peace.

Obviously, this information was passed on. The couple told just a handful of people, one of which was the writer who—as writers do, and I should know—figured that whether it was real or not, he might be able to do something with it. As indeed he did, passing it off as the fiction we know today. The fiction I read about when I was much younger and became gripped by. Consumed by. Yes, consumed, that's as good a word as any for what happened.

When did it start to take over my life? I don't actually remember, but my work at the paper began to suffer I do recall that. Getting called into the office of the editor and being chewed out for not focussing on my job properly. It was like being back at school again in the headmaster's office. In the end I quit altogether. A bit of money had been left in a trust fund for me by my parents for when I turned eighteen, and I'd barely touched that—preferring to work my way through uni doing various menial jobs. So I decided to use it to bankroll my research into this subject. Maybe I had in mind a book,

186

or documentary? Something that would make spending all that dough worthwhile.

That never happened, clearly. You'd have read about it if it had, watched the documentary on a streaming platform somewhere. But I do feel like it was worth it in the end, amassing those casefiles like the ones I told you about. Following the leads, getting to the truth like my old journo tutor used to say at uni.

Getting to the heart of it all, because that's important. Our heart's desire. That's all those people were after, even the ones who wanted something really wrong. Down the line, all around the world, wherever the item ended up next. I've gone back and mapped it all. There's a timeline on the wall of my small flat if you don't believe me.

Oh, I know there was some talk of destroying the thing with fire in the story—but like I said, some of the details are questionable. It *can't* be destroyed, you see. You can burn it, or try to, but it'll just end up back in your pocket—or someone's pocket—untouched. It *wants* to be used, just like the fakir wanted it to be used, but it all got out of control. It's touched so many people's lives, not just the ones who picked it up and clutched it in their right hands. All those poor people affected...

Those *paw* people.

That's not even funny. The amount of misery that thing's caused, the person who created it long gone now. I know it all, I've compiled it all. Years and years of my life, forgoing a partner, a family. Nothing mattered but this, tracking down the answers. Following the trail until...

Hasn't been a waste, it really hasn't. Because last week I found it! Of all the places it could possibly be, in a little second-hand antiques-stroke-collectibles-stroke-general bric-a-brac shop you might find on the high street. Except it wasn't on the high street, it was tucked away down a back alley. Run by a strange little man by the name of Mr Mendleson... "With a L. E. S. O. N," as he informed me.

Yes, he knew the piece I was talking about—a collectors' item he'd recently acquired. And yes, he was more than happy to sell it to me for the right price. It took all I had left, after selling up pretty much everything I owned and taking out a loan, but in the end the man agreed, and he disappeared into the back room only to return moments later with a bag. I didn't even look inside, because I knew it was in there. I could *feel* it. I realise that sounds weird, but then look at the thing we're talking about here. I could feel its power, could even sense that everything I'd ever discovered about it was correct, even the more outlandish stuff.

The smile he gave me as he wished me "farewell" was both chilling and full of woe, as was the "good luck" that followed me out through the door with its tinkling bell.

I'm not sure whether *I* found *it*, or whether eventually *it* found *me*. They do say that it comes into the possession of those desperate to use it. And I'm so very desperate. After all this time, all this searching, I know I'm going to use it. I can't resist it forever, even as it sits on that table in the corner of the flat, still in the bag.

But then, why should I resist? I didn't hunt for it this long just to leave it lying there staring at me. My dreams have been filled with images of that simian face since I brought it home, the one also long gone, the owner of the appendage. It's willing me on, forcing me to think about all the good things I could do with my requests, my asks... Oh, all right, my fucking wishes! (I really hate calling them that.) All three of them.

You could bring them *back*, it whispers to me. My folks, my parents. My situation is a reversal of the original tale, the son left alive and the mother and father dead. But if the state of their child was so bad after just ten days, imagine what my folks would look like! I could be specific, that's the key. Bring them back as they were, when I was just seven. Dad lifting me to sit on his shoulders, mum covering my face with kisses, wrapping me up tight.

Fuck, this is so hard. I know the dangers and yet still I—

It won't work, I keep telling myself that. I've been telling you that this whole time. It has never worked... Although maybe this time. Maybe. It's a chance, a risk. A risk I'm willing to take.

No. Don't. You can't!

So why is it out of the bag, why am I staring at it? That mummified thing, more bone than flesh and fur now. Why is it in my right hand, as I gather my thoughts to make that first, all-important—

But it's not the only thing that can play tricks. I'll get my parents back, just not that way. You see, it wasn't their fault the building caved in. Wasn't even God's at the end of the day. It was a wish, after some terrorist got his hands on the item: a wish that brought the place down. His will that caused the destruction, and all in the name of what he called "freedom". Should never have happened, like so many things this blasted paw is responsible for.

Should never have happened.

And now it won't have. Because I don't need three, I only need one. It can't be destroyed, but I can ask that it never existed in the first place. That it was never given such incredible power by the fakir, that it hadn't been passed on to the guy who asked to die, to the sergeant major. That it hadn't fallen into the hands of that family, so they were tempted and lost their son as a consequence. Then left the paw in the house when they moved, for it to carry on doing what it was designed to do.

It's moving, wriggling around now like a snake in my grasp. Working away to undo... not the original wish now, but everything. All the harm it's ever done. Like that woman with the demon, wishing away all the evil.

Deus ex machina they call it in stories. "God from the machine". Ha! Only this time the thing that'll fix the problem is the one that caused it in the first place. The ultimate cliché, but I know it *will* work. It can't resist me, or what I'm asking. Mum, Dad... All those Paw People. Everything reset.

Well, what would you do? What would you ask for? Just think about it for a moment...

That's how it gets you.

That's how this works.

189

THICKER THAN WATER

Meeting the family, it was a big step: a watershed.

Was there any wonder Naomi was getting cold feet now? Was getting jittery, even though it had been her who'd insisted they should make this trip? That it was about time, after almost eight months of seeing Gerry? Only now the day was here, she wasn't so sure. What if they didn't like her? What if they hated her, in point of fact? Thought she was no good for him? Couldn't stand the idea of her being with their Gerry? Couldn't stand the sight of her?

Calm down, Naomi told herself. *Look at the scenery and relax for Heaven's sake!* And it was beautiful, it had to be said: all greens and yellows, rolling by the passenger window of the car as they drove along idyllic country lanes. In a year which had seen one of the harshest winters this country could remember (followed by devastating floods in its wake), spring had finally arrived—indeed, it was so late it was almost giving way to the summer months.

She always did this, Naomi reminded herself when she found she still couldn't settle. Built things up, imagined the worst-case scenario. Whatever could go wrong, would. Claimed she wasn't a pessimist, but rather a realist (painfully aware of the irony that every single pessimist in history had said the same). Couldn't allow herself to think things might work out, that she might well be happy this time, because of all the crap she'd been through before. All the heartache...

The abandonment.

Naomi shook her head. No, not today. She wouldn't allow it. Those dark thoughts could just go away, like dark clouds chased off by the sun. No rain, no storms today, or at least she hoped not.

It wasn't something she was used to doing, if she was being honest: hoping. Not anymore, not these days. Well, not until Gerry came along anyway. Hadn't started out that way, she'd been quite a hopeful child she thought, always looking to the future but enjoying the present. However, losing both parents in quick succession at an early age—one to a debilitating disease and the other to suicide, she was told—tended to shake your confidence in the world. Destabilise you. A series of orphanages and foster carers later (no real homes, no real families) and she was out there being battered by the cold, harsh reality of life. Always the quiet one at university, then at work. The outsider. Never getting into the madness that was around her: the nightclubs, the drink and drugs... the casual sex.

Naomi told herself it was because she was better than that, she had more respect for herself than to get into the whole "one night stand" or "try before you buy" thing. And there was an element of that involved; *of course* there was. Saving herself, they used to call it. But she was also scared. Scared of the consequences of letting go, of losing herself, of opening up—opening her *heart*—to someone.

There had been boys, naturally. Someone who looked like she did was bound to get hit on (a natural beauty, apparently), and there were some she'd genuinely liked—those she thought liked her back for who she was. But when it came right down to it, none of them had waited until she was ready to *be* with them. To give herself to them. And the few times she had been stupid enough to almost—

Let's just say she'd learned her lesson, but good. Real life wasn't a fucking Disney movie. You put your trust in people, they invariably let you down, deserted you.

Until she'd found Gerry.

She looked across at him now, sitting there in the driving seat of his sporty silver BMW, shifting gears as they crested a hill, and Naomi couldn't help smiling. He'd been good for her, Gerry. Was perfect for her. Naomi's smile faded at the thought of that word. Nobody was perfect, let alone someone who might be interested in her.

Might be interested? He adores *you, you idiot!*

Still, nobody was perfect. But he was just so, so... perfect! She couldn't think of another word that adequately described him. The fine blond hair, which matched his eyebrows. Perfect cheekbones, pouting lips any male model would think themselves lucky to be blessed with, such penetrating eyes. And that body of his...

It had been the first thing she'd seen of him. Sleek and lean, yet well-muscled, he was the only thing Naomi had noticed as she'd walked out through the back doors of the hotel at the tail end of last summer; part of the holiday she'd promised herself and saved up for after another miserable few months.

In front of her was the pool she'd been intending to read and sunbathe beside—though she was hardly likely to get a tan when she was mostly covered by that sarong and floppy hat. But absolutely no swimming, she hated getting wet... or was it just the stripping off to a bathing suit? Anyway, when she looked up, she'd been expecting to see the usual gaggle of children messing about, the older folk splashing around as they did their lengths for exercise. But instead she'd seen *him*, Gerry, gliding through the water arm over arm, as fluid as the liquid he was immersed in. Flesh glistening in the sunlight, making him look as oiled as those strippers she'd witnessed once at a colleague's bachelorette party. But as impressive as those guys had been, they had nothing on Gerry—as she soon saw when he reached the other end of the pool and climbed out.

Realising she was in the way of a couple who were also looking to find a recliner, she'd taken a step—a couple of steps—only to almost trip and stumble. Naomi had never been the most spatially aware of people, never been one to mind her surroundings, but distracted like this... *Get a grip!* Naomi had told herself. She'd continued on to a seat nearby, trying not to make those glimpses through her sunglasses so obvious. Stealing glances at Gerry (not that she'd known his name then), aware that many of the other ladies present were doing the same. A woman walked past him with breasts that looked like they'd been pumped up at a garage, barely contained in that minuscule bikini top, skin as tanned as leather. But, as she'd taken her seat, Naomi had been impressed and pleasantly surprised by the way he'd hardly noticed that bimbo—continuing to towel himself down after the dip. The woman had walked on by, looking back only once with a frown, clearly not used to being ignored.

Naomi had settled down with her book, looking up a few times to see what the man was doing, sighing when she saw him heading to the bar on the other side of the pool. Resigning herself to the idea that he was probably meeting someone: girlfriend, fiancée, wife. Which seemed to make sense when she saw him with two drinks, two green cocktails with fruit and straws sticking out of the top.

But as amazed as she'd been by his ignorance of the plastic woman, she was even more surprised when he walked over in her direction with those drinks. *Oh no*, she thought, *please don't be one of those cheesy chat-up guys! Don't ruin such a* perfect *fantasy for me, that inside you're something more. That beneath the surface you're—*

Then he'd walked right by her, just like the enhanced woman had done with him, and it had actually physically pained Naomi. She felt that loss so deeply. Worse than finding out he was a dick would be not knowing him at all. So, when he'd skirted around, doubling back and placing one of the cocktails on the table beside her, she let out another sigh—this time of relief. When they talked about this afterwards, Gerry would always say that he'd been aware of her as soon as she appeared—though she knew he couldn't have seen her, he'd been too busy swimming, head in and out of the water as his arms propelled him further away from her. But that was his story and he was sticking to it.

During that first conversation, after he'd asked politely if he could sit on the recliner next to her, she'd found him confident but not overly so. Charming, though not to the point of nausea. But, most importantly, very easy to talk to—and an extremely good listener. That was worth its weight in gold. He hadn't used any lines, hadn't overly flattered her, he'd simply been Gerry. And Gerry had been lovely.

In the time between their parting and the dinner date they'd arranged for later at a nearby five-star restaurant, she'd wound herself up again, thinking of all the things that might be wrong with him. He was cheating on said girlfriend, fiancée, wife—had kids, a family he wasn't telling her about. He was a rapist, a multiple murderer with a string of convictions to his name... He worked in the seedy underbelly of the city, pimping out his women to slavering perverts and was going to get her hooked on heroin so she could be next!

All ridiculous, as she'd discovered later. Gerry worked in shipping, imports and exports, above board with legitimate offices, which he offered to show her around (proof enough, she thought to herself, that he had nothing to hide in this department). He negotiated deals, travelled a fair bit, and was also doing very well for himself, thanks (she saw just *how* well with that first piece of jewellery he gave her, a gold necklace—an unusual design, but she liked it). He hadn't needed to save up for the hotel, no siree! Not that any of this mattered to her, she'd never been impressed by wealth. It was merely a bonus that he might be a good provider.

She'd found out then that Gerry had been determined to do well, help out his family who—in a reversal of his fortunes—hadn't been doing so brilliantly of late.

"Only *just* keeping their heads above water, as a matter of fact," Gerry had told her sadly after finishing his salmon en croûte, staring down into his glass of Perrier as if to further illustrate his statement.

"Oh, I'm... I'm really sorry to hear that," she'd told him, at the same time envious of this connection he had to them; something she'd never really known. Naomi sensed a closeness when he talked about them, his mom and pop, his older brother. His childhood, being taught to fish from the jetty off the side of their house—it sounded idyllic. But she also felt that sadness when he'd had to go out into the world to make ends meet, that he hadn't been able to stay closer to home. In the end, after much deliberation, they'd made his choice for him, insisting he went out there and did them proud.

"You must be happy that you're now in a position to help them out though, surely?" Naomi had said, starting her dessert of chocolate torte, and he'd nodded.

"Yeah, I guess." But he'd shaken his head at that point and moved the conversation along, asking her more about herself; her life, her job, her hobbies. "I want to know everything about you, Naomi Jackson." His smile spoke of genuine interest. Nobody had ever wanted to know *everything* about her. Nobody had ever been that bothered. So she'd talked, figuring what did she have to lose?

Hope? She could lose the hope that was starting to build inside of her, the hope that had continued to build all this time. Since she'd found Gerry. Since they'd found each other.

Girlfriend, fiancée... wife? (Family?)

The hope she still had as she sat in the car, travelling towards their destination. But all that could be dashed, everything they'd been through in the last few months could be undone if Gerry's clan didn't take to her. It might change everything, leave everything in ruins. She asked herself again, why had she insisted on this trip?

194

Especially when Gerry had been so uncertain himself.

Maybe she shouldn't have asked him what was wrong when he'd looked so down that day. But Naomi had to know, wanted to make sure it wasn't something she'd done or said. "No, no. It's just that... Well, my folks have been in touch and... Naomi, I hadn't told them about you yet. I just wanted to keep you to myself a bit longer. Now they want to meet you."

She'd be lying if she said she didn't feel hurt by the first bit, but figured she could sort of understand it. All this time together, just the two of them, had been wonderful—the best of her life.

"I didn't want to... Not till I was absolutely sure about you. About how I felt."

"And?" she'd asked, biting her lip.

He'd looked at her blankly then, questioning.

"How *do* you feel?" she'd clarified.

"Oh." He'd smiled then. "That's easy. I worship you, Princess—you know that." The use of his nickname made her melt inside (just like Disney), especially used in that context. "You should do. I've never... well, I've never felt this way about anyone else."

Anyone else, all the others she'd been instantly jealous of as soon as he'd told her. There had been girls before, were bound to have been, but Gerry promised never anything serious, they hadn't really meant anything to him. Not like this. Now he was with her exclusively—which made her happy. She didn't want to share him with anybody. And it had been his idea to wait, not rush her—though they'd come close a few times, *really* close; her closest yet—because, as Gerry said, they were about more than that.

Never felt this way about anyone else.

Now she just wanted to feel that connection to his family as well, that belonging. Wasn't too much to ask, was it? But, as Gerry had warned her, meeting them would definitely "change things". The next big step (girlfriend, fiancée... wife; giving her that family), which could go either way.

"It's just that they can be a bit set in their ways," Gerry had informed her again only the other day. "Old fashioned, holding on to the past."

"Anybody would think you don't *want* me to meet them or something?" Naomi had said.

"It's not that, it's—" Gerry nodded. "Hey, I'm sure they'll love you as much as I do. You're very special, you know."

She'd beamed at that.

But here, now, those doubts—fuelled by Gerry's words—were resurfacing. Worst case scenarios: the mother thought she was a gold-digging whore; the father said they'd disown Gerry if he didn't tell her to get lost; the brother was a monster, was everything she hated in a guy—

No! She willed away the dark thoughts. Easier said than done, when the weather seemed to be turning against her as well. Clear, bright blue skies had now given way to a dull grey horizon with ink-blot clouds that looked like shadows. Even the pretty fields that she'd been staring at in a daze had become strange bog-like stretches of land. When had that happened?

"Enjoy your nap?" asked Gerry.

Naomi didn't even know she'd been asleep. She'd been worrying about what was going to happen when they arrived and then... Telling herself to relax, she'd obviously relaxed a little *too* much. Now she'd woken up and everything had taken on a strange dull cast, as if the film of her life had just switched from technicolour to black and white.

"How long was I...?"

"Not long. But it's actually not that far now," Gerry informed her. She couldn't tell if he was pleased about that or not. Naomi knew he was looking forward to seeing the brood again, but maybe under different circumstances? Maybe not with *her* in tow. Perhaps they were mad that he'd kept Naomi from them all this time? Moms in particular could be like that, couldn't they? Not that she'd know. Not that she'd ever really known her mom properly before she'd—

(Blood, water. The razor... How she always pictured it in her head.)

No, stop it. You're doing it again. Stop that right now!

The car carried on, and through the window she spotted the coastline—the angry sea running parallel to them. Rain suddenly started up, striking the windscreen and causing her to jump in her seat.

Battered by cold, hard reality.

"You okay?" asked Gerry, flicking on the wipers, and she gave a small tip of the head.

196

But she wasn't. Far from it. The downpour was making her even more anxious, doing little to calm her nerves. By the time they were driving down what Gerry called "Federal Street", the rain had settled into a steady drizzle and it was almost dark—in spite of the fact it was only afternoon and the nights were supposed to be getting lighter by the day.

Dark clouds, dark thoughts... dark place.

Gerry was going to take her on a little guided tour first, he informed her. Naomi wondered if he was just putting off the crunch time, but that was okay—she wasn't in any rush to sink their relationship (she'd already decided in her head by now that this whole thing would be a washout). He pointed out landmarks such as the old churches that surrounded the New Church Green, the hall on her right where the townspeople used to hold gatherings, the old town square and what had once been the refinery, before they passed over the bridge which ran across the Manuxet River and he drew her attention to the lighthouse in the distance. When he spoke about his hometown, it was with such a sense of pride, of belonging, and Naomi wished that she could experience that as well. Because all she saw was a place that might have been really nice once, but was currently in a state of disrepair and ruin.

Everything in ruins...

Gerry was clearly seeing all of this through rose-tinted glasses; as if through the eyes of a child. And that smell! Naomi did her best not to crinkle up her nose, but the aroma was so strong. A distinctive stench of the ocean, of fish.

Touring round the town square, Gerry showed her the old fire station, the Gilman Hotel, a couple of stores and what had been his favourite restaurant when he'd lived here. "Makes the best calamari in the northeast," Gerry stated; he did so love his seafood. It looked like a bit of a dive to Naomi, but she said nothing.

Gerry's family lived down by the sea itself, she knew, and Naomi peered over when he pointed to exactly where. It looked like some of the worst houses were situated down there, wood and brickwork plagued by rot. He hadn't been kidding when he said they were barely keeping their heads above water... in every respect. She couldn't help gaping across at him then.

"Your parents live down *there*?"

"Ahuh," he said simply.

She looked again, thinking maybe she was missing something—but she wasn't. If anything this closer scrutiny showed her that the problem was even more severe. Some of the houses were tilting, as if they were about to simply fall into the waves and be swept away.

I know Gerry said they weren't doing brilliantly, but this is ridiculous, thought Naomi. All that money he earned, how little of it must he have been sending back home for them to still be living in such squalor? In such a town as this?

A ghost town, for in all the time they'd been driving around, Naomi had yet to spot one person. Yes, it was raining and she didn't blame anyone for staying indoors in such poor weather, but that didn't explain why the buildings all looked deserted as well. There were no lights on, nothing. It was almost as if they wanted to purposefully give the impression here that nobody was home.

She was about to mention this to Gerry when he suddenly turned and said, "I guess we'd better be heading off to see them then."

Naomi nodded slowly, feeling her guts tying themselves into knots. Gerry steered the BMW down a couple more streets, then parked it up by the side of the road, telling her they'd have to walk from there.

"You're kidding?" she said, looking up through the window. It was pouring and she hadn't thought to bring either a coat or an umbrella with her; it had been such lovely weather when they'd set off. Her summer dress would be drenched in seconds. But Gerry didn't appear to be thinking about that, probably more bothered about what his family would think of her—plus it wasn't his fault he couldn't get any closer. In any event, he was out of the car now, slamming the door, so she followed him.

Gerry had his head tilted back, eyes closed. He seemed to be relishing the water on his face, unlike her. She coughed and he finally noticed her, standing there soaking. "Sorry," he said and came round to escort her down the path.

She almost slipped once or twice, especially in those shoes she'd chosen for the occasion—nothing too flashy, but they did have heels. Naomi was grabbing on to Gerry for dear life by the time they arrived at the house: a ramshackle affair that looked like it was on its last legs, with slates missing from the roof. While off to the side was the small jetty he had mentioned: uneven and held up by posts, it dipped and tilted and apparently led nowhere but *into* the sea itself.

Once again it looked like there was nobody at home.

Naomi got under the cover of the porch, but the rain still wasn't bothering Gerry. Her hair and make-up—which she'd taken so long over—would be ruined now. So much for first impressions. "Oh Gerry, whatever are they going to think of me?"

"You look wonderful to me," he replied. "Perfect."

Nobody was perfect, especially not her. She must look like a drowned dog.

"It's just a bit of water, they won't mind."

Naomi stared at the battered door. "I'm not so sure this is a good id—" she began, but it was already opening with a creak. Or maybe it was just finally collapsing, hanging there as it was on one hinge. The thought crossed her mind again that Gerry should be sending them more money, either that or relocating them completely. Getting them out of this godforsaken hole.

"Let me go in first," said Gerry, which she had no problem with at all. Then he was gone, swallowed up inside that darkness...

Dark place, dark house.

...and Naomi realised she was standing on the doorstep, what little there was of it, on her own.

Abandoned.

When she did peer inside she saw that there was a light coming from somewhere, flickering and casting shadows. The faint glow of a candle? Maybe there had been a power failure? Or it had been cut off for lack of payment? The putrid paintwork of the place was peeling, or perhaps it was just trying to flee the walls—she knew how it felt. The carpet she was treading on was damp and squishy, but there was little wonder as the rain was finding its way into the house from above. Perhaps that was what had caused the power to go off?

"H-Hello?" she called out, her eyes readjusting to the gloom.

Then she saw them, standing there in the hallway, Gerry next to a woman who was smaller than him, her outline dumpy. Some might say "mom-shaped". The dress she had on covered most of her body, made from a thick material. Her hair was tied up in a bun on top of her head, but various strands had leapt out and floated on the air,

199

giving her a look of being submerged. Her smile was warm, though, welcoming. It was her who had the candle, stuck inside some kind of ornate holder.

"Over here," Gerry said, unnecessarily.

Naomi continued to make her way inside, passing a set of what looked like the most rickety of stairs heading to an upper level.

"Mother, this is my... special friend. Miss Naomi Jackson."

Naomi frowned. She'd been wondering how he would introduce her, when the time came. Is that what she was, then? His friend? You worshipped your *friends*, did you? She was savvy enough to know it was because of the old-fashioned thing, however; the being set in your ways. At least he'd called her special.

But still, *friend*?

The woman stepped forward, stooping, shambling almost in a way that made Naomi want to cover the distance between them to save her the trouble.

"Gerald's teld us so much about yer," said the woman, free hand out.

Naomi shook it tentatively. "Really?"

"Oh yes." Her strange accent made it sound like "yersh". Her eyes twinkled in the light from the candle as she looked Naomi up and down.

"I'm really sorry about... I must look such a mess," she said to the woman.

"Naw, yer beautiful, dear," said Gerry's mother.

That made Naomi smile. "I hate to ask this when I've only just arrived, but I don't suppose there's anywhere I can, you know, freshen up at all?"

"'Course," said the woman. "Yer've had a long drive." She pointed to the stairs. "Just at the top there, oh and yer'd better take this."

She handed Naomi the candle, which she took with a thanks. Then they went off, leaving her alone again, standing there staring up the stairs she'd have to negotiate. Naomi took her time, very nearly putting her foot through one slat, but eventually she reached the top. The bathroom was opposite, just as Gerry's mom had promised, so she carried the candle through and locked the door behind her.

Water was dripping on her from above, but ironically when she'd placed the candle down and out of its reach, she couldn't get any to come through the taps attached to the chipped sink. The pipes just rattled and gurgled. Naomi sighed when she looked in the cracked mirror in front of her, it was like the Joker staring back. So she picked up a towel in an attempt to dry herself—only to realise that they were just as sopping as she was. Naomi could at least use it to wipe away the worst of the make-up, she told herself.

As she was putting it back on the rail, she found herself gazing across at the old bath in the corner. Naomi's mind went immediately to her own mother, as she pictured her in one very similar, water slopping over the edge as she held up the razor. Drawing it across veins, redness dripping into—

Blood, water. Water, blood.

She shook her head, snatching up the candle again and leaving as quickly as she could. The whole exercise had been a bit of a waste of time really, she looked almost as bad as when she arrived.

Naomi had one foot on the step to come down, when a big splash from the ceiling put out the candle, with no way to relight it. She swallowed hard, then left the candle and its holder on the stairs, as she figured she'd definitely need both hands now. By the time she was halfway down she was on the verge of tears. None of this was going right at all, and to make matters worse she could hear raised voices coming from what had to be the lounge—where Gerry and his mom had retreated. She strained to listen, but couldn't tell what the argument was about. All she could make out were male voices, one of them Gerry's.

Though in her heart of hearts Naomi knew it had to be about her. Everything she feared was coming true.

When she reached the bottom and stepped off (a big step) her foot landed in a puddle of some kind. "What the..." she managed. Instead of just damp, the carpet was now under a couple of inches of water at least.

Naomi swished through this...

Was there any wonder she was getting cold feet now?

...feeling her way around into the corridor again: aiming for the lounge. The arguing stopped when she reached the doorway and turned the corner. There were a couple more candles in this room, but these were no match for the murk inside. She could just about make out the shapes in there: Gerry with his mom again; and next to her was a seated figure, a man. Naomi squinted, thought that he had no legs at first, then realised he had a blanket over his knees. He was sitting next to a table which had one candle on it, so he was better illuminated than the others.

He was dressed in a suit that looked like it had seen its better days in the previous century—*early* in the previous century. The skin on his face was tight and shiny, as if it was about to rip at any moment, especially at the corners of his downturned mouth—except for the flesh underneath his eyes, which hung in bags below two white, bulging orbs. He was virtually hairless, didn't even have eyebrows, but then, thought Naomi, what kind of hair could possibly grow on that head anyway?

Gerry's father, had to be.

"Come on in girly, don't be shy," said the man, beckoning with a hand. He sounded like he'd been gargling with those words, before spitting them out. "Let's have a look atch-yer!"

Gerry said nothing.

Naomi ventured in a little further, suddenly all too aware of how her dress was clinging to her, especially when the man's bulbous eyes lingered a little too long on her breasts. What started off as folding her arms across her chest soon turned into a hug she was giving herself, and not just because she was freezing.

"Ahh," gurgled the man. "Preddy you are." He licked his lips; it made Naomi feel physically sick.

"Now, now, Benjamin," said his wife. "Stop that."

No, stop it. You're doing it again. Stop that right now!

"Yer scaring the poor lass."

"N-Not at all," said Naomi, struggling to keep the hitch from her voice.

The woman picked something up from the table with a rattle and a clink. "Would yer like a cup of tea, dear?" she asked Naomi, obviously deciding that the girl was going to get one regardless. "I've just this minute made a pot." Again she was shambling across the space, forcing Naomi to meet her halfway, taking the chipped cup and saucer from her hands.

Naomi looked down at the tea. It was thick and gelatinous... and, though it was hard to tell, there looked to be a greenish tint to it. The woman was waiting there expectantly. Naomi grimaced, took a sip. It was cold—very cold—and tasted brackish, but she forced it down with another hard swallow. It almost came immediately back up when she saw how the remaining liquid had settled back in the base of the cup, like mud in a river.

"Somethin' to eat, p'haps?"

Naomi thought of the calamari back at the restaurant Gerry had talked about and held up a hand. "Oh, no... no thank you. I'm really not—"

"So whet d'ya think of our little town then?" This from the father, who practically coughed out the last of his phlegmy question.

"Erm, it's... er..."

"Bin around since the seventeenth century, it has. A hugely successful seaport at one time or annuther."

"It..." Naomi was struggling for something to say. "Forgive me, but it seems to have fallen on... dark times of late."

All three of them looked at her, practically in unison—and as if to silently say that they might never, ever forgive her.

"There's bin darker," said Gerry's mother, pulling back to join her son and husband again, wading through the water.

The older folk splashing around...

"But we endure," her husband added. "We endure. Like as after that nasty business back in the '30s, the persecutions. Some hid, some escaped. But if it hadn't a bin for the War comin' along when it did... people forgettin'." He shook his head. "We survived those hardships anyway. What few of us were left, we endured."

"Let's not terk about all that," Gerry's mom cut in, trying to change the subject. "Let's terk about yer two. All very excitin', I have t'say."

More than just a friend then, if it was exciting?

"I'm... That is, Gerry's..." Naomi began. "You must be very proud of him, all he's achieved."

"Aye," said the mother, "he's a good lad. Loyal, y'know?"

She nodded; Naomi knew that. Everything else aside, all this aside, she was well aware of that. "Proud of how well he's done for himself out there, with his business and everything?"

The man in the chair laughed suddenly, a sort of strange gurgling noise. "For 'imself?"

"Father," said Gerry. "Please don't."

"You think 'e did all that by 'imself."

"Benjamin!" This was the mother again. "Now's not the time nor the place."

"I'm sorry, but I can't go on pretendin'," said the father. "'im there thinkin' he could just keep her to 'imself like that." He coughed that watery cough again.

Naomi was frowning once more. So they *were* mad about him keeping quiet? Was that what the argument had been about?

"Thinkin' we'd be all right about the two of 'em!"

No, this was all about her not fitting in again, wasn't it? Just like uni, like work. About her being an outsider, not being accepted. For God's sake, if you couldn't even be accepted here, by these people... But how would Gerry feel about that, she could see the way he... worshipped this place. Had basically been forced to leave it so he could try and bail his folks out—the water rising, up to her calves now—but what did his dad mean when he said Gerry hadn't done it on his own?

Naomi was already going through what would happen now in her head. The long drive home in silence, promises to call her when they got back and then never seeing Gerry again. Her ringing and leaving messages on his phone, getting increasingly desperate. Alone, deserted.

No girlfriend, no fiancée, no wife... no *family*.

Taking the razor, following her mother's lead?

Blood, water...

She couldn't have been more wrong. Couldn't have thought up this worst-case scenario in a million years.

"Neglectin' his duties, his responsibilities," the father continued on with his rant. And Naomi found she couldn't bite her tongue any longer, no matter how things transpired.

"Gerry is the most caring, responsible man I've ever known!" she blurted out. "I love him—and he loves me. Don't you?"

Gerry remained silent.

"*Caring?*" said his father. "Did yer care about them other lasses yer brought back here, eh? About what happened to 'em?"

All the others, the ones she'd been so jealous of. So they'd been brought back here too? And what had happened with them, he'd

204

dumped them when he got bored? Gerry had told her she was special, that's why she'd wanted his family's approval so much. But now she wasn't so sure, about him or them.

Real life wasn't a fucking Disney movie. You put your trust in people, they invariably let you down.

Their relationship was sinking...

"Naomi, it isn't how you think," said Gerry, finally finding his voice. Making to move towards her, then stopping.

"Aye, you know the way it has to be, boy. I teld yer. You've known all along how this ends, yer were just kiddin' yerself."

"Breedin' or sacrifice," said Gerry sombrely, his tones starting to match his family's.

Pimping out his women... His mother thinking she was a gold-digging whore.

Rapist... multiple murderer.

Yer scaring the poor lass.

"*What?*" shouted Naomi, thinking she'd misheard.

"It's just like I taught 'im, just like fishin'," gargled the father. "'Cept young Gerald's the bait now. We sent him out there, funded him with what was left of the town's gold. He brought back what we needed."

A good provider. Worth its weight in—

Naomi stared across at Gerry's mom now, and she nodded. "It's true I'm afraid, dear."

Town's gold? Naomi's hand went to her necklace and its symbol.

"Well, we couldn't send out his brother—lookin' the way he does. As natural as thet might be." The father pointed behind her and Naomi turned, screamed when she saw what had risen up out of the water.

Never been one to mind her surroundings.

Devastating floods in its wake...

Blood, water...

So close she could do nothing *but* see him: the naked thing in front of her. He had the same bulging eyes as the father, but these were much more prominent in the middle of a face that could only be described as hideous, framed by fine, slicked-back hair. Lumps and bumps covered the skin, while a set of flapping gills opened and closed on his neck. The mouth was much wider than any normal person's, framed by blubbery lips, and when the "man" parted these he revealed row upon row of needle-like teeth.

Gerry's brother, the monster.

Natural-looking...

"Came on 'im powerfully quick, it did," Gerry's pop continued. "But it gits us all in the end."

Naomi tried to run past the brother, had to save herself, but he grabbed her, spun her so she was facing the room again—then wrapped two strong arms around her, the webbed fingers gripping.

"Be careful!" shouted Gerry. "Don't hurt her!"

"Yer still don't get it, do you? She's not yours!" snapped Gerry's dad.

"Not *just* yours," corrected Gerry's mother.

Didn't want to share her...

"Yer..." She pointed at Naomi. "Yer belong to all o' us. And yet to none o' us. He wasn't lying when he said yer were special, y'know."

"You freaks are all mad!" shrieked Naomi. She was still asleep in the car, hadn't woken up—and this was all some bizarre dream, some nightmare brought on by her fears. Or something in that horrible tea she'd been given? Maybe she'd been poisoned?

"Can't you feel it, child?" the woman asked her. (Inside you're something more... Beneath the surface you're...) "It's how ye two found each other, it's why yer felt the way you did."

The connection? Was that what this crazy bitch was talking about?

Was aware *of her as soon as she'd appeared.*

Always the outsider...

"Yer blood, dear. It's in yer *blood!* Yer heritage is the same as Gerald's."

Her father's disease? ("Natural as that might be...") Her mother not being able to live with the consequences?

Blood in the water...

Some hid, some escaped.

Escaped and carried on with their lives elsewhere, loving other people, having families, having children! She'd never known her grandparents, had barely known her parents, but what if—

The woman shambled back over again and held Naomi's necklace up to examine it. "The symbol of The Order. He would be pleased. *He* will be pleased. The one yer have been saving y'self for all this time."

"What... what the fuck are you talking about?"

"Yer know. Deep down yer know, child... Princess."

Girlfriend, fiancée, wife... family.

Naomi fought against the knowledge, just as she fought against Gerry's brother, but the woman was right. About the blood, about her family. She'd always wanted one and now she'd got it, hadn't she. One who adored her, in fact. It just hadn't been what she'd expected. And she realised then, that she hadn't been abandoned after all.

"A fine catch," burbled the father.

He'd done them proud.

She was perfect.

The older man's blanket was slipping from his lap and Naomi could see the many tentacles he had for legs, writhing and sliding over each other. She almost screamed again.

"And thers much to do," said the mother. "A festival t'prepare for, an end of the dark times to look ferward to."

Dark times, dark clouds. Dark shadows... They had hung over this place for such a long time, and would continue to do so for many years to come. Nothing they ever did would change that, not even giving her to—

A big step... a watershed.

She suddenly felt very, very scared: of letting go, of losing herself, of opening up to—

She'd feel the loss so deeply.

Naomi tried to imagine what would happen to her, the worst-case scenario, but nothing would come. It couldn't, it was beyond her imagination.

All she could see now in her mind's eye was the redness, so thick. Thicker than—

Water... The water *and* the blood.

The blood and...

The water.

THE GREY ROOM

My name's Dodgson, but some people call me Dodge.

Not a great nickname when you're in the painting and decorating trade, let me tell you. Not a great nickname for doing anything, I'll be honest. I could have been an astrophysicist and still not be taken seriously. I've had all the cowboy jokes, all the Dodgy Dodgson stuff (imagine if I'd been an accountant!). Blame my late dad, as I followed him into the family business... And I'm not knocking what I do, believe me. I make a decent and honest living. A normal living, a normal existence. It's just that, well, I keep thinking about how there's more to life than that. More things in Heaven and Earth than most people care to see, or want to know about.

It's one of the reasons why I'm doing this little side project, in my spare time. I'm hoping something might come of it, that it might fulfil some kind of ambition of mine from when I was younger. I was always creative you see, in one way or another. Loved to draw, paint (with oils and watercolours rather than emulsion), make things, models usually. Good with my hands. Had a go at writing, but was never really any great shakes. Trying to copy those horror authors I loved, you know the ones I mean: who wrote books with lurid covers. Skulls or guys with fangs on them, dripping with blood. Make believe, fiction. When the most frightening stuff of all is—

But also I think it's important to chronicle all this. If I don't, nobody else will. Tom's certainly not going to bother, he's much more interested in getting out there and doing all that weird shit than writing it down. It would bore him to tears, I reckon.

He's given me permission, of course. I wouldn't be doing this without his blessing. You can't do anything anymore without ticking those boxes; can't even go on the net without giving consent to this and that, let alone record someone, or write about them. There's just one stipulation: it can't see the light of day till he either retires, when his "good work" is done, or something happens to him. So these are just my notes really, gathering everything together. Getting things straight, planning. Jotting down my recollections.

I just wish I'd started doing it sooner, but you don't think, do you? Maybe we'll go back and hoover up all those other encounters he's talked about like "The Noving Fur" or "The Black Veil", although that might still be a bit raw for him. It's one of the reasons why he ended up in such a mess here, the fact he was so down about Aster.

Oh, right. Before we get into all that, maybe I should tell you a bit about how I came to meet him, the bloke I'll be telling you about. Whose adventures I'll be chronicling, I guess you'd call it. I first bumped into him, quite literally—rounding a corner and walking into each other—at my local college. I bloody loved that place! Apart from being a right laugh, getting to hang out with some of the best people I've ever known, the General Art and Design course I took gave me a chance to try out all those things I was just talking about. I had some stupid idea that I might get into galleries eventually. Make my mark, make millions. Yeah, right. I think my dad just saw it as practice, getting me ready for the firm.

I even enjoyed the theory side of things, mainly because our tutor was really laid back and showed us old movies at lunchtimes. But I needed to do a lot of planning, research; more than most, who'd just wing it. That's what I was doing in the library that day, getting out books to do a piece about Surrealism so I could get my grades. This was before you could look everything up on your computer, or even your phone .

So there I was carrying all those heavy books on Dalí, Magritte, not really looking where I was going, when I turned a corner and walked straight into him. I apologised, but Tom said that it was as much his fault as mine. That he had things on his mind and wasn't really paying attention to where he was going. As he helped me pick up my load, I noticed some of the photocopies that he'd dropped; newspaper clippings relating to a certain abandoned asylum not far away from the college. A place that was reportedly haunted by the spirits of patients who'd died on its wards.

I found out later that the head librarian there allowed him access to the archives section in the basement, for a fee of course. I asked

209

him if he was researching the place for an essay of his own, maybe a design project, and he just looked at me and smiled. I didn't know it at the time, didn't know until after the fact, but he was actually planning on breaking in and spending the weekend there. Rather him than me, was my first thought when I found out. Still is usually.

He had this goth look to him, Tom, even back then. Black trousers—not jeans, never jeans like the rest of us scruffs—black T-shirt or jumper, long black coat. Wasn't his intention, he always said, he just preferred wearing that kind of thing because it meant he didn't have to think about his wardrobe much. Like Einstein and all his suits, the same thing every day. Plus it meant that he could blend in when he went out to all those spooky locations late at night in the pitch black.

Once I'd met him, I couldn't help spotting Tom around campus. I never did find out what he was studying, he was always a bit evasive about it, but in the end it didn't really matter because he dropped out anyway before he could graduate. I used to see him in the local pubs quite often back in the day, would go over and have a few jars with him.

That turned into drinks with several of my mates as well, who didn't really know what to make of him at first, I don't think. But they were just as fascinated by his wild and wonderful tales as I was, he was quite the showman back then, quite the storyteller when he got going. Drew a crowd.

Often this would go on long after closing time, especially at The Crow, because we knew the lad whose family owned the place, Lumley. Tom would tell us about how he'd driven out to some spot because the residents reckoned they'd seen the spectre of a huge glowing cat prowling the streets; how he'd once spent a night in a cave on the coast and almost drowned, simply because—as legend would have it—the spirits of long, lost souls resided there. Or spent time camped out on the moors because of some photographs taken by a guy who'd gone missing—and which apparently showed a procession of the dead roaming the land...

We'd sit there opened-mouthed at all this, taking it in. Sometimes he saw things, experienced things; sometimes he didn't. I don't know if we fully believed him back then, or were just having fun, getting into the spirit of the thing—if you'll pardon the pun. Fiction, like those horror books I used to love so much. Halloweens were the best time when Tom was around, I have to admit.

But then college ended, life took over. Like I say, I followed dad into the decorating trade because it was steady work—unlike being an artist or writer or whatever—and it was always what I was going to do, I suppose. I got engaged twice, married and divorced once (my old mum would say I was too good for them, but in hindsight it was probably the other way around)... No children, which some might say was a blessing. Most people I knew from back then drifted away, but a few of us stayed in the area. I still drank in The Crow, which Lumley took over from his own folks. And I don't think I ever thought about Tom in all that time, in all those years. I can't even remember saying goodbye to him, it was sort of as if he just vanished like a ghost himself.

Only to crop up on social media, friending me on InstaFace or whatever it's called these days. I mean, I knew who it was straight away—there aren't many people with that name, it's even worse than mine—and so I accepted the request. He only had a handful of other friends, none in common (one of which was Aster), but there was very little about them in their information. Very little about Tom himself, actually. But we got chatting, as you do.

"Hey TC, it's been a minute," I said. "How're things?" He'd always hated that nickname, same as I do mine. Thought it made him sound like that cartoon cat, which in fairness it does. Anything's better than Carnacki, though, isn't it? I once asked him what it was: German, Polish? And he just shrugged. Typical Tom.

Anyway, he'd been travelling, seeing a bit of the world. Learning a bit about this, a bit about that. Mainly how things ticked, he said. He was back home now however, and looking to reconnect, touch base. So I suggested we meet up, me and him and a few of the old college guys (he could barely remember them, or their names, which was why they weren't on his friends list already; they are now). On that first night, at The Crow naturally, there was myself, Bierce, Chambers, Dee Nesbit, Hartley and Lizzy Asquith. Lizzy had always had a thing for Tom, I think, which was why she wanted to tag along.

We all met up, had a drink, reminisced about old times when our knees didn't crack, ate pizza, chips and curry, and generally had a really nice time. Throughout the evening everyone was trying to get

211

Tom to open up about what he'd been up to. Had to be more exciting than Nesbit and the old bangers she fixes up, right? Or Hartley's window cleaning round, or even Lizzy's work at the insurance brokers.

Little did we know...

He waited till it was almost closing time, as if knowing that Lumley would do another lock-in once we were in full flow, then he proceeded to tell us about an incident in East Africa a few months ago. An encounter he'd had with a "pretty nasty Mbwiri."

Yeah, that was our initial reaction as well.

Tom then told us how he'd helped one of the local shaman rid a young boy of a demon that had inhabited him. "He'd been misdiagnosed with epilepsy, but there were clear signs of possession," Tom informed us, matter of factly.

When Chambers started giggling, Tom turned and looked him straight in the eye, deadly serious. He went on to tell us how they'd driven it out, showing us photos on his phone of the rituals. I can remember exchanging glances with Bierce, not knowing what to make of it all. Surely it was just another tall tale, like the others?

Only it wasn't. Neither were the ones he'd told us before when we were back in college, I've come to realise. Oh, there are people who still dismiss all this as nonsense, who mock Tom for what he does. But I've spoken with some of the people he's helped, read the testimonies from others (you wouldn't believe some of the names on that list!). Seen the evidence he has in his own private archives that probably make the one back in that library look tiny by comparison. He's saved the lives of some people, and others have died as a result of his battles against malevolent entities. Tom might sound like those characters you've read about, like D'Amour, like Constantine, Dylan Dog, Felix Castor or Cal McDonald—whose adventures I've read and thoroughly enjoyed myself, I admit—but he's the real deal, take it from me. Don't call him a ghostbuster, for Heaven's sake. As Tom insists, he's a "finder". Whether that means he finds a ghost at the end of his investigations, or just the truth, it's what he is.

And, since he got back, he's made a point of gathering us together periodically to tell us about his latest case. He calls them cases, like he's on the trail of an ordinary criminal or something. Like Sam Spade in one of those old movies our theory tutor used to show us.

Some might say that he still needs an audience, that there's still some of the showman in him—and he does tell his stories as well as he ever did, with even more passion if that's possible—but I don't think it's that at all. Tom's not bothered about fame, fortune, any of that. The limelight. Like I say, he wouldn't even bother setting all this down if it was left to him, let alone try and get it out there into the world eventually. He's quite content to leave it at our small circle for the time being, just needs to tell someone outside of that work he talks about. The good work. I think it's a catharsis of sorts.

The most recent example of which was about a week ago, when he messaged our group for a meet. It had been a little while since we'd heard from him, but none of us were very surprised. After what had happened to Aster and everything... but I'll come to that in a bit. Let's just say he needed time to get over the previous incident, not that you ever really get over something like he went through—I'd imagine. We only really knew the bare bones of it (poor choice of words, Dodge) because going into detail had been too hard for him.

But it seemed like the way he'd dealt with it was to get right back on the horse, get back to that important work. Which was where he'd been, he finally told us after another night of drink and pub grub, answering the call of a client we'll refer to as "Anderson"; passed on by the friend of a friend of a friend.

"On the face of it," Tom said to us, once Lumley had locked the doors and we'd all been given a glass of the strong stuff (we usually needed it when Tom got going), "this looked like just another haunted house affair." He talks about those like they're commonplace, routine, which I suppose to him they are. "Well, I say house—when in actual fact the supernatural activity was confined to just one room.

"Anderson had moved back in with his mother not that long ago, after going through a bit of a traumatic divorce," Tom continued, and I couldn't help flinching at that. I knew all too well what those were like. "From what I gathered there was a custody battle over his son too, which he ultimately lost." Now those I didn't have any experience with, thankfully, but I could well imagine the upset. "Anyway, the house in question is a Victorian property that's been in the family since the late 1800s, about twenty miles or so from here. Nothing unusual about it, though: sandy-coloured brickwork; high-

213

pitched roof; ornate gable trim; brickwork porch... That kind of thing. Oh, and nice bay windows you can sit and read in, the perfect place to get over something as devastating as a separation. I certainly didn't get a sense of anything abnormal from it, anything... evil. And I have done with other houses like that.

"I was greeted at the door by Anderson himself, a tall man who looked like he'd been quite a strapping fellow until recently. But he was way too thin now, and pale at the moment, with sunken, almost black eyes. As I'd suspected, his mother—a sweet lady with dyed hair and a tight perm who seemed very exited I was there—told me he hadn't been eating much lately, and had barely been out of the house since he got there.

"'I keep saying to him, he needs to get out more. Mix with people of his own age again,' she said to me as we sat in the lounge and she brought tea, sandwiches and cake—none of which Anderson himself touched."

Sounded a bit like my old mum, that woman, especially given what she said next:

"'Plenty more fish in the sea, isn't that right, Mr Carnacki?'

"'Hmm, oh yes. I suppose there—'

"'You can't talk, you never bothered much after Dad,' Anderson cut in.

"'That was different, and you know it,' was her only reply.

"'Do you think we could talk a bit more about why you called me in?' I said, trying to shift the conversation away from Anderson's marital problems." Tom shifted about himself then on the bench in The Crow. For someone who had no problem talking about ghosts and demons, this one particular subject made him very uncomfortable: relationships. I never saw him with a girlfriend at college, not that there weren't interested parties—there still are, like I say Lizzy would jump at a date with Tom. And he's never mentioned partners in all the time he's been back. I just don't think that kind of thing interests him; certainly not as much as stuff like this. His kind of lifestyle would be pretty hard for someone to put up with, I'd imagine. It would take quite an understanding woman to be with him.

"'It's the spare room,' Anderson's mother told me. 'It's always been a bit... But it's been getting worse of late, especially at night-time.'

"'How do you mean, getting worse?' I asked her.

"'I mean, well, there's always been noises. The house settling, you put it down to, don't you?'

"'Do you?'

"'Well, yes. Especially old ones like this. The plumbing's not what it once was, Mr Carnacki. The radiators make a terrible racket sometimes, clanking away.'

"'But this is something else, something different?' I said then, pushing her on the subject.

"She nodded. 'The door, it...'

"'It keeps slamming, banging,' Anderson broke in again. 'All night some nights. We've checked the room for draughts, because you get those in old houses too. But there's nothing. The windows are closed, but the door keeps banging and banging. It's impossible to sleep, even with tablets.' Which of course explained his sunken and black eyes, if the divorce and subsequent troubles hadn't already.

"'We've had builders in, workmen looking at the room to see what they thought. None of them could help,' Anderson's mother told me. 'Couldn't get out fast enough, actually.'

"It was then that I asked if I could see the room itself, so I was taken upstairs and along a narrow corridor. On the left was the main bedroom, where Anderson's mother slept next door to the bathroom and toilet. Then on the right were two other bedrooms with their doors open—Anderson's and his younger brother's. 'Robert doesn't really visit any more,' Anderson's mother confessed. 'There was a bit of a... falling out.'

"I didn't ask about that at the time, but keep it in mind, my friends, because it will become significant. No, I was more keen to examine the room at the end of the corridor, the spare bedroom. I could feel a tug I couldn't explain, just put it down to wanting to get on with the inspection. Though the closer I drew, the more nervous I became. I felt a chill running right through me at even the thought of going inside, and almost turned to the pair I was with to ask if they were sure there were no draughts in this part of the house. There weren't of course—the coldness was down to something else altogether.

"Nevertheless, I went with them as they opened the door, allowing me a glimpse inside. It was an ordinary room, with a window on the

215

left—which let in very little light, I have to say, giving the whole place a grey look—a wardrobe and dressing table on the right, and a neatly made bed in the middle. 'There you are, you see,' Anderson told me, and walked into the room holding out his hands. 'Nothing. There never is, not in all the times I've been in here.'

"Except... there definitely was *something*. That feeling I hadn't had outside, or in the living room, or anywhere else in the house for that matter. A feeling of something... other. That it had been here, even if it wasn't at the moment. And I understood totally why those workmen hadn't wanted to stay in here a moment longer than they needed to. Taking out my handheld K2 EMF meter, I did a quick sweep but didn't get much of a reading.

"'Do you come in here a lot? Spend much time in here?' I asked Anderson, who shook his head.

"'No, not really,' he answered uncertainly. 'No more than—'

"'More than usual lately,' his mother corrected, then shrugged when he pulled a face. 'Well you do, love. Have done since the banging started.' I imagined him getting up at least to see what was happening with the door at night-time.

"'And before that?' I enquired, thinking about how eager I'd been to get up here and inside. Simultaneously couldn't wait, yet terrified at the prospect.

"Anderson shook his head, but it was hard to tell if that was a no or he just couldn't remember. When his mother spoke up again, we both jumped. '*Oh*, tell Mr Carnacki about the bedding!' she suddenly blurted out.

"'The bedding?' It turned out that every morning since the door's banging had started, they'd found the bedding crumpled up and in the corner of the room. Dragged from the bed and pulled across the floor, then bundled into that far corner. It was one of the reasons why they'd decided to get me involved. Why they thought it might be a haunting. I frowned and rubbed my chin, thinking perhaps this was another instance of poltergeist activity. Like in that asylum years ago, Dodge. Do you remember?"

I did, *of course* I did. It was back when we first met, as you know yourselves now. Angry spirits in torment, that's what poltergeist are, Tom had told me back then. There's even a film in case you're not familiar with the concept; Indian burial grounds and all that. Pissed

216

off dead people because they only moved the headstones before building the houses. More fiction, but *based* on an element of truth, which was what Tom was interested in more than anything. Finding said truth.

"So I asked if anything bad had happened in that room in the past, if there might be any restless spirits causing this? Any other unusual activity before. 'Not that we're aware of,' his mother offered. 'Nothing I've been told anyway. But then it was passed down through my late husband's side of the family.'

"'Late husband?' I recalled Anderson saying downstairs something about his father, but not that he'd died." Again, this was sounding more and more like my own parents, as my old mum never remarried either after dad passed on. Tom continued: "'Did he...' I nodded at the room to show what I was thinking.

"'Oh no, no. Cancer. He died in the General, Mr Carnacki, 15 years ago now.'

"'Right. I'm so sorry.'

"'It was a long time ago,' she said.

"'Okay, well I've seen all I need to for now, I think.' I wanted to get out of that room, honestly. Get back downstairs so I could fill them in on what came next. 'If it's all right with you, I'll stay for a few nights and try and work out what's causing your problems. I've brought some equipment with me, back in the car.'

"I was told that I could stay in Anderson's brother's old room, and as I was settling in I thought about what his mother—who was doing the pots downstairs—had said. The falling out she'd mentioned. 'So, your brother doesn't use this room much?'

"Anderson sighed. 'No, not much. Not these days.'

"'Are you two close?'

"'We get on, I suppose. But I don't think you could call us close.'

"There was a photo on the window sill in there and I left my unpacking for a moment to wander over to it. Picking it up, I saw a man who looked a bit like Anderson only more thick-set. He was standing next to a woman with ringlets, and at her side was a teenage girl dressed in a black mini-dress with tights and boots. Her hair was bright red and her eye-liner made her look like an Egyptian queen; even blacker than Anderson's sunken eyes. She had serpent tattoos on her arms and was wearing quite a bit of jewellery: a necklace

217

with what looked like a bat hanging from it; a nose-ring; bracelets... All silver. The only thing out of place was a golden ring on the third finger of her right hand. But it was more or less the uniform of a goth."

"You can't talk," Chambers shouted out at this point in the story, slightly merry, and Tom threw him another one of those withering looks that shut him up sharpish. Tom might be a lot of things, but a goth isn't one of them; not that there's anything wrong with that, you understand. Just a time and a place. He picked up the tale:

"Anderson joined me, jabbing a finger at the picture. 'That's what the falling out was over, Rob's step-daughter, Molly. Moll, she insisted.'

"'Oh?' I asked. 'Didn't she get on with Rob, or you guys?'

"'That was the problem, she got on *too* well. With Rob and Mum anyway, I don't really know her. Funny sort of kid, bloody emo if you ask me. He used to bring her to stay, I know that, especially when she was rowing with Rob's other half. Only one day about seven or eight months ago she ran off, and they got the blame for it. That cow said Mum and Rob had been filling her head with nonsense. Didn't need to from what I could see, listening to all that miserable music, reading all that death poetry. Like something out of *Beetlejuice* she was. Probably went off with one of those bands she used to follow around, just to spite her mother. They got the police on to it, went out looking for her themselves. No sign. But she'll turn up, I daresay. They always do, don't they?'

"I didn't really know what to say to that, missing people aren't my area, so I just nodded and put the photo back again. Then I carried on unpacking my stuff, asking if I could set up my equipment in the spare room and just outside the door. Video cameras with thermal imaging and a live feed running to my laptop, motion detectors, EVP recorders... the usual. Then, after a dinner of shepherd's pie that Anderson's mother kindly made—which her son just picked at again—and an evening of inane television which included the woman's favourite soaps, we all made our way to bed. If the other rooms had been empty, I might have sealed them just to make sure their doors weren't the ones making the noise the Andersons were talking about. But as there were people sleeping in them, I didn't need to; a camera trained down the hallway would soon tell me if they were slamming their own doors anyway, not that I expected them to be doing that. Neither of them struck me as the attention grabbing sort.

"Everything was quiet for a good while, and I was beginning to think maybe I'd had a wasted trip. I'd been keeping one eye on the wireless feeds to my laptop, but also doing a search into the house and the Anderson family to see what I could find out, which ended up being nothing. The owners stretched right back to Anderson's great-grandfather, the family line, but there were no records of anything untoward happening on the property that I could see. I made a mental note to get my tech guy, Fitz, to do a deeper dive.

"I think it must have been around half-two, three in the morning when it started that first night, because I admit I'd nodded off in front of the screen. I jerked awake with a start, though, when I heard that banging Anderson had described. *Just* as he'd described as well, like a door slamming repeatedly over and over. The bedroom was in darkness, in spite of the lights having been on when I dropped to sleep. All I could think was the power must have gone off.

"I checked the screen of the laptop in front of me, which I noticed was on battery power. The live feed picture was distorted—first snow on it, then wavy lines. Then that screen went black as well. If I was to see what was going on, I had to get up and check for myself. But a strange feeling of dread was washing over me again, which had nothing to do with the darkness—and I would have given anything to get out of going to the spare room at that moment in time. I'd been brought in to do a job, however, so I took out my phone, flipped on the torch, and forced myself to go to my own door, wrenching it open to see what was happening. There was little to no light out there in the corridor either; I could barely see a thing up the other end. And the blackness practically ate up my torch-light.

"I'm not sure I would even have budged then if it hadn't been for the scream, and flashing my torch to the side I could at least see that Anderson's bedroom door was already open. Realised that he must have gone to the room already to investigate.

"That got me moving. I rushed up the corridor, fighting back my fear, and saw all of my equipment in disarray, the cameras on tripods knocked over; whether it was Anderson stumbling into them that had caused it, I had no idea. But he was definitely there, my torch picking up his bare feet just over the threshold of the room... which bizarrely still appeared grey even at night. The door was fixed wide open now, not banging at all.

"But those feet weren't holding him upright anymore. I could see the soles, the toes pointing downwards at the floor—where he'd fallen over. I wondered briefly if he'd tumbled over my cameras, gone headlong into the room. Or had he just collapsed into there? In the end it didn't really matter, he needed my help, and I was about to crouch down to try and rouse him when I thought I saw hands on his body. Grabbing his arms, legs, torso. His head! Clawing at him, holding him down—and perhaps had even pulled him to the ground to begin with?

"I blinked once, twice, my vision still blurry from sleep. There was a second scream, more high-pitched than the first, and I tore my eyes away for a second to see another figure in the corridor practically on top of me. It was still in shadow, but small enough to tell it was Anderson's mother. By the time I looked back at his body again, the hands had gone.

"'Oh... oh no! What's happened?' she asked me and all I could tell her was that Anderson had fallen.

"'Stay with him, I'll call for an ambulance,' I told her. Which I did, saying it was an emergency. The medics arrived about twenty minutes later, by which time the power had come back on and we had light again. Morning wasn't far away either, but that didn't stop the paramedics being wary of going near that room too, especially when they saw all of my stuff littered around. They loaded the still unconscious Anderson onto a stretcher, though, and got out of there as soon as possible. I went down with his mother to see them both off—she promised to let me know if there were any developments— and when I returned to the house, to the room, I saw that all the sheets from the bed were gathered in the far corner. As with the door, it was just like they'd told me when I first arrived.

"I didn't hang around in there long, myself. Instead, I went back to my room and rebooted the laptop, which was charging. Then I wound back the footage from the previous night, to try to work out exactly what had happened. And to see whether my cameras had caught anything... odd."

"Like hands grabbing hold of him?" asked Lumley, who'd joined us sitting down by now.

"Exactly. But there was nothing. I spooled back the feeds, but none of them had captured the door slamming; just the noise of it. The cameras had fallen over by then apparently and all I got was a tilted angle. Then the distortion I'd seen the previous night, before finally showing the feet of the paramedics moving past when they arrived, shuffling into the room. The angles were wrong to be able to see what happened with the bedsheets as well.

"Yawning, I wandered down for something to eat—as Anderson's mother had told me to make myself at home, and all the excitement had given me an appetite, as it often does. I ended up scrambling myself some eggs, which I had on toast, washed down with coffee. I took another cup into the living room with me, sitting down on one of the comfy chairs there to message Fitz and get him to do that deep dive on the family, the house—and by extension the spare room. Once I was finished, I promised myself I'd only stay there for the time it took to drink my coffee, but regardless of the fact I'd made it incredibly strong, I ended up falling asleep again.

"I was woken by the house phone ringing at around midday—Mrs Anderson calling up with a progress report. Her son was in a stable condition, comfortable but still completely out of it. He'd had an MRI that morning, because they were worried about bleeds on the brain, but it had come back normal. They were, however, concerned about the marks on him. Finger-marks to be precise.

"'He had them around his throat too, Mr Carnacki. That's what they're saying caused the blackout, the lack of oxygen. Just before he fell.' She sounded suspicious, as if I might have had something to do with that. 'I think the police will want to speak to you,' she told me.

"'Okay,' I said, knowing I wasn't Anderson's attacker but having absolutely no idea how I'd prove it. Luckily, as you know, Dodge, the Chief Inspector owes me a favour or several because of what I did for his son-in-law not that long ago—so I called him up and explained the situation, that there were forces at work here I couldn't explain... yet. He promised to hold off the dogs, for now, which would buy me some time to get to the bottom of it all.

"I fixed myself a sandwich for lunch, then went back upstairs to check on my equipment. It was all intact, as far as I could see, so I

221

righted the cameras and set everything up again. I felt a little braver in the daytime about going inside the room itself, though only a little. It was just like it had been the first time I'd seen it, an ordinary room—except far from it—the only ostensibly strange thing being those sheets in the corner. I went over and picked them up, noting that there was nothing peculiar about that corner either. Just the painted wall, a skirting board... Shaking my head, I took the sheets back over to the bed and made it again. I still couldn't see the connection, why only the sheets were moving—and why into *that* corner?

"By mid-afternoon, I'd heard back from Fitz and it shed some light on why the room itself might be haunted. 'Someone died in there, boss, and under mysterious circumstances,' he informed me when he rang. 'Anderson's great-grandmother to be precise. Wasn't easy to find, as it had all been hushed up. Probably easier if I send everything over by email.'

"Which he did, and I sat there reading about how Anderson's great-grandfather had been accused of murdering her. Strangling her actually, something he protested his innocence about in jail—where he later took his own life by hanging himself. Edith Anderson was a lot younger than her husband and apparently wasn't too thrilled with married life. A lot of people married for stability and status back then, and in exchange she bore Theodore Anderson an heir. He—Anderson's grandfather—survived, little more than a toddler, and was looked after by his aunty and uncle until he could inherit the property. They were the ones who swept it all under the carpet, according to Fitz. After all, Theodore was never formally charged and it wouldn't exactly be a topic of dinner conversation within the family.

"So, a violent and sudden death—the very essence of a haunting or poltergeist activity. I figured that at last I might be getting somewhere in figuring this mystery out, finding out the truth. And I started thinking about things like a clearing, a blessing perhaps. Something to rid the room of the bad energy, that might see Edith pass on peacefully to the other side.

"I knew I'd need to be at full strength to perform something like that though, so I got my head down again for a while in bed. Too long, as it turned out, because when I woke it was already getting dark—not even nine o'clock, but then the days are still quite short at this time of year. And the room wasn't waiting until the middle of the night this time, its door banging again, which was what woke me up in the first place. It was as if it knew I was alone, and had been waiting for the light to drain from the sky.

"I clambered from the bed, trying the lights again in Robert Anderson's old bedroom. They came on but were flickering wildly. Once more, I felt that tug. The pull of the room. But at the same time I didn't want to go anywhere near it. That was why I took the chalk from my pocket and was starting to draw a circle of protection on the floor. I've talked before about how such circles can help ward off evil spirits, haven't I. Only this time I didn't get it done in time, was thinking about poor Aster and how stepping out of a circle like that one cost him dearly. If only he'd..."

Tom paused, pinching the bridge of his nose. He took a swig of the whisky in front of him and composed himself, before continuing: "Anyway, before I could protect myself, I realised I was walking through the door and back up towards the Grey Room—as I'd come to call it. Still thinking about Aster, about Anderson and what had happened to him the night before. I can't explain it, only that I lost time—and suddenly was in the room. Just standing there, not knowing what to do next. Not really able to do anything.

"I remember the hands again, seeing those hands that had been reaching for Anderson. That were holding him down. And I remember seeing a vision of Edith and Theodore arguing in that room—which, I admit, might have been down to the fact Fitz had put them in my mind. Nonetheless, I saw the man—bushy moustache, wearing old-fashioned clothes—shouting and screaming at his wife, his fists opening and closing. She was in tears, angry, clutching her hand, the ring on the third finger of the left hand.

"I couldn't help thinking I was being shown this, perhaps to help me understand what was happening. Rooms, houses even, can absorb negative energy—especially if it's over some length of time. And the fact that the final confrontation between those two happened in the Grey Room...

"Then I don't remember anything at all, which is hardly surprising. According to the person who saved me, I wasn't far off going the way of Anderson. That person, Anderson's mother, had returned to

223

the house and—after calling out and getting no answer—came to look for me. She found me in the room, standing there, and then I collapsed to the floor. Somehow she managed to drag me out, and down the corridor.

"The woman attempted to rouse me then, slapping my face. I remember being propped up against the wall while she fetched me a glass of water. 'Steady, steady,' she said, putting the glass to my lips and I almost choked on the first few sips. My throat was sore, and when I mentioned this, Anderson's mother nodded.

"'When I entered the room I found you with your hands at your own neck,' she told me. 'I-I think it's the same thing that happened with my boy.' Who had now woken up in hospital, and confirmed that I wasn't anywhere near him when the incident occurred which put him in that place. A place I should probably have been in as well; would *definitely* have been if Anderson's mother hadn't turned up. In hospital, or worse.

"'It's whatever's in there, isn't it?' she said to me, as she helped me down the stairs to the living room. She brought me more water as I lay down on the sofa, which I sipped again to ease my raw throat. My voice was hoarse, but I managed to tell her what I'd discovered about the room and her hand went to her mouth. 'Oh my... and you think it's Edith doing this? What does she want, vengeance?'

"'I don't know,' I admitted. 'It was my intention to try and help her move on, cleanse the room. Looks like she had other ideas.'

"The poor woman began to cry. 'I'm usually such a positive person, Mr Carnacki. Even when my Harold passed away, I tried to keep... I miss him, but I like to think wherever he is *he's* at peace. And I have such happy memories of living here with him, it's a comfort. Was a comfort, until...' She was crying freely now, more upset than I'd seen her since coming here. It was then that I felt it, another twinge from the room. Another tug, and I saw that she felt it as well. Thought for a moment she was actually going to leave me there and head back upstairs.

"I managed to get up and stagger over to her, patted her on the arm. 'Can I ask you something?'

"'Of course. Anything, Mr Carnacki.'

"'Did your husband spend a lot of time in that room?'

"The old woman thought for a moment or two before answering.

'Not so much before he found out about... well, that he was sick. But a fair bit afterwards, yes.'

"'And your son, after his divorce. You say he spent quite a bit of time in there, too.'

"She nodded. 'Why, what—'

"'And Molly, Rob's step-daughter? Did she used to spend time in there, before she ran away?'

"'Why, Mr Carnacki, she used to *sleep* in there. Always insisted.'

"I nodded. 'Mrs Anderson, I want you to return to the hospital. Your place is with your son.'

I saw Lizzy sigh at that line, holding her hand to her chest. Her eyes were glistening.

"'Don't come back to this house until you hear from me again, do you understand?'

"'I-I don't, but... Mr Carnacki, come with me. You need to be checked over yourself.'

"I shook my head. 'I still have a job to do, and I intend to see it through.'

Again, another sigh from Lizzy and she gazed at Tom longingly.

"Reluctantly, the old woman packed what she needed for Anderson and left. I spent the night downstairs, resting. Felt like now that I'd figured all this out, I could somehow resist the urge to go back to that room until the next day. Knowledge is, as they say, power. And finally I knew exactly what I was dealing with.

"My plan was a fairly simple one. I would prepare things in the daytime, ready to face the Grey Room that evening—as soon as it got dark again. Although it hurt to swallow, I ate, because I also felt quite drained and I knew it would give me strength. Bananas are especially good for that; they give you energy, as any professional tennis player will tell you. Mrs Anderson had no garlic in the house, so I had to make a trip to the local supermarket to pick some up.'

"Garlic and bananas?" said Bierce, pulling a face.

"The garlic wasn't for eating," Tom explained with a smile. "It was to help shield me from harm in that room. I would draw a chalk circle in there, you see, same as I was going to do in Anderson's brother's room the previous night but didn't get the chance. The garlic, smudged around the edge, would make for even better protection."

225

"What were you expecting," chipped in Hartley, "a vampire?"

Tom jabbed a finger in our friend's direction. "You're more right than you know, Hartley," he told him. "As you'll see when I head into the conclusion of this case. Only this particular vampire wasn't interested in something as ordinary as blood.

"Now, where was I? Oh yes, the circles. Chalk, garlic, and a circle of water inside that. Circles are powerful, rings within rings. And just for good measure, I made the Second Sign of the Saaamaaa Ritual within the water circle, then created an electric pentacle. Before you ask, that's simply a pentacle made up of strip flashlight torches. Battery-powered, so that if the electricity went off again the lights would stay on. I got that idea from Professor Gardner's 'Experiments with a Medium', a means to separate the material from the immaterial. Levels of protection, at any rate. Because, my friends, I would need them.

"I then sat inside, cross-legged, waiting for darkness to come. Not that it ever really became dark in there, just grey upon grey. But outside, night-time. I waited for the door to start banging once more. And I waited, and I waited.

"It was like the watched pot syndrome, never boiling when you're looking directly at it. I was waiting for something that had happened when I wasn't around twice on the trot the last two nights, but seemed shy for some reason that third night. I grew bored, even though I had my phone for company, to flick through; and the connection, I have to say, was superb inside my little 'shelter', the best it had been since I got there.

"I should probably have had someone else with me, or at the very least in the house, but after Aster I didn't want to place anyone in that amount of danger ever again. One thing to take the risk myself, quite another to ask somebody else to do the same, no matter the cause.

"Just when I was beginning to wonder if it would happen, there was a sharp bang. I whipped my head sideways to see the door to the Grey Room had closed then opened again—so quickly I hadn't even caught it. Suddenly I sensed movement in front of me and I turned again, just as the door slammed once more.

"The movement turned out to be those hands again. Grey hands in the Grey Room, coming out of the floor and reaching upwards. Then

226

out of the wall in front, to the side of me—reaching around the wardrobe and dresser, the bed. Now behind me, and I looked over my shoulder to see hands, arms stretching out from that wall too. From the floor behind me, growing like bizarre, grey plants. Then above me, coming in from the ceiling. Hands, fingers reaching for me from every angle.

"But when they hit the circles, they stopped. Their fingers prodded the invisible barriers, testing for weaknesses but finding none. I was safe inside it, as I'd thought. Even from the top, the protections formed a sort of dome around me, over my head—stopping the hands and fingers from grabbing me.

"That was when I started to hear the voices, the whispering. They were voices I recognised, voices from my past. From all the people I've ever let down: my parents; my teachers and tutors at college; my friends..."

Tom looked at us each in turn, knowing that when he left without saying a word it had affected each and every one of us to some degree, even if we hadn't known it.

"Finally, Aster. If I'd kept him inside the circles of protection during our encounter with the Black Veil, perhaps he would still be alive today. My fault, my sadness, my anger and grief. The voices were bringing it all to the surface, perhaps in an effort to coax me out so it could get at me. I wouldn't give it the satisfaction, though.

"It was then that I saw the bedsheets moving, being dragged from the bed. One of the hands reaching out and tugging at them, from the corner of the room. I noticed a flash of gold on that hand, before I was distracted again."

"Edith?" asked Lizzy. "She was doing all that because she'd died... *been killed* in the room?"

Tom shook his head. "I've seen some powerful spirits in my time, but none that could conjure up what was happening inside that room. This was something else entirely, the place belonged to the grey hands and fingers. The grey *thing* that had taken over the room completely, that had been called by people's sorrow, that had broken through using a gateway of dread and despondence. An entity that was causing the room, the very floor to shake now.

"Suddenly the hands all around me vanished, pulling back and withdrawing for some reason I wouldn't find out until moments later.

227

Not until the floorboards I was sitting on rocked, and exploded beneath me. The creature, the *monster* had found a way inside, tunnelling up underneath the circles to get at me. And it manifested itself next as a giant hand, made up of lots of smaller ones.

"It shunted me upwards, huge fingers snapping closed to try and trap me. If I hadn't leaped sideways at the same time it struck I'd have been caught inside its cage. As it was, I ended up outside of the protection circles, rolling over and landing on the floor on the other side. There was nothing to stop it from getting to me now, either inside or outside of my little invisible fortress. Except it wasn't coming after me...

"It had paused, was looking down at the object I'd dropped when it attacked. An object I was using to check on the news sites, as I often do, looking for strange phenomenon. The huge grey hand was looking—or as much as a hand *can* look—down at my mobile, fascinated. Then, as suddenly as it had appeared underneath me, it dove *into* that phone like a swimmer exploring the waters of a cove.

"I gaped at this, not really understanding what was happening—and only snapped out of it when I noticed movement off to the side of me again. The bedding, still being dragged. The hand, the arm still in the corner. A hand with a ring on its finger, but not the third finger of its left hand—rather on its right! The arm, tattooed with a serpent. Acting purely on instinct, I grabbed the bedding before it could be pulled into that corner, before the hand could disappear again, and I tugged, standing as I did so.

"Through the fissure in the corner came more of the arm, then a shoulder. Black clothing, a hint of dyed red hair. I pulled and pulled with all of the strength I had left, and eventually out fell a body, before the opening closed in on itself once again.

"Molly, the missing teenager..."

I looked around then at my friends, all with their mouths open. All just as confused as I was to begin with, before Tom explained everything.

"She was a bit disorientated, but otherwise fine. Had no memory of what had happened to her, or for what reason. Couldn't understand why she'd been taken, while others had... It was the ring, you see. The ring she'd found in that very room, jammed between the floorboards in the corner. A family heirloom, forgotten about, and which I remembered from the vision Edith had tugged off her finger and flung at Theodore. If only she'd kept it on...

"Why?" asked Dee Nesbit.

"Well, all rings, all circles have power, remember? But this one especially... I don't know where Theodore picked it up, but I recognised it when I got a proper look. It's an ancient ring of great power." He stared at Chambers, no doubt expecting some crack about it being "my precious" but the man kept quiet, as mesmerised as the rest of us. Tom continued: "Protection in and of itself. The Grey was brought here by Edith's torment, sensed it like a shark after blood. That vampire thing you mentioned before, Hartley. But it wouldn't have made her kill herself if she'd still been wearing that ring."

"So she killed *herself*?" said Lizzy. "It wasn't Theodore?"

Tom shook his head. "I'm not saying her life was great, because it wasn't, but on that score he was telling the truth. He was innocent, it was the Grey that forced her own hands to her throat, just like it had done with Anderson and myself. Our grief, our distress fuelled it, gave it power. You see it feeds on that, can't exist without it. Probably fed on Anderson's father's sadness too, might even have caused his illness to get worse. But the one person it couldn't get to was Mrs Anderson because of her positive attitude. The only time it became aware of her was after Anderson ended up in hospital."

"But it spared Molly?" asked Bierce, still not understanding.

"Because she was wearing the ring, like I said. She might have been depressed, listening to that miserable music as Anderson told me, writing poetry. But it couldn't get her to kill herself because she'd found that ring and put it on, thank God! Instead, it took her back through to the other side. To its home. It had been slowly feasting on her all this time: her anxiety, her neuroses, the works. The only upside to all this is that she's a much happier person now, is even reconciling with her mother. It's brought the whole family back together again, as it happens."

"But what about the Grey?" Dee wanted to know. "What happened to that thing?"

Tom grinned. "It was attracted to the doom and gloom of our world, the things being reported on a minute by minute basis. The anger, hate and misery on the news, on social media. It just couldn't resist. So it entered via my phone."

"You mean... it's still in there?" This was a shocked Hartley.

"It's... I turned off the phone and that's now in a secure place, so there's no way back for it that way."

"Light is green, the trap is clean," said Chambers with a snigger. Tom shot him another one of those furious glances.

"But couldn't it just come out through another device?" asked Hartley, looking down at his own phone nervously, prodding it with a shaking finger.

"It's possible, I suppose, but why would it? There's enough to feed on in there to last a million lifetimes. It's trapped, but in a trap of its own making. A snake eating its own tail. Who knows, maybe it'll make the 'net a better place—'cure' it like it inadvertently helped Molly. Burn itself out? But I've told her to keep that ring on, the only thing that saved her. I've also suggested the family sell that property, move on. But as Mrs Anderson said to me, it belongs to the boys. It's their inheritance. Their birthright. A better one now that the Grey is gone from that room, I must say. Since the light has been let back in. They shouldn't have any problems moving forwards."

Tom clapped his knees then, the story pretty much finished—it was all we'd get out of him for the time being at any rate. Until the next event. So we all said our goodbyes, hugged (Lizzy's hug with Tom went on a little longer than he was probably comfortable with) and that was that.

And this is this. The first of his adventures to be transcribed, with maybe a little embellishment—I have always been a creative person. Good with my ha— Maybe not.

As for me, I'm just waiting for the next time Tom gets in touch. The next gathering when he tells us what he's been up to since our last lock-in. Our last meeting. Tom Carnacki, TC—as he hates to be called. A terrible nickname, I admit.

Like Dodge, for a painter-decorator, though some people call me that. *He* calls me that.

But my name is Dodgson. And if you've learned nothing else today, you now know life can be anything but normal for some.

That there's more to life. More things in Heaven and Earth—not to mention the spaces in-between...

Than most people care to see, or know about.

ABOUT THE AUTHOR

Paul Kane is an award-winning (including the British Fantasy Society's Legends of FantasyCon Award), bestselling writer and editor based in Derbyshire, UK. His short story collections include *Alone (In the Dark)*, *Touching the Flame*, *FunnyBones*, *Peripheral Visions*, *Shadow Writer*, *The Adventures of Dalton Quayle*, *The Butterfly Man and Other Stories*, *The Spaces Between*, *Ghosts*, the British Fantasy Award-nominated *Monsters*, *Shadow Casting*, *Nailbiters*, *Death*, *Disexistence*, *Scary Tales*, *More Monsters*, *Lost Souls*, *The Controllers*, *The Colour of Madness*, *Traumas*, *Darkness & Shadows*, *The Naked Eye*, *Tempting Fate*, *Nailbiters – Hard Bitten*, *Zombies!* and *Even More Monsters*. His novellas include *The Lazarus Condition*, *RED* and *Pain Cages* (a #1 Amazon bestseller). He is the author of such novels as *Of Darkness and Light*, *The Gemini Factor* and the bestselling *Arrowhead* trilogy (*Arrowhead*, *Broken Arrow* and *Arrowland*, gathered together in the sell-out omnibus edition *Hooded Man*), a post-apocalyptic reworking of the Robin Hood mythology. His latest novels include *Lunar* (which is set to be turned into a feature film), the short YA novel *The Rainbow Man* (as P.B. Kane), the critically-acclaimed and award-winning *Sherlock Holmes and the Servants of Hell* from Solaris, the sequels to *RED—Blood RED* and *Deep RED*, recently collected in an omnibus edition—*Before* from Grey Matter Press, *Arcana* from WordFire Press, plus *Her Last Secret*, *Her Husband's Grave* and

The Family Lie from HQ/HarperCollins (as P.L. Kane)

He has also written for comics, most notably for the *Dead Roots* zombie anthology alongside writers such as James Moran (*Torchwood, Cockneys vs. Zombies*) and Jason Arnopp (*Doctor Who, Friday the 13th, The Last Days of Jack Sparks*) and as part of the team turning *Clive Barker's Books of Blood* into motion comics for Seraphim/MadeFire. His stand-alone comic *The Disease*, published by Hellbound Media, was also a 2016 Ghastly Award-nominated title in the "One Shot" category. Paul is co-editor of the anthology *Hellbound Hearts* (Simon & Schuster)—stories based around the mythology that spawned *Hellraiser*—*The Mammoth Book of Body Horror* (Constable & Robinson/Running Press), featuring the likes of Stephen King and James Herbert, *A Carnivàle of Horror* (PS) featuring Ray Bradbury and Joe Hill, *Beyond Rue Morgue* from Titan (stories based around Poe's detective, Dupin), *Exit Wounds*—a crime anthology featuring the likes of Lee Child, Val McDermid, Dennis Lehane and Jeffery Deaver—*Wonderland* (a finalist in the Shirley Jackson Awards) the bestselling*Cursed* and its sequel *Twice Cursed*, #1 bestseller *The Other Side of Never: Dark Tales from the World of Peter & Wendy* and *In These Hallowed Halls* (the first ever Dark Academia anthology), the last six also from Titan.

His non-fiction books include *The Hellraiser Films and Their Legacy, Voices in the Dark and Shadow Writer—The Non-Fiction. Vol. 1: Reviews* and *Vol. 2: Articles and Essays*, plus his genre journalism has appeared in the likes of *SFX, Fangoria, Dreamwatch, Gorezone* and *Rue Morgue*. He also co-wrote the afterword to the PS edition of Stephen King's *Night Shift* collection. He has been a Guest at Alt.Fiction five times, was a Guest at the first SFX Weekender, at Thought Bubble in 2011, Derbyshire Literary Festival and Off the Shelf in 2012, Monster Mash and Event Horizon in 2013, Edge-Lit in 2014, HorrorCon, HorrorFest and Grimm Up North in 2015, The Dublin Ghost Story Festival and Sledge-Lit in 2016, IMATS Olympia and Celluloid Screams in 2017, Black Library Live (Warhammer 40k) and The UK Ghost Story Festival in 2019, delivered the keynote speech at the 2021 WordCrafter conference, as well as being a panellist at FantasyCon and the World Fantasy Convention, and a fiction judge at the Sci-Fi London Film Festival. He is a former Special Publications Editor of the British Fantasy Society, has served as co-chair for the UK arm of the Horror Writers Association, and was co-chair of ChillerCon 2022 in Scarborough.

His work has been optioned for film and television, and his zombie story "Dead Time" was turned into an episode of the Lionsgate/NBC TV series *Fear Itself*, adapted by Steve Niles (*30 Days of Night*) and directed by Darren Lynn Bousman (*SAW II-IV* and *Spiral*). He also scripted *The Opportunity*, which premiered at the Cannes Film Festival, *Wind Chimes* (directed by Brad "*Hallows Eve*" Watson and which sold to TV), *The Weeping Woman*—filmed by award-winning director Mark Steensland, starring Tony-nominated actor Stephen Geoffreys (*Fright Night*)—*Confidence*, directed by award-winning Mike Clarke (*A Hand to Play, Paper and Plastic*) which stars Simon Bamford (*Hellraiser, Nightbreed, Starfish*), and *The Torturer* directed by Joe Manco of Little Spark Films, now streaming in over 100 countries. Loose Canon/Hydra Films have just turned Paul's novelette *Men of the Cloth* into a feature called *Sacrifice* (aka *The Colour of Madness*), starring *Re-Animator* and *You're Next*'s Barbara Crampton. His work for audio includes the full cast drama adaptation of *The Hellbound Heart* for Bafflegab, starring Tom Meeten (*The Ghoul*), Neve McIntosh (*Doctor Who*) and Alice Lowe (*Prevenge*), and the *Robin of Sherwood* adventure *The Red Lord* for Spiteful Puppet/ITV, narrated by Ian Ogilvy (*Return of the Saint*). You can find out more at his website www.shadow-writer.co.uk which has featured Guest Writers such as Dean Koontz, Olivie Blake, Robert Kirkman, Charlaine Harris, Paul Tremblay, Catriona Ward and Guillermo del Toro.

Also Available from Black Beacon Books

In a broken world, lighting a match is an act of rebellion...

For news, reviews, competitions, author interviews,
and exclusive excerpts

Visit our website
blackbeaconbooks.com

Like us on Facebook
facebook.com/BlackBeaconBooks

Join us on Twitter
@BlackBeacons

Find us on Instagram
instagram.com/blackbeaconbooks

Subscribe on Patreon
patreon.com/blackbeaconbooks

Discover All our Social Media Links
https://linktr.ee/blackbeaconbooks

www.ingramcontent.com/pod-product-compliance
Lightning Source LLC
Chambersburg PA
CBHW020607180626
46810CB00007B/2686